AFRICAN WRITERS SERIES

Editorial Adviser · Chinua Achebe

98 Dominic Mulaisho: *The Tongue of the Dumb*

6^{-31}

The Tongue of the Dumb

Dominic Mulaisho

HEINEMANN
London · Ibadan
Nairobi

Heinemann Educational Books Ltd
48 Charles Street, London W1X 8AH
P.M.B. *5205, Ibadan* . P.O. BOX *25080, Nairobi*
EDINBURGH MELBOURNE TORONTO AUCKLAND
HONG KONG SINGAPORE KUALA LUMPUR NEW DELHI

ISBN O 435 90098 6

Printed in England by
Cox & Wyman Ltd
London, Fakenham and Reading

To my wife Esther Nanda without whose patience and advice this book would not have been written.

To my children Mkando, Nyawa, Kamuvwi and Simukani for neither allowing me a dull moment nor a moment for thought.

Chapter 1

Many years ago, at the turn of the last century, when the people of Kaunga were running away from the Chewa in the Eastern Province, they spent a whole year wandering before they finally settled down in the Kaunga Valley. As a result of their nomadic life the people were not used to growing maize, so they forgot to pray to the Rain Spirit and offer sacrifice to it. When they finally settled in the Kaunga Valley, which up to then had been known for its fertility and plentiful rains, the rain did not come. For many years nothing came except a brief drizzle at the beginning of the rainy season and a brief shower at the end of the season. Later on, however, once in every five or so years, there was real rain and the crops grew, and the people had enough food to last the next few years. Because of this favour which the spirits were beginning to show to the valley, the people prayed again, hoping that, with the passage of time, the Rain God would forget their sins of omission and give them rain regularly.

Nineteen forty-eight was a year in which, if the cycle was repeated, the valley would be full of rain and the crops would grow. Dulani, Lubinda and many others in Mpona's village and in the other villages of the kingdom were working hard to tend them. Already in this month of December the rainfall had been good, and everywhere one looked there was a mass of green leaf fluttering in the wind. The maize was doing well and vegetable relish was plentiful. Unless something untoward happened (and the whole kingdom had offered enough sacrifices to prevent this), 1949 would see a bumper harvest.

As he tilled the soil to free the maize of the thick under-growth of leafy grass, Lubinda's thoughts went back five years, to the time when the Chief had been finally reinstated and cured of his madness. The return of the Chief had been followed by a bumper harvest. Would this year also be the same he asked himself? The hoe kept at its job, weeding out the grass. He still had a long way to go, but he was not giving up. The future of his many wives and children depended upon his keeping at it. He wondered at the way the people forgot the past. At one time there had been a lot of talk against him, blaming him for the Chief's madness; but now all this had died down and, what is more, the Chief himself trusted him and confided in him. He tried to picture the young girl Ngoza, who had been the Chief's wife. He could see her only vaguely in his mind, but he remembered her challenge to him clearly. He sighed. The whole affair was long past. The midwife had died before she could reveal the secret. Ngoza had fled the kingdom, and people now feared him because he was the real power behind Chief Mpona.

Thinking of Ngoza reminded him of Natombi. His pulse quickened. He knew that the child Dulani had had by Natombi was Dulani's own. But it did him good to tell people, just a few that he trusted, that the child was not Dulani's, but his. After many years of childless marriage Dulani had approached him for the purpose of 'employing' him, but when he had gone to Natombi and told her why he had come, she had insulted his manhood and clawed him. He remembered how lust had welled up in him, how he had pinned her to the ground with his powerful hands and how she had kicked him back; and yet the following year she had had a child.

'Good, the child is dumb,' whispered Lubinda to himself. 'I am still going to get her. I am Lubinda: I can't be beaten by a girl from a small village like Cakuwamba. I conquered the Chief's wife. What is she? What is she? Lizard only, only . . .' he swore. Then he returned to his work.

The sun was rising high, quickly. The corn was glinting as the cold fresh wind blew across it. A lonely cicada was singing among the corn. Lubinda, partly to stretch his back but also to see if he could find the cicada, walked forward and peered among the leaves. He smiled as he saw it. 'Even they too,' he said to himself in a low voice, and walked back. As he again bent down to his task, he heard the deep tones of drums from the village. As he listened he felt his heart lifting with joy. Then he remembered that tonight the Chief's daughter was coming of age. The three months since her first menstruation had passed so quickly. Why was this giving him so much joy? he was wondering. Then he remembered that as Councillor he would be acting as host to all the headmen who were coming. Moreover Dulani would be busy with dancing and drumming, so he might get an opportunity to slip out. 'Natombi,' he muttered. 'I am going to see her tonight.'

A voice called out.

'Woo,' replied Lubinda.

'You are asleep, eh?' It was Dulani's voice.

'What?' asked Lubinda. 'Come and see how much work I've done. You young men of today don't know how to work.'

Dulani was glad of an opportunity to relax. He liked old Lubinda very much and he confided in him. He was sure that without him he would never have had his child. If it had been someone else he would have long ago disgraced him; but Lubinda always behaved with discretion in the presence of Natombi. There were times when Dulani hated Natombi for having, as he thought, given in to Lubinda, even though that had been his wish. But when his wife asked him why he was looking at her in that way, he would be embarrassed and say nothing. It was more important, thought Dulani, to have a child than to quarrel about things gone by.

'How are you, Dulani?' asked Lubinda.

'I am well. Oh, you are still a strong old man, eh?' replied Dulani, surveying the portion Lubinda had cultivated.

3

'Don't forget we have a feast tonight,' Lubinda reminded him. Then he asked in a low voice, 'It is true what I hear?'

'What?' asked Dulani.

'Come on, what do you hear?' prompted Dulani. 'Where there is dew there is water.'

'That old Simbeya is going to marry the Chief's daughter,' replied Lubinda.

'What!' exclaimed Dulani.

Lubinda noted Dulani's exclamation. It even went beyond that of a person who disapproved because Simbeya was old, older than Mpona, and a leper. He knew at once what was happening. 'If it was a young man like you, one would understand,' said Lubinda, 'but an old and decaying cockroach like him, hu! Is the Chief mad again?' Lubinda looked at Dulani. 'Listen, my friend. She is a nice girl. If I were still as young as you, I would try my luck. Tonight, drum near her. Don't leave the place, otherwise Simbeya will creep there. Then tomorrow tell me how she looked at you, and . . .' He broke off. 'You know I have influence with the Chief,' he said finally.

The fact that Dulani did not protest, but merely smiled, confirmed Lubinda's diagnosis. His mind was working fast. Then he surveyed the clouds. 'We shouldn't have prayed for the rain yesterday,' he said simply.

'You think it'll rain tonight?' asked Dulani, a shadow of disappointment flitting across his face.

'Let's bet,' said Lubinda, laughing at Dulani. 'You don't know Kaunga, eh? It will rain tonight.'

'What will you bet?' challenged Dulani. 'I haven't seen any red insects coming out of their holes, so how can it rain?'

Lubinda laughed. 'You remind me of my children, Dulani. You want to see the lion's tail before you can believe it is a lion. These insects come after the rain. All right, I will give you the Chief's daughter, that beautiful one.'

Dulani chuckled, but remembered what he had called Lubinda for.

4

'Friend,' he asked, 'when black ants cross your path, what does it mean?'

'Oh, you saw black ants cross your path?' asked Lubinda. The laughter stopped and he became pensive. 'That is strange,' he said, 'because I've also seen something odd. Black ants!'

Dulani too was not laughing any longer. 'What did you see?' he asked.

'Two cicadas mating. I've never seen that before. Were these ants marching in single file, head to end?' asked Lubinda.

'Yes,' replied Dulani, somewhat surprised.

'And making a roar like fermenting beer as they passed?' asked Lubinda.

'Yes,' replied Dulani.

Then Lubinda stood pensively. Dulani could see that there was fear and worry on his face. Then, 'Look there,' gasped Lubinda, pointing at the masau tree near by. 'Look, look. There's an owl there. Don't chase it away,' he said, arresting Dulani's hand as he tried to throw a stone at it. 'What you saw, my friend, and what I saw and what we see now is taboo. It means that something bad is going to happen today. Maybe tonight. Maybe in the village. And maybe somewhere else.'

What is it, I wonder? he was asking himself. Maybe it is this Chief's daughter? Maybe someone like Simbeya wants to stop others from trying their luck? Maybe, maybe . . . Then something dawned on him. 'I hear this new teacher from the mission, he and his wife don't get on well together?' he asked Dulani.

'I don't know,' replied Dulani. 'But why would that be bad luck?'

'And that the teacher's wife brings you game meat?' asked Lubinda.

'You mean that the teacher might want to bewitch me?' asked Dulani, afraid. He had heard of the strong magic, medicine possessed by people from Petauke, where the teacher came from.

'No, no, my friend. People don't bewitch others for eating their meat. Does the teacher not know your wife?'

'No, if that's what you mean, no,' replied Dulani emphatically. But as he was saying it doubt and anger crept into him. Did he really believe what he was saying?

'Friend, be home early today. I wouldn't stay too long here. Something is going to happen,' advised Lubinda. Then they parted company, and Dulani went back to his job.

Later on in the afternoon, Dulani sat sprawled out after the day's work. He was crunching at his nsima like a pig that had not eaten for many days, and lapping at his water like a dog. There were a lot of things that Natombi did not like about this man of hers, and this crunching of his mealie-porridge like a pig simply sent her mad.

'It is taboo,' said Natombi after listening to her husband's account of the black ants that had crossed his path. 'Is there anyone sick in the village?' she asked.

'Nobody that I know of,' replied Dulani.

'I know who it must be,' she said as she washed up the pot. He had said some rude things to her that morning, and now she felt anger welling up inside her.

'Who is it, Natombi?' asked Dulani earnestly.

'You know there's only one person you can be so worried about,' she said, a taunting note in her voice. 'If it's her,' she continued, 'I'm sure she is well. Doesn't she tell you how she is in walale (town)?' His wife was clearly back on her hobby-horse. This step-sister was a sword which divided them.

'Natombi,' said the man, 'how many times have I told you that I do not know your step-sister. Why do you accuse me?'

'I don't accuse you,' she retorted. 'It's the people. All the women of this village laugh at me because of your ways. Since the girl went away you have gone about your work like a bereaved person. I too can see what I can see.'

Dulani stood up. Somehow she always succeeded in spoiling his food by bringing up this story. But this time he was going to fight back. Lubinda had told him something about her and the teacher. When he told him that he had no enemies in the village who could have sent the black ants to him, Lubinda had asked about the teacher. 'Did he give the game meat to you or to her?'

'Why, you fool,' Dulani had said, 'isn't it the same thing whether it's to me or to her?'

'To some people he and she are one and the same thing,' Lubinda had replied. But he had refused to be drawn further. That could have only one meaning.

'You know the teacher, and Lubinda has told me so,' said Dulani, threatening violence.

'You lie. And you know Lubinda lies,' replied the woman. 'The teacher gives us meat because he is a good man. Lubinda has been troubling me for some time now. He wants to sleep with me and you send him to me.' She broke into tears. 'Am I a bitch to sleep with every man whom you send to me while you go about with other women? Why did you marry me? To sell me to your people? Let me go,' she shrieked. 'I am tired of this! I am ashamed of having put up with you for all this time. This is your child, your own child, but you won't believe it.'

'You have always told me otherwise, woman,' bellowed Dulani.

'Yes, because that is what you want to hear, that he is not your child. Isn't that so? Then why don't you let me take him away with me? Mwape is not your son!' she shrieked into his ears. 'Do you hear?'

Lightning began to flash as the dusk crept up. Clouds raced across the sky like waves upon the sea. A cold wind smelling of rain blew across the field, and the corn fluttered in the breeze. Mwape, the boy, looked from one parent to the other, confused. He was a small but robust boy. He looked every inch like Dulani. He had a well-rounded face, with large eyes, and a mouth that was always at the point of provoking a quarrel. But the people who said that they knew what they knew said that he was not Dulani's child. His former wife, whom he had lived with for five years, had died childless, and yet before he had married her she had had a 'bush' pregnancy, which had not held. How was it that after only two years of his marriage to Natombi he now had a child, and anyway, why a dumb child, of all things? This is what people had been asking ever since Mwape was born.

It was dark as they made their way to the village. As they drew near they could hear the vibrations of each throb of the drum as the drummers put the final touches to the preparations for the big occasion. Their pace quickened with the rhythm and, for a moment, in the excitement of anticipation, each of them forgot the quarrel. Now they could hear the voice of the famed dancer Cazunda yodelling his voice to prime it. Soon the women would ululate to announce the transition to maturity. They must hurry, because all the other people were already in the village, waiting for this occasion that comes only once in the lifetime of a girl. And the girl was a chief's daughter, at that.

At the village, in the falling dusk, the elderly women were busy with the maiden who was about to come of age. Natombi had not been invited to assist at this ceremony because, although a woman, she was still young. Also, since this was a royal occasion a girl from a common family, and a foreigner at that, could not be invited even though she was married to Dulani.

Mrs Lubinda senior marked two lines on the ground in the small hut. Then she set a calabash of water on the girl's head. The girl put her feet in between these lines. Mrs Lubinda demonstrated the dance. Slowly her hips swayed from side to side. Then the movement increased, and the women in the hut began to beat the drums until she was like a trembling reed in a fast current. The girl danced after her, putting all her energy and concentration into her movements. If her feet strayed a single inch beyond the two lines she knew that she would be slapped. If she spilled even a single drop of the water from the heavy jar she knew that she would be beaten. She

8

danced on. Now every part of her body was trembling like an electric fish.

'That isn't how to do it!' rasped Mrs Simbeya, the old, grey-haired, red-eyed woman, smacking her hard on the back.

So the young girl danced on until she was writhing like a snake. The women struck up a song:

> *Namwali, namwali bvina*
> *Kuti atambala aone*
> *Kuti wakhwima*
> *Khwi! Khwi!*

'Young maid, young maid, dance so the young men can see you are of age. Go on with the dance.'

Then Mrs Lubinda sat the young, shy girl up. She slapped her again, and all the elderly women began to rain blows on her. She had been trained not to cry; if she had cried she would merely have been making matters worse. Instead she sat meekly, her fly-switch in her hands.

'When your husband is angry with you,' said Mrs Lubinda, 'give him good food.'

The other women said, 'True, true.'

'When you are at the monthly period, do not touch your husband's food. Do not put salt in his food, and when he has to eat do not hand the food to him yourself. Give it to your child or leave it on the floor. If you do not observe this his chest will open and it will be full of blood and he will die.'

'True, true,' chorused the other women.

'Do not look into your husband's face; that is not modest. Always look at his stomach. Once the stomach is full then everything will go well with you.'

'True, true,' replied the other women.

'When your husband beats you, do not run to your mother, because one of these days he will beat your mother up.'

'True, true.'

'Do not "jump" your husband – do not run about with other men. If you do so you will have difficulties when giving birth to your child, and maybe, if you do not reveal all at that time, you will die.'

9

'True, true,' replied the women. The instructions continued.

In the flickering light of the fire, while the rest of the people, including the mother, the Chief and headman waited outside, the induction went on.

'Tonight you will hear the hyena open your door,' continued Mrs Lubinda. 'Do not cry or call for help, but let the hyena in. If you do not let him in then you will not be regarded as a real woman, and you will lose this man who has been chosen by us to become your husband.'

'True, true,' said the women.

The initiation group in the hut was just preparing to come out, bearing the young girl shoulder-high, when Natombi and her husband Dulani reached the house, anxious to join the other people in the festivities. But when they arrived, they discovered that the boy Mwape had disappeared. Could he have disappeared into the group of children that they had just passed, the group playing hide-and-seek in the dark?

'Natombi, where is Mwape?' asked Dulani.

'You were with him in front. How could you lose him when you know that he can't talk?' she answered. 'He must be somewhere near here.'

'Mwape!' called Dulani, 'Mwape!'

The lightning flashed in the darkness and an enormous rumble took up the hue and cry. Why did it have to rain this night, of all nights, thought Chief Mpona, as he surveyed the many jars of beer which had been brewed for the feast. He looked anxiously at the sky. Maybe it might clear. But the others who sat around, Simbeya, Lubinda, Yuda, Banda, and the visiting headmen and dignitaries from the whole valley, also wondered whether there would be any celebrations.

'Don't just say he isn't there. You must find my child.' Natombi was getting anxious and angry. 'How can you say that you don't remember whether he was still in front of you when you passed the well, as though he was a dog? You must find him.'

Dulani had already slipped away to continue his search. He

ran around calling, 'Mwape, Mwape'. Only yesterday two lions had been heard chasing each other near the village. Impulsively, Dulani headed for the maize fields. It is better to search farthest first. He called for the boy as he ran.

The lightning flashed along his path, and he caught the glint of eyes close to him. 'Could it be my son? What is it?' he muttered to himself. He called out in a deep roar above the din of the thunder, 'Mwape!' There was no reply.

'Who goes there in the road?' he challenged. Then he saw a movement, and suddenly he realized that it could be a lion or a leopard. Instinctively, he picked up a stone and, charging like a madman, he hurled it at the object. An animal sprang away, calling 'Woo-wee, woo-woo-oo, woo-wee.' It was a hyena.

Dulani swept past, now fearing the worst, calling 'Mwape! Mwape!' Lightning flashed again, and this time the rain came tumbling down from heaven, so thick that Dulani could not see ahead. Yet he went on calling, 'Mwape, my son. Mwape, Mwape.' If only a voice would answer.

A voice seemed to answer from within so strongly that he turned to follow its direction. 'Go home, Dulani. Mwape is no more,' the voice seemed to be saying. Dulani ran on and on, calling the boy's name, 'Mwape, Mwape, Mwape my son.'

The raindrops turned to hailstones and pelted his head until it was one great bee-sting. He ran on, still calling out to the boy, so fast that he could not hear the floods rushing behind him.

At the village the dance warmed up. Upon hearing that Dulani had gone in search of the child, Banda and his brother had volunteered to take his place at the big drum. The initiate was hoisted on to a platform, where she sat, head bowed, while the people showered gifts on her. Then it was her turn to dance for them, to dance in order to thank them, but also to dance to show them how she could dance for her future husband.

At first the big drum beat slowly. The girl swayed her waist slowly, in tune to the drum. Standing there alone on the platform she looked half asleep. Then the smaller drums joined in and the pace began to quicken. She swung into the rhythm. Quicker and quicker the rhythm went, and faster and faster she swayed her waist until, in the end, with arms delicately raised up, she looked once again like a graceful reed in a current. In the reflection of the fire her body was smooth, lithe, and beautiful. This was a great moment for the Chief, as it was for whoever was going to marry her.

The hour was getting late, but Dulani had not returned. Lubinda, noticing Natombi's absence, quietly slipped away, and in a moment he was whispering 'Odi!' at Natombi's door.

'Who are you?' asked Natombi from within.

'I am Lubinda,' whispered the man outside. 'I have come to find out about Dulani. Are he and the child back yet?'

Natombi felt frightened. There was something which told her that this man was not come to help. Yet she was anxious. Dulani had not returned after all this time, although the child had been found shortly after he had left. She had asked his brother Banda to follow him to the fields to tell him that Mwape was at home, but Banda had said that Dulani would soon return – he was not a woman who would lose the way.

'Isn't he at the celebrations?' asked Natombi.

'No,' replied Lubinda in a whisper. 'Let me in. I want to help you.'

'Then tell the Chief my husband is missing. I must tell the Chief.' Natombi opened the door to rush out. Lubinda held her firm in his arms.

'Tonight, Natombi, you are mine. Tonight . . .' he whispered.

She shook him off and ran shouting, 'My husband, my husband, my husband is lost.'

The drumming stopped. The dancing stopped. All the men scattered to the fields to look for Dulani. The raindrops once again changed to hailstones. Lightning flashed more fiercely and thunder roared. As the rain became thicker, the search for Dulani was given up and the men picked their way back, by the frightening light of the flashes. A cloud of fear and anxiety more terrible than the hailstones settled on the village and snuffed out the air of celebration.

Lightning struck the tree outside the Chief's house. The people ran out to find it ablaze. They ran back to huddle together. Natombi was weeping in her hut. Banda, her brother in-law, was with her.

'My husband, my husband! They have bewitched him,' she was crying.

'Don't cry,' urged Banda. 'That would give him misfortune. Dulani is alive. I know that.'

'Then go and find him. My husband, my husband!'

In this village she stood alone if Dulani was not there. It was he who had brought her from Cakuwamba, he of the royal family and she a commoner. She had never been welcomed as one of the village. It frightened her to think what would happen if, if . . . 'No, no,' she was telling herself, 'Dulani is coming back.'

The rain pelted on and lightning flashed more and more; the circle of sympathizers began to increase until Banda had been joined by Lubinda, Yuda, several headmen and the Chief himself. They were all waiting for the rain to stop before resuming the search.

'Where is the teacher?' asked Lubinda. 'He may know where Dulani is.'

'He must be asleep,' replied Banda. 'Dulani told me that the teacher would not be at the coming-of-age ceremony because his religion forbids it.'

'His religion forbids it!' exclaimed Lubinda. 'Somebody go and tell him his friend Dulani is missing. His religion forbids it indeed!' Lubinda spat before him. 'Why doesn't his religion forbid him other things? There are strange things happening in this village since this teacher of yours came. Only yesterday I saw two cicadas mating and Dulani saw a procession of black ants.'

Someone held Lubinda by the arm. 'Did you see black ants then?' he asked.

'Black ants,' replied Lubinda, 'and now lightning has struck the tree under which we pray to the spirits for rain, and Dulani is missing.' In the dim reflection of the wood fire could be seen the huddle of frightened faces; for them black ants could only have one meaning.

The cock crew. Thunder and lightning ceased almost immediately. The rain eased into a drizzle and the men went out again. Natombi sat weeping. Soon a cry came from one of the leaders of the search party. 'Water, water! Floods! Kaunga!'

True enough, Kaunga had broken its banks and its flooded waters were rushing past the village, which fortunately stood on a higher site. They all rushed back to the village, because for as far as one could see, in the red light of dawn there was nothing but water.

'Floods, floods!' they were shouting.

Just then the hail started again. Dulani in a last effort renewed his call for Mwape. By now his head had become sore. He ran on still calling for Mwape, until suddenly, without warning, he found himself surrounded by water, rushing at him from all directions. 'Floods!' his heart exclaimed. He made to escape, but not knowing where he was going, he lunged full tilt into the masau tree in his field. In a moment the floods were roaring over his unconscious body.

Next morning they found Dulani washed away by the floods, his body anchored against a submerged anthill. Thrust into his nostrils were two red fangs which filled both the nose and mouth with a slimy liquid. The body was limp and boneless and the skull cracked. Sprawled out parallel to his body and meeting it at the head was a python.

Chapter 2

There was no shrill cry, ululation, or the happy note of a high-pitched drum to announce the defloration of the girl when early that morning Mrs Lubinda, the mistress of ceremonies, emerged from the girl's hut. Even though the sun was already shining brightly, the day was like a drum muffled in sorrow. A man had died in the village. There was a corpse in the house. And there was also a python whose head had been cut off by Lubinda, the medicine man, in order to concoct a prescription to protect the village against these things happening again. By midday virtually all the men and women from the twenty or so villages in the valley – Cikokola, Ciwera, Cakuwamba, Sipopa, Mkando, Kanaventi and the others – had come to Mpona's village. As each group neared the village the women started to mourn. 'They have bewitched our man – these people are cruel. Mpona, your village is going to finish us. Mpona, Lubinda, is this how you rule us now, sending us to share a deathbed with pythons, the pythons which are being sent by the spirits because we no longer remember our ancestors? Mpona, our world is coming to an end, children are now growing upper teeth first like goats, and snakes are mating in our presence. They have eaten our man . . .'

The crowd of men under the tree near Dulani's house sat quiet and huddled as each procession of mourners arrived. It would have been proper to challenge their accusations, but not until after the funeral, since in a moment of sorrow each man must say what is in his heart. Afterwards the group would join the rest of the mourners – the men under the tree and the

15

women in the house of the widowed woman where Dulani's body, covered in a discoloured white cloth, lay grossly swollen by the water. Then the new wave of arrivals would stand up to go and see where it all happened. They would not challenge the widow there and then in the presence of the corpse. But as soon as they were on their way to the death spot they would say, 'Did you see how little she weeps? Why did she send her husband to look for a child whom she knew to be in the village? They say that someone overheard them quarrel at the garden yesterday. Yuda heard them. This new teacher in this village from Petauke, the one they call Aphunzitsi, they say he knows this woman. If that is so then this man has been bewitched or has died because the woman has "jumped him".'

'My friends,' whispered Cakuwamba to his people as his party went over to see where it had all happened. 'This girl comes from my village, our village. These people in this village do not like her; they hate her. Why, ask me? I will tell you. It is not Aphunzitsi who has caused this death. Lubinda wanted this woman and this woman was always in sorrow, in much trouble because she would not agree. Was it not last year when she nearly left to come back to our village? Let us not be deceived. There are rings within rings in this matter.'

The people of Cakuwamba were the traditional asabwira, or undertakers, for any member of the royal family, and Dulani was a cousin of the Chief. Since arriving they had been cutting reeds, measuring the body and weaving the mat in which it would be wrapped. None of the people of Mpona could speak to them and they, in accordance with tradition, brushed them aside, saying 'Get away, this is not your business. We are here to cast away the rubbish that you produce, you dogs.' No harshness was intended.

In the afternoon the body was bathed and wrapped in a new black cloth and then put into the reed box. The asabwira led the procession to the grave while the women mourned. At the grave Lubinda touched the coffin and protested at the direction the head was going to face. An argument sprang up.

'Shut up! It is none of your business how we bury people.

16

The head must always face the east so that if he is a witch he can pack his bags before the sun rises,' said Katundu.

'Where did you see a person facing the west?' asked another one from Cakuwamba. 'That is why you people of this village are witches.' There was silence among the other people. But the asabwira, because it was their traditional duty to make this heavy matter look light, began to laugh. You could not say they were happy, because it was a hollow laugh, and they felt the loss as much as anyone else.

'Some of you look happy; tonight we know you will come back to dig this body up. Beware,' said the headman Cakuwamba. 'We have already sprayed the corpse with medicine. He who eats it dies right here on this grave.' The people of Mpona mumbled to each other. This was going too far, but what could they do? Cakuwamba continued: 'As for some of you who have your red eyes on the widow, we are going to take her away with us.' Katundu looked at Lubinda, all eyes following him, and when he saw that Lubinda was uneasy he laughed.

After the burial the people returned home to Mpona. At the entrance to the village they all washed their hands to stop them carrying misfortune into the village. Immediately the women set up a wail. 'Dulani has gone. Witchcraft of this village has killed him. They have killed him so that they can use his blood to multiply their crops. You have left us alone, Dulani; we are confused. You were here yesterday and today you are dead. The snake of this village has consumed you. These young women you bring into the village, these women have two hearts and ten eyes, Dulani, they have despatched you to your death. We told you, we told you to marry your own, and now see what has happened. Dulani, you are wayward. See how you have left us.'

The widow remained in the house. She would not be allowed to go out. Holding on firmly to Mwape, her dumb son, she was weeping silently. Now and again words broke through her sobs: 'Father of Mwape, you have left us alone. See what you have done. I speak to you, you cannot even answer. I lived well in this village because of you. Now they will cast me away and they will take your son. Dulani, do you hear me? Why did you do it? Why did you leave us alone? Mwape, you will grow without talking to your father. Your father, like you, my son, cannot talk any longer.'

Mrs Lubinda senior cut in, 'She cries only because Dulani used to keep her like a white donna. She does not sorrow for him, only for the things that he gave her.' Natombi kept quiet, but she went on sobbing. 'As if she ever cared about him when he was alive,' repeated Mrs Lubinda.

As the sun set two huge fires rose, one for the women and the other for the men. All the people who had come to the funeral remained to keep the wake, because to go away without a gesture to those in sorrow would not have been correct. The asabwira were hard put to it to lighten the occasion. But in the end, and with the help of some beer and stories, they were succeeding. 'Now, let us see how many of you are awake, especially you sleepy people of Mpona,' said Katundu. 'Your father's bald head. What is that?'

'A rock,' answered Lubinda. He too as Councillor had a job to enliven the atmosphere.

'Ah! He's thinking of the rock he will use to cut up Dulani's body!' said Katundu.

'You rascal!' said Lubinda. They all laughed.

'Your father's bald head. What is it? Quick, or your time's up. Time's up!' said Katundu.

'All right. You gravediggers think you are very clever. Here's one from me.' It was Lubinda. 'The sweet things of the ladle.'

'Your toothless woman!' replied Cakuwamba. Again there was general laughter, but Lubinda did not appear too amused. 'Come on, time's up!' The people laughed at the indecent haste. 'Now, what was the answer to your's?' asked Lubinda of Katundu.

'Your father's bald head? Pumpkin, of course. Have you ever seen a hairy pumpkin?'

The people thought this was very clever, and they laughed.

'Now here is ours,' said Cakuwamba. 'Chief Mpona is beating the drum and Chief Mphuka is dancing.'

Everyone said that it was simple. Then Yuda gave the answer, 'It is the water and the reed. Don't you see how the reed dances in rushing water? Now have mine.'

Cumba, also from Mpona, interrupted Yuda and said, 'Wait, I will fix these fellows. My father has a big pond but there is only one fish!'

The people from Cakuwamba could not answer.

'Now,' said Lubinda, 'the sweet things of the ladle are – sleep.'

After a run of successful answering, the Cakuwamba people failed and it was Cumba's turn to explain his conundrum. 'That? Well, it is Cakuwamba's mouth. Don't you see that although it is as large as that of a huge frog it has only one tongue?'

More beer passed round the fire and as everyone, including Cakuwamba, was laughing, Cumba kept saying, 'It is true, his mouth is even larger than his grandmother's. It is, of course, much larger than his eyes, which look like bubble fish . . .'

When you are bitten by a snake you panic first, then you realize what has happened, and afterwards you feel the pain of the poison wriggling up from your foot to your head. The death of Dulani was a sudden and unexpected tragedy, especially as it came right in the midst of festivities. Although it appeared outwardly that the people had accepted it, in fact they were all still very dazed. No one could understand what the village had done to deserve all this.

For his part, since hearing the news Mpona had said not a word, being too overcome by the loss of his cousin. Why did they who had bewitched him have to choose that time, of all times, when he was celebrating his daughter's coming of age? His thoughts went back to the past. This was yet another misfortune. Someone in the village was responsible for this. Some people were already saying that this thing had come because of the school he had allowed the white people to set up. Was this possible? Mpona thought of the way in which his youngest son appeared to be enjoying this thing called schooling. Every evening he came back with amusing stories of all that they did at the school. The teacher was teaching them, by looking at a piece of paper, to understand the words of a man who died many years ago. How could that be? Could it be that this teacher communed with the dead? How could what happened in the past be known without someone actually telling you? Then there was that story which his son never tired of, the story about a young child who was born in a goat-shed. What was strange about this, since even here one lived together with goats? If this young man rose after death, then surely he must have been a ghost. Were all these white men not ghosts? If this person had been a man, black, he would have been a spirit. Could it be that all these things were happening because of this ghost?

As Mpona was sitting quietly on his stool, all by himself, Lubinda came to see him. By then the night had become very old and the Milky Way could be seen in the sky. For a long time both men kept quiet. It was the way to express the sorrow of the country at what had happened. Then Lubinda opened the conversation: 'Is this new man that you have allowed into this kingdom sick, or is he established in this village?'

'Which one?' asked the Chief with irritation. 'If you mean the teacher, I wasn't the only one to allow him into this village. You all received the cloth which the white one at the mission brought, didn't you? Didn't you accept the white man's medicine?' asked Mpona.

'But he's never been seen. What kind of a man is he who doesn't mourn with others when they are in difficulties? It is because we have accepted the coming of the white man's religion into this village that all these things are happening. When I ruled this country in your absence, the other white man who died some years ago tried to establish his church here. We all refused and we did not have misfortune. How can the spirit hear our prayers for rain, for rain that will not destroy, when we admit the worship of an unknown spirit in our own village – the centre of the kingdom?' Lubinda was feeling annoyed because Mpona did not appear to be making any effort to listen. 'That is what the headmen gathered at that fire are saying. They have sent me to tell you that this man who does not come to sorrow with others must go.'

'But the teacher went to the house of the widow. I saw him there with my own eyes,' commented the Chief.

'Yes, to the house of the widow. The house of the widow. Whose funeral is this? Is it hers or ours? Was he at the grave-yard? Was he there at the fire with us? Is he keeping the wake? No! He belongs to the white men and not to us. He even told the children, our own children, not to join in pagan mourning. That is what his religion says,' replied Lubinda.

Mpona cleared his throat. Lubinda was always organizing pressure groups to get him to do this or that. 'He thinks that I'm weak,' the Chief said to himself. 'I suppose it's my fault; I've given him too much say in everything.'

In his mind, Lubinda, as he went away, felt satisfied that he had planted the seed for the removal of the teacher. But he knew that if he was to reap the fruit he would have to keep cultivating the ground, because Mpona was incapable of action. There was danger in letting the teacher stay in the village. If he stayed, then the white men would establish themselves in the kingdom. Those white missionaries could become too powerful, and whoever they supported could also become very powerful. If Mpona was left alone he was bound to give in some day. But that was only if he was really left alone.

In another house where the fire had long died down and the occupants might be assumed to be asleep, the teacher and his wife were in fact still sitting up, unable to rest. The first cock had just crowed, but they still sat huddled together like rejected market fish. Outside the moon was in full bloom, washed clean by the torrential rains of the previous night. There was something serene, something peaceful and kindly about the face of that moon slowly creeping up the sky, with the rabbit on its face urging it on. You would not have thought that only the previous night it had been hidden by the tumult of quarrelling clouds, thunder, lightning, and rain. Looking at it on that night was like looking at the deep Kawe pool in the Luangwa river. It never looks more peaceful than when a crocodile has just pulled a human being into its inner caverns.

Outside the hut stood the wooden mortar into which the teacher's wife had been pounding groundnuts to add to the pumpkin leaves for relish. Standing with the pounding stick in it, it looked as though the woman at the mortar had just gone back into the house to add more fire to the pot. A little way off in the same yard was the low, long roof of the mud shelter which was the school. The walls had just been filled in and plastered with mud and the mud still smelt raw. A child or a pregnant woman who has eaten ant soil will know how the raw smell of the damp clay fills the nostrils. Tomorrow, if it had not been for this tragedy, he and the school-children would have been making the earth mounds where the children would sit. The small blackboard smeared into the wall still carried the legend of the alphabet.

Nanga uyu ndani?
'A' wamkulu, 'A' wamkulu
Dzina lace 'A'

('Who is this one? It is capital A, capital A. His name is A, capital A, capital A.')

That song, sung at the beginning of the class in the afternoon, was a rallying song. It was what attracted the pupils to the deep shade under the tree, which was the school until this new building was completed. The children loved to come to this place where they could shout and sing their heads off in screeching noise. The teacher, popularly referred to as Aphunzitsi, would be there among them exuding encouragement, mystical joy, and satisfaction. Even though he was new to the village he had come to love this school of his so much.

For him the construction of the new low mud-walled shelter was the fulfilment of a dream. It was his design; he had put everything that he had into this building, and to him it appeared to bubble with his soul. Every night he walked round it as he recited the rosary. He prayed God to bless every particle of mud that went into the building, every pole, every blade of grass. Some people had accused him of isolating himself from the adults of the village. But what did that matter to him? He was a shy man and one who would not dare impose himself on these people.

But tonight the sky, the school, and everything else stood in mute silence. And in the hut Nyalutila sat with his wife and his thoughts. The people had learnt to call him Aphunzitsi, which means 'teacher'. He had already, in the short period that he had been in the village, inspired so much reverence that to call him by his real name – Nyalutila – would have sounded disrespectful.

In a certain kind of way he was one of the village, and yet there was a manner in which he was not one of them. He was one of them because the Chief and some of the people had come to accept and respect him for the good man he was. Now and again, when he was allowed to, he joined in the people's mirth, and when the village was in sorrow he would join in the people's suffering – you do not need an invitation to sorrow with fellow men. But he was also an outsider because there were people who did not like his presence, people who felt that as a foreigner from Nyimba, when he came to sorrow with them he came to mock their misfortunes. He was not a son of the soil. He worshipped a strange god. Even if he might come to the sick-bed, what was the use of letting him stay there if he could not ask the spirits, in the language of him who was sick with suffering, to heal him, to let the poor man live? Instead Aphunzitsi came to the death-bed to remind a man that he still held to a pagan religion. The man had lived all his life that way and the teacher came, just when he was about to give up his ghost into the hands of the spirits of his ancestors, and said: 'You have worshipped the wrong god and unless you change in these last few seconds you are damned.'

Aphunzitsi was still asking himself the question, why did it have to happen this way? 'It is very bad, very sad,' said his wife for the hundredth time. She knew just how much her husband was suffering. She had just begun to be accepted into the community, and now this had happened and once again all the women in the village who had been so friendly to her were keeping to themselves. Is it not strange how, when people are in sorrow, they retreat from those who are not part of their family? They look at you with defiance, with fear that you might dilute their sufferings by trying to share them with them.

But in this instance the people of Mpona had gone even further. Upon hearing the news that early morning when Dulani's body was discovered, Aphunzitsi had gone straight to where the people were gathering, and his wife to the house of the widow.

But as soon as Lubinda had seen him, he had started to say things: 'Some people only come now because it is daylight. While we scoured the countryside for Dulani last night, they slept peacefully because they didn't want to be disturbed. How can we regard them as new friends?' The teacher had sat quietly but uneasily.

'Yes, this is true. They weren't even at the initiation ceremony, and yet the Chief thinks they are his special friends,' said Yuda.

'This village should know its friends. A friend is one who comes to comfort you in the darkness of difficulty, not when the sun has broken through the sky and the storm is no more,' continued Lubinda.

'If it's us from Cakuwamba that you're talking about, you rascals, we shall beat you up,' said one man from Cakuwamba, taking advantage of his being an asabwira.

'No, it isn't you,' said Lubinda. 'There are people here whose religion does not allow them to sorrow with us, because we are pagans. I know that they will not even be at

24

the funeral today because it is a pagan burial. Why don't they just go away now, back to the home their white missionaries have built them?'

The teacher did not move and continued to sit with his head cast down. After a while he stood up, and Lubinda said, 'Let him go. We don't want him here.'

When later his wife followed him, with the fowl which she had meant to offer to the mourners still in her hands, he found that she too had been humiliated. No one in the house had talked to her, and when she had pulled Mrs Lubinda aside to offer the fowl she had rasped, 'This is our sorrow, our funeral. We don't want your presents.'

That was why they were still sitting up into the early hours of the morning. That was why they did not dare go out to join the other men and women in keeping the wake.

'It is very bad indeed,' whispered Aphunzitsi in reply.

'You should try again.' said the wife after some silence. 'What will the people say if we continue here and do not join them?'

'I am a Christian,' said the Aphunzitsi. His temper was rising, and he was saying that he no longer cared. 'I am a Christian. I cannot mourn in the pagan way. They refused to allow me to pray for his soul, and now when we tried to give them our sympathy they spat on us.'

'What has your Christianity done for us since we came here? Who gives me salt when I have none? Is it not the women of this village? When did your priests ever give me salt?' Aphunzitsi kept quiet. His wife was right in what she was saying. This was not the time to quarrel with her. So he let her go on. 'When our child died at Nyimba, who buried him for us? Did your priests from Naviluli dig the grave or make the coffin? Did they even come to the funeral?'

His heart stirred like a fish as the woman began to weep. He clasped her hand in hand and the two wept silently. 'Namwase, mother of Mwase, you are right,' he mumbled. 'My son!' But in his heart he knew that it would have been wrong, a sin, for him to have gone to a pagan funeral. That was what the priests had taught him. It is a sin to attend the funeral of a pagan. It is a sin to join in or watch pagan dances. All these things are sins. Had Father Chiphwanya, who knew everything, not emphasized these points before sending him to this village? But it was these people, the thought kept coming back to his heart, who would bury his wife if she died, and not the white missionaries. So he stood up.

'You are going?' asked his wife's eyes as she watched him stand. He nodded. He walked to the tree under which all the male mourners lay spread out around the dying fire, feeling like a string of dowry beads about to be rejected. He had hardly sat down when the third cock crew and Lubinda returned from his early dawn interview with the Chief.

Shortly after that, when it was almost daylight, the people from the other villages began to leave. Just then, right out of the blue, literally out of the clear blue sky of the morning sun, there was a brief shower of rain. As the people went their ways, they were saying to each other, 'It is because a member of the royal family has died that it rains so.'

When the shower stopped, Mpona came out of his house. He surveyed the clear skies briefly and his eyes followed them to the horizon, where they became tucked into the ground. For a moment his eyes lingered over the rough-hewn precipice of the hills in the misty distance. His small nose sniffed at the horizon. He could smell the heavily-scented flowers and the hazy mist from the distant hills.

He looked at the rocks tarred with the dark brush of age and worn into furrows by the merciless hammering of the rain and the streamlets of water chasing each other into the valley. Then his thoughts turned back to the Kaunga river, the river that bounds the valley on the fourth side, the river that creeps along with unobtrusive quiet during the dry season. He thought of its calm, clear, water, of the fish turning their fat bellies down into the bottom of the clear water. Then of the peace of death that would descend upon the quiet waters and of the surface that would be carpeted with the fat bellies of sweet river bream. This was the Kaunga, which became a

26

vicious and vengeful terror during the rainy season, which had become clouded with the mud of turbulence and roared and galloped downstream in a mad bid to seek revenge. 'Dulani,' he sighed to himself.

He wondered whether the kingdom would remain the same after what had happened. He wondered about the teacher, the school, and the white men. He also wondered about the floods. Although the water had largely receded in the last two days, the maize plants did not seem to be standing up. They were all still like the grass in the elephant's path. But for the moment the main issue was Dulani's death.

Chapter 3

At the mission, activity was mounting. Within a week it would be Christmas. The crib had been prepared by the Father Superior, prepared with his own hands. It was a beautiful crib with dry grass, little carved animals, a bearded Joseph and a Mary aflame with beauty. Between them, lying in the crib with tiny hands held up high, was the infant Jesus. For Father Gonzago each year's crib was the result of thorough research, and it was quite different from that of the previous year. This year the infant Jesus, Mary, and Joseph had been painted black. This decision resulted in much acrimony between Father Oliver, popularly known as Chiphwanya, and the little Superior.

'You must not distort truth,' Father Chiphwanya had urged. 'Jesus was white, not black.'

'Father,' replied the soft-spoken little man, 'Jesus became Man. This is the most important mystery of the Nativity. It is as Man I am going to portray Him and it so happens that here in the valley – nay – I would go further, here in Northern Rhodesia, here in Africa, the majority are black.' The little man's eyes had shone with enthusiasm. They always did when he warmed to an argument. Then the eyes reminded you of a little rabbit glaring into the torch-light of the hunter. They looked so ardent and so innocent.

'Nonsense, Father Superior,' Chiphwanya retorted. 'These black people of yours must be taught that they owe everything to the white man – their health, their salvation from slavery, their salvation from hell. Do you realize that only five years ago the Cikunda were terrorizing these Nsengas? Do you realize that without us, the white men, the gospel would never have spread? Jesus had to be born white. No civilized person would have listened to a black Jesus.'

'Jesus did not have to be born at all. Jesus did not have to be born white. But He was born Man. That is the mystery for which we are grateful.' The old man always lifted his helmet at the mention of the name 'Jesus'. This up-and-down movement of the helmet and the quiet voice would have signalled to anyone else but Father Chiphwanya the feeling of determination in the man.

But Father Chiphwanya went on. 'That's rubbish. Rubbish! I have cause to know. You don't know a thing about it. You just sit here making your crib. This is your annual pilgrimage to Mecca. You are cultivating a false sense of pride in these people.' Father Chiphwanya clenched his fists. In shirt-sleeves his arms looked as big as thighs. The cloudy beard jutted out. In that split second, he was like a baroque statue of energy. The little Father Superior withdrew quietly, to continue with his work at the crib.

The little boys at the mission were practising for Christmas. Brother Aruppe, the small elderly brother who was the dogsbody of the mission, was sitting before the piano leading the choir practice:

> *Ku Betelehemu ku Betelehemu*
> *Mthenga wabwino*
> *Virgo Woyera, Virgo Woyera*
> *Anabala mwana*
> *Wabadwa Klistu*
> *Momboli wathu*
> *Angelo onse*
> *Amlemekeza*
> *Abusa aimba, Mafumu agwada*
> *Anthu onse akondwera.*

('From Bethlehem there is a joyful message. The Holy Virgin gave birth. Christ is born, our Redeemer. All the angels worship. The shepherds sing. The Kings kneel before him and all the people rejoice.')

Brother Aruppe was a small man with a weather-beaten scaly skin, hairy arms, and a back curved into a bow from lifting heavy bags and stones. His head was pointed, and only at the apex was there any sign of visible hair-growth. He was so light and small that sitting there before the enormous organ he looked like an ugly little sparrow treading on a heap of maize. He was warming up to the music, to the children's throaty singing. Sweat was shining through his thick khaki shirt, and although one did not normally laugh in church, he was smiling with glee as he bounced up and down on this enormous machine. You could feel Christmas approaching: the large crowds that would come to the mission, the goats that would be slaughtered by the missionaries as a special treat, the plentiful supply of mealie-meal, the large succulent mangoes that were being gathered in to ripen so that they could be distributed to the people, the sweets, the sports that would follow – the brother's enthusiasm reminded the small boys of these and many other things. It reminded them of how the church would fill up at the evening prayers before Christmas, how they as the alapazi, the boarders, would walk into the church in a march, with their uniforms labelled 'Katondwe', and how the villagers, some of whom had come from as far away as beyond Mpona would look at them and admire. This was Christmas. Then there might be rain on Christmas Day itself and if that happened they might run back to their dormitories, to sing and jabber among themselves. Maybe if the teacher was not there, they could run into the rain for a brief shower. But it was the rich goat-meat, the prospect of much nsima and all those other things that made Christmas so different from other feasts. Besides, tomorrow on Christmas Day they would be able to go to the priests and say, 'Kisimisi box, Father' and the priest would have to give them something.

Father Chiphwanya was busy in other fields. He had already

sent out more than a hundred Christmas cards to friends all over Europe, and to a few in Northern Rhodesia. All along the wall of his room were many more cards which had found their way to the world-famous man hidden behind the forgotten world.

Brother Aruppe's eye caught the Christmas cards in the Father's room as he walked from the church after the final rehearsal before Christmas. He stood at the window, gazing at the cards. There was one which attracted him most. It was a simple picture of a child looking at a crib. In the crib the little Jesus was sitting up with outstretched and eager arms, and the child was running towards the crib. So eager they both looked! Squeezing his nose to the glass pane, Aruppe could read the writing on it. 'A Blessed Christmas. I am the food of Life.'

He had not seen Father Chiphwanya in the room. So when the priest shot up to the window and called out, 'What is it, Aruppe?' the little brother was embarrassed. He walked round to the door, and after knocking, was admitted into the room, which had been completely transformed.

'They are beautiful cards,' said Aruppe, after some time, 'Beautiful.' Father Chiphwanya did not reply. He went on writing and whistling to himself as though there was no one in his room.

'Father,' said Aruppe, after walking round the room. 'This is a beautiful card.'

'You like it, eh?' asked Father Chiphwanya without looking up.

'Look at the curves, the idea of speed, and the eagerness of the two.' It was the same card that the brother had spotted through the window. Father Chiphwanya looked up and found Aruppe's thick hairy fingers caressing the picture.

'Take your fingers off that card!' bellowed Chiphwanya.

'I'm sorry, Father,' said the brother, too absorbed to understand the full venom of Chiphwanya's words. 'They are so beautiful, these cards, Father,' he said, turning to him, 'why don't you put some of these in the dining-room? I could go in there and see them without disturbing you. I have no cards, and I am sure Father Superior would be pleased with these.' Father Chiphwanya knit his brows. He could no longer concentrate, even though he was merely addressing envelopes. 'Go away, Brother!' he said. 'You might as well ask me to hang up a Michelangelo on a village tree among these primitive Africans.'

Brother Aruppe stood quietly. 'Father Oliver is an important and clever man. Maybe I have disturbed him,' he said to himself. So he walked out of the room carrying with him the longing memory of the child and his Jesus, the shining stars, the snow-capped landscapes, the beautiful churches, and the crucifix built into the Christmas tree with its leaves and lit branches. These were the things that the well-to-do did with Christmas in his country. It was so beautiful.

Father Chiphwanya settled down to his job of writing. He had finished with the cards. They would not reach their destination until long after Christmas, but he had written them. He was now writing to his sister in Cracow: 'Imagine a young man on the dust heap. He sees many young and happy men and women pass by and rush on to festivities. That is me, Anatolia; being in Africa, especially in this part of the world, is like being on a dust heap. Even for me, renouncing all the pleasures of the flesh, it is difficult. Tomorrow is Christmas. There will be nothing to look forward to except the hordes of half-naked unwashed natives begging for presents. And my so-called colleagues at the mission? Well, they are Europeans of course. But they have an advantage over you and me for this kind of life. They were never brought up in a castle. One of them I believe was an illegitimate child. Perhaps I should not be talking in this way to a laywoman. But, my dear Anatolia, you know that you are my only window upon the world, the only one to whom I can open my heart. Well, I will miss you a lot tomorrow, but think of me. I am praying for you and I know that my friends here have been praying for you ever since I told them you were going to be operated upon. I am so glad to know you are better.'

Father Chiphwanya turned over the page to write on the other side. His thoughts were thousands of miles away. He thought of the chimes that used to break over Cracow at midnight to announce the arrival of Christmas, of the many Christmas trees that used to glitter and grace the windows of the houses, of the tinsel decorations upon these trees and the load of presents that would bend the branches down. He thought of the turkey dishes and the rich Christmas cakes. He thought of himself there at the altar saying the midnight mass before a packed congregation of dignitaries. There he could speak his true thoughts and be understood. There he could use his oratory in the service of God. Then there were the babies in lily-white baptismal gowns to be baptized on Christmas Day. His thoughts reverted to the midnight mass. He would stand before them all in his white vestments streaked with red-gold borders, and calling out loud and clear he would announce the birth of the infant Jesus.

A lizard clambering up the wall fell with a heavy thud. This brought him back. He looked through the window. The strong light of the hot sun made him blink after the cloudy scenes of a snowy Christmas. There was an old emaciated man in dirty rags walking towards the house. From the manner he felt his way with his stick he appeared to be blind. The old man carried something, but Father Chiphwanya could not see, in the sudden glare of the light, what it was. He stood up to go and drink some water in the dining-room. There he saw a solitary card on the wall. It was from the Monseigneur in Lusaka. That and his own cards were the only cards in the mission. As he drank his water, he saw a kind of Christmas tree in the corner of the room. It was just an ordinary twig covered in cotton wool. Brother Aruppe had scrawled a 'Happy Xmas' and put it round the twig like a halo. Father Chiphwanya laughed to himself at the rough drawing of a child and Jesus in the crib which Brother Aruppe had put in the middle of the branch. As he was returning to his room he saw the old blind man.

'Father Superior?' asked the blind man as he heard Chiphwanya's footsteps.

Father Chiphwanya looked at the figure. 'Beggars, all of them,' he said to himself and went off.

'A fowl for Father Superior,' cried the beggar after the priest who had just passed. 'It is my Christmas present to him.' Father Chiphwanya did not look back.

Christmas passed quietly. In the evening, as the religious community sat down for the meal – which was the remains from the luncheon – Father Superior turned to Father Chiphwanya.

'Father Oliver, have you heard?'

'What?' asked Father Chiphwanya, his glasses resting on the bone that he was doing justice to.

'There was an old man here yesterday. He brought me a fowl,' replied the Superior.

'This isn't the chicken we are eating?' exclaimed Father Chiphwanya, stopping eating. He was about to spit the chicken out when the Superior said, 'No, that one has been fattened, but it was a good chicken. The blind man talked about Mpona. He told me that there was a strange death in Mpona's village a week ago.'

'Oh, somebody bewitched, no doubt. How interesting,' replied Father Chiphwanya.

'No,' replied the Superior, 'someone died of drowning and constriction by a python, both at the same time.' Father Superior was thoughtful. He had read a lot about magical deaths in Africa, but this one was odd. 'Strange, isn't it?' he asked finally, looking up at Father Chiphwanya.

'I suppose if he had died first of drowning and then of constriction, you wouldn't have found it strange,' Father Chiphwanya chuckled, beard shaking. He had become so ill-tempered of late that, when Father Superior saw him chuckle, he too laughed aloud. Brother Aruppe joined in. He raised a mug of water and toasted, 'A Merry Christmas.' Immediately a cloudburst of ill-temper descended upon Father Chiphwanya's bushy brows. 'They don't understand cynicism,' he

34

muttered to himself. 'Look, Father Superior, there is nothing strange about what you are saying. It is no more unnatural than you here dying from over-eating,' he said.

'But that is not my point, Father,' replied the old man. 'There is a vital matter about this business which I thought would concern you.' The waiter passed the large plates of chopped-up sugared oranges around. First to Father Superior, then to Chiphwanya, and last and least, of course, to Brother Aruppe. Tonight they were having a special treat – a brew of American coffee, which had been sent all the way from the States by an admirer of Father Chiphwanya's.

'You see,' resumed Father Superior after thanking the waiter, 'the people think that this man was bewitched. Right now they have their knife in the teacher, your teacher, and unless something is done they are going to chase him away, or kill him. You have heard of ritual murder, haven't you? There is plenty of it among the tribes of the Union of South Africa, and also among the Lozi of Barotseland. By killing the teacher in this way, they hope to mix his blood up with the grain and, although it is now too late to plant, normally if they did this there would be a bumper harvest. The floods have apparently swept away all the maize.'

'But they can't do that to a Christian. They can't do that to one of our men,' protested Father Chiphwanya, at last beginning to see the seriousness of the situation. 'Who are these men? I will have them arrested and charged under the Witchcraft Ordinance.'

Brother Aruppe was listening intently. For him there was no doubt that there were witches in Africa. He had lived too long in Africa not to know that this was truly the case. Had he not, some years back, found the body of one of the mission staff who had died and been buried, cut up, and partly roasted? If that was not witchcraft, then what was it? Father Chiphwanya looked at Aruppe. He read fear in his eyes, almost a pleading that he should not be sent away.

'Go away, Aruppe,' ordered Father Chiphwanya. In doing so he was certain that he was protecting him from temptation.

Father Gonzago remained quiet for some time. He was thinking of Mpona. It was a long while since he had last seen him but he could still remember the slight frame, which looked like a rich green banana leaf that had been seared by a wild fire over and over. Then there were the ribs on his chest, which stood out like the bars of a xylophone; and the booming cough and the thick phlegm that tumbled out of his jaws like a clot of blood. He remembered the attentive ears, forever pricked, and the distant eyes listening for sounds beyond this life. He wondered about Mpona. He wondered what the news of this violent death would bring to the kingdom. In his mind he saw the lush green vegetation, the strong scent of the many tropical shrubs, and the hot damp air in the pit of the valley. He remembered how enervating it had felt but also how blissful it must be to swim day in and day out in the liquid of the placenta that was the valley. He wondered whether this thing which had just happened would shatter the peace of the valley.

Would Mpona be safe? He asked himself the question again. For him the gospel was to be brought through the old people rather than the children. It was the old people who stood nearest to the Day of Judgement. Anything learnt in childhood was bound to be forgotten in adult life unless there was a connecting ladder between the old and the new. Mpona could be such a ladder (even though he might die a pagan) because he was a good man. The Father Superior sat quiet for a long time thinking about the strange death of Dulani. Would the affair end suddenly, just as it had come, or would the people finally march to the Cave to throw into its bowels those that they thought had bewitched Dulani? The people talked of there being a long white snake, bees, and a one-armed giant in this Cave, he recalled. It was of course only superstition, he reminded himself. But he remembered how frightened the people had been when he had tried to enter the Cave, from which it was said no one returned alive.

Very early the following morning Father Chiphwanya was on his motor-cycle, speeding away from the mission at

Katondwe to Mpona, twenty miles away. Incensed by what the Father Superior had told him the previous night, he rode on down the Luangwa river, into which the Kaunga pours its muddy tempest.

Katondwe Mission stood half-way between Mpona's village and Feira Boma, and although it was within Mpona's area it was not part of his kingdom, because the white men inhabited it.

The mission stood on a knoll in the great Kaunga Valley. This part of the valley was rocky and arid and the mopani trees, which normally belong to the hills, had to push their roots deep down into the ground to avoid drying up. On the highest point of this rocky knoll stood the little chapel. Built of red brick and large, smooth rocks, it was a beautiful example of Polish architecture. The Gothic dome capped by shining aluminium was a miniature St Peter's, proclaiming loud and clear to Jews and Gentiles alike the arrival of the white man's religion in a land of heathens.

A mile away from the mission proper could be seen a low muddy wall with a plain cross before it: the cemetery for the burial of white men and Christian natives. You might think this the greatest outrage against nature, that the dead should be buried among the people, as if death was nothing! If you had entered the cemetery and turned left, you would have found there a small house into which the white man shelved the bodies of all his fellow white men who had died. Here in this hut you would have seen an archbishop, who had died on his way from Zumbo and whose remains had been brought thither; the body of Father John, still lying tall and erect; and a young man who had died of malaria, trying to carry the Gospel to as many as possible. When his body had been dressed up and he lay in the church, the rosary beads woven round his fingers, the biretta on his head, and the chalice in his hands, how much like a living man he looked – yet he was dead. Dead at thirty-five from the malaria from which he had cured so many people.

Move on to the other bodies on the shelves and briefly look

at the death-grimaces that were once human faces. You would see the scraped skulls and the bones stretched out and you would ask what the purpose of life really was. By the time you have finished with your inspection you would have counted twelve skeletons, the toll which malaria had extracted from the white man in two years.

This macabre sight would have so frightened you that if you had looked up and seen the insignificant form of a little, dried-up old man pacing up and down among the graves and reciting the breviary, you would have recoiled with terror, for he too should have been in this house of horrors, and yet he was not. In 1948 that man would be Father Gonzago, the Superior of the mission and the most regular visitor to the cemetery. He had been at this mission for close upon ten years now. What he was now, what position he had at the mission, he owed entirely to the workings of nature. All those who could have led the mission, all the men of action, had died.

Father Gonzago was retiring, blissful in prayer and happy to obey. Thus it was that although he was saluted every day as Father Superior, the real ruler, commander and general of the mission was Father Paul Oliver, known as Father Chiphwanya by the natives at the mission. He was tall and roughly built, and he had a stormy temper. His white cassock was tightly filled out, tattered, and patched. He had bushy eyebrows and a face clouded with the grimness of thunder about to explode. But perhaps these external features belied the inner man; he might have been one of those people who are ashamed to weep in public, and yet will break down inwardly?

Such a man was Father Chiphwanya, S.J., the man who met the few schoolboys and workers at the mission as communicants in church, as servants at table, and as pagan souls to be instructed in the classroom. Now and again a worker died. With the preoccupation of a man thinking of higher things he mumbled blessings over the starved body and sprayed holy water across it with the glumness of a spitting

38

cobra. Afterwards he would roughly turn to the people and order them to bury the remains, and then stride off to take his four o'clock tea. The people might not understand how a person could leave the graveside before a body was buried, but they had come to accept that the white man was not an ordinary man like themselves, that he was a superior being and could do anything he wished.

Father Chiphwanya was erudite. He read Shakespeare with the same ease that he recited his breviary. Every month scores of letters poured into the mission, offering this or that donation towards his work. Without him, as he was often wont to remind the little Father Superior, the mission would be dead and he, Father Superior, would be forced 'to feast off the skulls of those mummies' in the cemetery.

Did Father Superior know that most of what the mission had, did not come from the Pope in Rome, but from Father Chiphwanya's friends in Poland, in Britain, Ireland and America? He chuckled away at their invitations. 'If only they knew,' he said ruefully to himself, 'that those who come to Katondwe never return.' This was Father Chiphwanya, Ph.D., D.Sc. (Cracow), an eminent scholar, a brilliant correspondent and a scientist of world renown, now reduced to the management of two small catechism classes, and to having to put up for the rest of his life, with the company of a blissful idiot, as he called him, of a little Superior, Father Gonzago; and a little illiterate Brother.

He owed the Monseigneur in Lusaka a grudge for having sent him to this lonely outpost after he had been his private secretary. What had he done to deserve this? He reflected deeply on the Jesuit vow of Obedience. Ignatius Loyola, that pathetically simple and uncomplicated soldier, he said to himself, had never foreseen how some of the Superiors would use this stick to entrench their positions. Jesuit discipline was all right, so long as those who exercised it were worthy men. But on the other hand, he was grateful for the opportunity that this posting had given him. With an aged man for a superior all that happened at the mission could only happen because of him, Father Oliver. Soon enough those in Lusaka would be forced to acknowledge his work.

To him the work was clear. It did not consist simply in baptizing people, but also in curing them. Curing them of their bodily diseases as well as the ills of their minds. The natives had to be forced into becoming Christians. They also had to be forced to abandon superstition. He was appalled by the Father Superior, who would rather have let the natives go on living as they had always done. He was appalled by the District Commissioner at the Boma, who seemed to do nothing to force the people to change their ways. But he had a plan of his own for them. Already he was striking at the heart of superstition and witchcraft. He had sent a teacher to Mpona's village itself to destroy superstition and teach the Gospel. That was why Father Chiphwanya had hope. That was why he had contempt for the people who could not act, and that was why he had transformed the mission into a commando post. That was why, above all, he did not waste any time in the indulgence of a Christmas Boxing Day holiday, but sped on to Mpona, tearing and roaring through the intervening villages like a whirlwind.

In his heart, Father Chiphwanya was saying that he would fix that native of a chief. After all that he had done for him and his people, how could he stab him in the back by closing the school? What right did he have to threaten the tacher? There was no need to draw up a plan of his strategy. Mpona simply had to be told.

The cycle dipped into the Kaulungu stream. He was tempted to stop a while there and rest under the cool shade of the leafy tree. The water in the stream was sparkling clear as it gently flowed under the low make-shift earth bridge which the people had been forced to construct a year ago for the white men at the Boma at Feira. But he went on. Just before reaching Mwabvi's village, he rode off into the bush in order to avoid a crowd of people. Father Chiphwanya was very angry with them for not giving way. But when he realized that they were carrying a corpse to the burial place, he relented and simply asked, 'A Christian?'

'No,' said the man at the head of the procession.

'A pagan!' yelled the priest, 'why didn't you call me to baptize him? Satan! Satan! If you don't bring your sick to the mission, I will tell the D.C. to imprison you.'

'Yes, bwana,' replied the leader meekly.

'Where's the graveyard?' asked Father Chiphwanya, whose anger had not as yet subsided and required propitiation. The leader pointed his folded hand in the western direction.

'Ah, yes,' hissed the priest, 'I have caught you out. You believe in witchcraft. You think I don't know why you fold your hand? You think that if you point the graveyard out with your straight finger you will become lame, don't you?'

'Yes,' replied the leader. The crowd was hushed and cowed. Even a dead man had to give way to the European.

When Father Chiphwanya went off, the people started to whisper among themselves.

'This is what I was saying,' said one. 'At the edge of the village the tree collapsed in our way. Now we meet a white man who speaks to us as though we are going to a dance.'

'This is taboo, I tell you. I will not be surprised if, when we try to bury this man who has left us, the body will rise up again,' said another.

Father Chiphwanya sped on through Cusowe, Ntalasha, Kasinsa, Ciwera, and then he turned left to Mpona. He found that the children had already been alerted by the sound of his motor-cycle and were excitedly awaiting his arrival. Upon seeing him, the men quickly made their way to Mpona's court until there were there not only Mpona and Lubinda, but also Yuda, who limped to the place as quickly as he could, Banda, Cumba, Simbeya who hobbled thither, Simtowe, Silwamia, Simoni and many others in the village.

The men were sitting quietly and glumly, but there was fear in their hearts. Only Lubinda appeared to take the situation in his stride. 'We shall see what he wants. If it is the school, we don't want it here.'

When Chiphwanya had come to Mpona for the first time he had been received with pomp and ceremony, and borne skyhigh by the singing crowd. Today there were only the children. So Father Chiphwanya knew that something had gone wrong.

'Where is the Chief?' Father Chiphwanya inquired of the children. 'Where is the teacher, Aphunzitsi?' was his next inquiry.

'Why is the school not open, teacher?' asked the priest, after locating the teacher, who was sitting disconsolately at his house. The teacher could not answer. In the last few months the teacher appeared to have shrunk to half his former size.

'Why is the school closed?'

'Father, these people here do not want the school. They are pagans and they want to kill me,' whispered the teacher.

'Is it true a man died here? And is that why you did not come to the mission for Christmas mass?' asked the priest.

'I am not feeling well, Father. I have been vomiting and my body trembles, so I could not come,' replied the teacher. 'But I prayed in my house.'

'That is not good enough. Mass is mass,' replied the priest rather angrily.

'Yes, Father, I am sorry. A man died and they say it was I who killed him. Can you take me away, Father, back to my home?' pleaded the teacher.

The men at the court saw Father Chiphwanya stride towards Natombi's house. Even the goats seemed to know that this man was white, because as he approached them they ran away, bleating. Natombi was in the house. She had been inside ever since the funeral. Only at night did she come out to breathe some fresh air. The teacher reluctantly said, 'Odi', and it was only after some persuasion that she came out of the hut and knelt down at a distance from the two men. The people at the court observed what was happening.

Father Chiphwanya looked at the frail frame of the woman kneeling before him. She was tender and greatly emaciated. Her cheek-bones stood out and the little flesh left on her face was tightly stretched over them. Her eyes, when now and again she looked up, were deep and sunken from sorrow and hunger, and the arms were those of a skeleton. Father Chiphwanya looked at her. Somehow she reminded him of his sister in her structure. Sorrow clouded his chest and instinctively he took a step towards her, clasped her hand in his and said, 'Woman, I am sorry for what has happened to you.'

Abashed, the woman ran trembling back into the hut. The men beckoned to each other. They could not believe what they were seeing. But the women also were peeping at this scene through the urine holes in the huts.

Then the priest marched towards the court. The men at the court prepared themselves for the worst. The teacher followed reluctantly several steps behind.

'I hear you are in sorrow,' said the priest.

'Yes, it is true,' replied Mpona.

'But the school must open,' said the priest.

'Do not agree,' intervened Lubinda, not giving the Chief an opportunity to speak. A momentary flush of anger passed over the Chief's face.

'You must not agree. It is his teacher who has caused all these things. Before this school came here and the white man came, such strange things never happened here. We do not want a school and we do not want your church here. We can worship in the way that we have always done.'

'Mpona! Do you hear me? The school must open,' said the priest.

'The school will not open. Tell him that. We have all agreed already that it will not open. To open the school so that this white man can teach our boys to hold hands with girls the way he has been doing with that woman? How can a woman who has lost a husband agree to this, and in the open before all our eyes? We do not want the school here, it has brought witchcraft. Does this white one know how his teacher has been behaving here?' asked Lubinda.

A whirlwind formed in the corner of the village. Slowly at

first, then gathering momentum, it sucked up loose grass and leaves. Quickly it sidled towards the court, and without warning it swept off the roof of the court, leaving the council covered in dust.

'Mpona, I want to hear from you. The school opens tomorrow or else I will tell the D.C. about it. If you do not allow the teacher to teach religion, I will punish you. This village will have plague. The fire of God will descend on it,' said the priest.

The Chief looked at Lubinda. Lubinda looked at the others in turn, at Simbeya, at Yuda; he looked into the face of Banda, of Simtowe, of Silwamia. He looked straight at Cumba, at them all. But they were all cowed and silent. They were not going to speak out in the presence of the white man. Lubinda shot a glance at Aphunzitsi. 'If you leave this man here we shall see what we shall see. He bewitched our man because of this woman, the woman with whom you have been touching hands. You despise us, and you do not respect our customs. This village is going to be destroyed by the spirits of our ancestors if we agree to this.'

'School tomorrow! And anyone who does not send his child to school will hear from the Boma,' said the priest, turning to go away. In his heart he felt rather pleased with the way things had gone. He had expected more hostility, perhaps even a spear. After all, this was what the School of Oriental Studies had prepared him for in its orientation programme in London. He remembered the advice of one of the lecturers who had himself been a D.C. in Kenya: 'Always be firm with the native.' It seemed that policy would pay. As he sped off he chuckled to himself. These natives would go to endless trouble to explain the whirlwind. Scientific in a curious way, weren't they?

'Go and tell your mother and your grandmother to open the school for themselves,' Cumba shouted after the priest, long after he had gone. The atmosphere eased and the group laughed. But the Chief remained pensive and withdrawn. His distant eyes looked even more distant now.

44

Chapter 4

Simtowe was sitting on one side of the shed that was used as an arts and crafts centre for all the men at Mpona's village. It was a large, round, grass-thatched shed built around a tree which was still growing. Every afternoon the men gathered here after their labours in the fields to repair their hoes, sharpen their axes, weave new baskets, both for their women and for catching fish, and do many other odd jobs. Sometimes the nsaka, as the place was called, was full to capacity and many of these self-taught craftsmen would spill out into the sheds of the other trees near by. Sometimes, like today, there were only a few people because some would be at their fields still, putting in the last ounce of energy that might make all the difference between starvation and plenty.

Simtowe was carving an axe handle out of a hardy piece of mupani wood. He had completed all the rough work, and the outline of the handle could now be seen. Only the smoothing off was left to do. He ran and re-ran the sharp, carved, iron blade sensitively over the head of the handle. A grin of satisfaction broke across his mouth. The handle felt firm and smooth, and he gripped it as if he was about to cut a log of wood. He beckoned to Silwamia, who was busy near him at his furnace. The furnace was a goat-skin bag with two open slits where the handles fitted, with a clay pipe which led to a shallow hole containing charcoal at the other end.

'See,' said Simtowe, 'I told you it would be good, didn't I?' He held up the handle for Silwamia to see.

'Beautiful,' replied Silwamia, who went on blowing the

furnace. 'Now you really deserve a new wife, even though you do look like a porcupine.' Simtowe laughed. The flame shot through the charcoal, first an uncertain blue flame, then red, and finally white hot.

'Put my rod in there, I want to bore a hole for the axe. That is what you have to pay me for laughing at my pretty face,' said Simtowe.

'Those two don't always seem to agree, do they?' observed Simtowe as he struggled with the red-hot rod burning into the axe. 'But the school has re-opened.'

'That was a childish thing,' said Silwamia, pausing. 'You can't oppose a white man like that. The trouble with this village and this kingdom, my friend, is that we all want to be chiefs,' he added in a whisper. 'But Mpona is watching all these things and one day he is going to strike. These people have forgotten what Mpona really is. Before he went mad, my friend, Mpona was a terror even to his court and the headmen. That's why they bewitched him and he went mad. And don't you find it strange that the Chief became mad within the first few months of Lubinda becoming his Councillor?'

'Is it true that it was Mpona who did not want Lubinda to become Councillor?' asked Simtowe. He had stopped pumping the bellows and was now leaning sideways towards Silwamia to capture every word.

'It wasn't only Mpona. None of us was very happy with Lubinda. A long time ago, Lubinda's people came from the land of the Lozi. They have a lot of witchcraft there and that's why he's the village medicine man today. Also, there is some doubt about whether he is legitimate. It seems that he is a bush child. Lubinda knew that the Chief was not happy with him. Maybe that's why he decided to fix him by carrying on with the Chief's young wife.'

'And the Chief knows who it was?' asked Silwamia.

'He's not foolish. I tell you, one of these days he's going to strike. Mpona, if he is still the same man, is a cobra. Don't deceive yourself. I swear by my daughter Kasimbi that you will see what you have never seen.'

'You think, then, that he too has medicine?' asked Silwamia.

'Medicine? Why do you think Lubinda can't touch him? He has tried to topple him. The other night – was it a month ago? – he went to the palace. But, just when he'd entered, the whole place was covered with a thick mist like the fulele on top of Kaongole hill. So he couldn't do his work of bewitching the chief because he couldn't find him. Instead, the Chief caught him, stark naked.'

'Yah!' was all Silwamia could say.

'Why do you think the Chief is more often with Simbeya than Lubinda, his Councillor? Have you ever seen a leper like Simbeya become such a close friend of the court as in this village? Simbeya is the anchor of his canoe. He trusts Simbeya because he protects him from witchcraft. You will see how the Yudas, Bandas, and even Ciwera are going to perish with Lubinda. Here comes Cumba. I wonder what he's going to laugh about today.'

Silwamia tucked his black loin-cloth further into his stomach so that it rubbed tightly against his thighs. His bare back arched over the bellows and, slowly at first, he began to move his arms up and down like rusty pistons. Then he picked up speed and the furnace, which had died down, once more became a halo of white flame. Perspiration coursed down his narrow, lean back as his shoulder-blades pushed the hands down, only to be pushed out at the next movement. Looking at the massive, rock-like hands and the shoulder blades separately, they seemed like a man struggling with a crocodile in the middle of the terrible Kawa pool in the Luangwa river.

Simtowe had also resumed in earnest his work of boring a hole through the axe handle. His head was cocked on one side and the head of the handle was almost diagonally opposite his eyes. That was the only way in which he could look at an object squarely, by putting it away from his direct vision. Many years ago, at birth, he had had clear and straight eyesight. But it was said that when the child was given to its grandmother for her to see it, she put some medicine into its

47

eyes, and within a few days both eyes squinted. When he grew up Simtowe had been struck by a further misfortune; the left eye had developed a cataract which now covered the whole pupil. He thus had a sideways and blank look about him which reminded people of the old one-eyed, one-haired, one-legged woman of the folk stories who begged from the young men, who, when they did not give her alms, suddenly found that their wives had become one-eyed, one-legged and one-haired. He wore nothing but a torn black loin-cloth. Unlike Silwamia, whose head looked as hard as a dried coconut, his head was soft and well-shaped, with luxuriant grey hair.

With much sighing Cumba set down his load – a block of wood a foot square hewn from a tree trunk. He wiped the sweat from his brow. The other two did not look up. He sighed again and this time they both looked up.

'Simtowe,' called out Cumba, 'why do you look at me as if I were muck? Look straight at me instead of looking at me like a wounded buffalo.'

'You see what I said?' said Simtowe to Silwamia. 'He's always making fun of others. And what's this great load you're carrying Cumba?'

'This? It's nothing,' replied Cumba. 'My mother-in-law, she thinks I married a beauty. She doesn't see the pock-marks on her daughter's skin, the marks which make her look like a rotting hippo that has been pecked at by crows. Even her nose is like a hippo's. So she keeps on giving me job after job. Make this for me! Make that! Do this! Do that! One of these days I'll make her coffin and I'll be glad of it.'

The conversation turned to the maize. They had feared that the whole maize crop would be ruined by the floods that had killed Dulani. However, one by one the maize plants were standing up again and the fields were green once more. Most of the crop had been spared, since the floods had receded so quickly. Now the flowers were beginning to shoot and soon the fields would be a golden sea. So the people did not worry unduly about the floods. It was one of those things; no rain beyond a brief shower for many years, and when it came, floods. You just had to wait. After all, you could be dead before the harvest, bewitched by someone. So why worry?

The three men packed up their tools. All the other people had gone already. The sun was a raw red wound, its clear rays were still stabbing the sky as if they were staging a last act of defiance. Suddenly an excited cry came through from the village.

'Zombe, zombe!' the children were shouting.

The three men looked at each other in horror. Had they all heard what each one had heard?

'Zombe, zombe!' shouted the children again.

The men's knees trembled and fear masked their faces. They looked up into the sky, and there was a brown sheet of locusts sailing across it. The sheet rolled over to the ground and they could now see, against the setting sun, how large a swarm it was. These locusts could be going to one place only – the maize fields. The cloud of despair, which had lifted after the maize had begun to recover from the floods, was descending again upon the village; it was a nervous people that gathered at the Chief's court, to plan a strategy against this new invasion.

The children were as happy to see the locusts as they were to see a downpour, in which they would stand until they were soaked. Locusts had last visited the kingdom seven years ago. Few of these children had been born then, and certainly none of them could remember the visit. Already they had improvised bows and arrows and were busy shooting at the insects that settled near the village. The village was full of the shrieks and laughter of the children. Tonight they would fill their frying-pans with them. If the insects tasted like nthonthwa, the small, fat green grasshoppers, then they could wish for no better delicacy.

At the court some of the elders had assembled, and a number of rapid actions were being planned within the royal enclosure. The Chief was sitting on a stool, with everyone squatting on the floor before him. Now and again he would stand up to look across the fence at the further hordes of locusts flying in. He was impatient, even jittery, as his eyes flitted from one fence to the other.

'These locusts must be fought here and not allowed to go farther into the kingdom. Those blue hills they have flown across must be the last hills they see,' he said after listening to the debate. 'Silwamia, go to Mkando and tell all the people there to come and fight the locusts from the east side. Banda, go to Ciwera, and Simtowe to Kanaventi. Lubinda, you will take charge here. When the first cock crows you will all go to the fields, men and women, and attack the vermin.' It was the old Mpona come to life again, the old Mpona impatient of debate, ruthless, quick to take action. 'If we don't catch these insects, even the little maize which has survived the floods will go.'

By first cock-crow, when the earth turns quiet and the night cold, the men and women of Mpona, of Mkando, of Kanaventi, and of Ciwera were in the fields of Mpona village, shivering, sweeping the locusts off the maize stalks and tree branches into their baskets and jars. You don't need any incentive to catch locusts, because once you fill a jar with them you will have relish for a long time to come. They harm the maize but, on the other hand, once they have come you can't just catch them and then destroy them as if they were snakes.

Thus, what had set out to be a counter-attack on the locusts, actually became a pleasurable harvest. There was even something exhilarating about going into the deep of the maize stalks in the dark hours of early dawn with the cold green leaves washing against one's bare body, the locusts drumming into one's jar like a landslide into the water, while all the time they were chewing up the leaves. One didn't worry about the sharp, prickly legs of the insects; one just pushed them into the jar until it was full, and then fetched another jar.

The villagers did not notice the passage of time. They did not always remember that they had come out to crush dangerous insects. From being a crucial battle, it turned into a sport; then into a hunt for food if they were in need of relish. Only when full light broke upon their activities did they discover the full horror: every leaf had been eaten, and even stalks had been chewed. There was nothing but desolation. This time hunger had come. The marauding cloud went from one village to the other until, in the end, the whole kingdom was a scorched battlefield of blackened maize stalks.

In Mpona, people were dazed. There was no longer any point in continuing to work when what had been saved from the floods could be so tragically wrenched from their labour-blistered hands. Who could see any hope for tomorrow when rains were not likely to come for another five years? There might be a shower next year, but what use was a shower? You cannot put out an underground fire with a shower.

'These things surprise me,' said Mpona to his confidant, Simbeya. 'What has this village done to deserve all this? First there was the strange death of Dulani, my own cousin, and that after so many strange things had happened. Then came the whirlwind, a whirlwind which went straight for my roof. And now the locusts! It was my field they settled on first. What can all this mean? Do the spirits want me to give up the throne? If I stay, Simbeya, there will be more disasters until we are all dead.'

'But if you go, who can rule? There is no one else that the people in this village and the people in the kingdom trust,' replied Simbeya.

The old man was like a wizened owl. He had come to value Mpona, who could be trusted, and had the interests of all at heart. Also it was because of him that Simbeya was still in the village. It was Mpona who had decreed that lepers should not be treated in the same manner as people with smallpox. So he was in the village instead of in the cave outside the village. He could sit in his house or outside it, and play with his grandchildren, knowing that soon enough his old wife would come to join them and bring food. He knew that his grandchildren would feed him even when the time came when he had no fingers left. To know that one could continue to enjoy the warmth of domestic love as if one were whole was something to be grateful for. That is why Simbeya cared for the Chief; that is why from the bottom of his heart he was saying, 'You cannot go. Who will rule if you go? You must fight against this bad luck.'

'But you know I cannot fight,' replied Mpona. 'This village is possessed with ill omen. This kingdom is doomed. I can fight one man. I can fight two, many more and even the whole kingdom. But I cannot fight the spirits of our ancestors. I cannot.'

Mpona, with his distant eyes, was looking earnestly into Simbeya's eyes. Many times before now it was the old man who had resolved crises for him. Even his being chosen as Chief had been determined by Simbeya's insistence.

'That is where you go wrong. The spirits of our ancestors are all good spirits. They do not torture goodness. I may be an old man, Chief, but I see what I see. Someone in this village is doing all these things to embarrass you because he does not want you here. It is this someone that you must fight. Fight, fight! That's the only answer. And in the end, and if this fails, do not despair. You must call in a witch-diviner. If you leave it to others to do so then it will be you, Mpona, that the diviner will find guilty. There are witches in this village. Do you think that Natombi is innocent? Do you think that Aphunzitsi is innocent? But there is an even greater enemy that you must fight without fear.'

'Who is that?' asked Mpona. Simbeya looked back to see if they were overheard. Lubinda had entered the palace grounds and was already within hearing. Simbeya kept quiet, and as soon as Lubinda sat down, he hobbled out.

The sun shone bright and hot and in Lubinda's face could be seen the marks of a sleepless night spent killing locusts in the fields. He could see that, although the Chief had not been out in the fields, he too had not slept. For a moment he felt sorry for the frail man seated before him with the black kalimadole cloth hanging more loosely than ever from his thin shoulders. He could see from the fiery glances that the weary man shot at him now and again that he was reaching the end of his tether and, like an imprisoned bull, was impatient to get out but too weak in body to struggle. The Chief darted another glance at Lubinda; his eyes followed the furrows of sleeplessness on his face, and then the smooth curves of his well-filled shoulders and the rest of his body. There was something about Lubinda which inspired strength in the Chief whenever he saw him. Simbeya inspired pity rather than courage.

'I have come about these things which are happening to me,' said Lubinda. 'I am a very unfortunate man.'

'Yes, we are all unlucky: you and I and all our people,' replied the Chief.

'But you are the Chief. You are chosen by the spirits of our ancestors. It cannot be that they are angry with you. It is I, Lubinda, that they are angry with. I have suffered much in my waking life and in my dreams to save this village, this country, from this ill luck. First the spirits made you mad so that I might suffer in doing your work. You don't know how I suffered and prayed that you should be well again. And now, when my prayer is answered, these things befall us. In the first real rains since your return a man dies, your roof is blown off, and now these locusts.'

'Yes, these locusts. They have finished us off,' replied Mpona.

'I must leave you, so that the people can choose someone whom the spirits like. I cannot go on like this with that hill there on the horizon tied round my neck.'

'But you cannot go, Lubinda. This is a difficult time for me and for you. The people will accuse us, as I am sure they are already doing, of causing these things. But if you go . . .'

'Yes, if I go what will happen? You have other people who can advise you. Simbeya for instance: he knows everything, doesn't he?' asked Lubinda.

So far the conversation was going well.

'He is only an old man. You are young, and somehow in your presence I feel that we can rule this country well. Simbeya is there to be ruled and not to rule.'

'But that is what he is telling everybody, Chief,' said Lubinda. 'You ought to know what your people are doing in this kingdom. I will help you if you will protect me against those who speak evil of me.'

'How can this be done?' asked Mpona, puzzled by what Lubinda was saying about Simbeya, but brushing this aside.

'There are witches in this village who wish to see me fall because they want others who do not care for you to exploit your goodness. These are the people you should do something about. I want you to continue as our Chief,' said Lubinda passionately, 'but you must expose the witches.'

'Who do you mean?' asked Mpona.

'Do you think that the python that killed Dulani went there on its own? I heard Dulani quarrel with his wife the day that thing happened. I am told that only yesterday Natombi burnt the cloth which Banda's wife gave her for Mwape to cover himself when he sleeps. They say she burnt it because that is the cloth Nanyawa – Banda's wife – used to carry her child in, the one who suffered from mumps only a month ago. How can a woman who is not a witch burn the cloth which another woman used for carrying her child, as if that child was dead? Is that not to wish the child ill-luck and death?

'They say that the boy Mwape was bewitched and that that is why he doesn't speak. But by whom was he bewitched? It was not by the grandmother, even though some people who want to hide the truth have been saying this.'

The Chief nodded; he was listening.

'And now about these locusts. They came from Nyimba. Only one person in this village comes from there. The last time that they came, it was after Mwalilya had been through here from Nyimba, collecting our men for forced labour. I don't know what this means, but I think that you should know what the people are saying. You mention Dulani's death and the whirlwind. The missionary and this new religion

54

and school. Some people say that when the white man first came to this village and we resisted accepting his goods and the founding of the school here, he shook the dust off his feet and said, 'Unless you agree, I will send fire to this village and kingdom and all houses will be destroyed.' Since then, Simbeya has contracted leprosy – the fire of God. Yuda has also got it now. Your house was nearly razed to the ground. All kinds of things are happening that never happened before.'

'You think then that the white man is against us?' asked Mpona. This was a sore point with him, and although he sat there listening intently to Lubinda's explanations, he had not forgiven him for coming out openly and in public against him when the missionary last came to force the people to re-open the school. But Lubinda appeared to sense this.

'No, Chief. Don't do anything to the white man. What I said then I said because I thought your position was in danger. But it isn't, and you understand his doings best. That is why, when you sought my advice later, I said we should re-open the school.'

Mpona kept silent.

'What shall we do then to stop these misfortunes?' asked Mpona after some thought.

'The people are asking for a kamcape to come. Only the witch-diviner can tell us why all these things are happening. So many things have happened, and it is time that we found out why. If you delay, the people will begin to talk. If you feel you cannot call the kamcape yourself, then allow me to do so. I want the truth to come out,' replied Lubinda.

Mpona thought about all the gossip that connected Lubinda with a plot to bewitch him. He thought of what Simbeya had just told him, and of the other story about Lubinda coming to the court at night and finding nothing there but thick fog. Was Simbeya right in all these claims? Was it really Lubinda who . . .? Even in his mind the question could not be completed. He thought of Ngoza, his young wife, the girl whose whereabouts even he as a Chief could not ask. She had offended against royalty by committing adultery. The law, he was certain, had taken its own course.

Lubinda stood up. It was the first time for a long while that he had had an opportunity of discussing matters of state with the Chief. Since his return, the Chief had grown remote, and even though Lubinda was his Councillor there had been moments when he had felt insecure.

Chapter 5

When your husband dies, it is not really your funeral and so, although you as the widow are expected to be sorrowful, it will only be *your* funeral when your brother or sister dies. When this terrible thing happens, people will pity you and do everything possible to make your comfortless life cheerful. But their real sympathy will always lie with the relatives of the dead one, because it is they who will suffer most from the death. Moreover, you as the one who was his wife, are expected to have known what was happening to your husband. So, if you did not tell his relatives of what was happening to their own and he suddenly dies, surely you must take some of the blame.

So it was that a few weeks after the death of Dulani, people were already talking. Natombi caught bits and pieces of the gossip that was circulating round the village. Her fellow women-folk stopped visiting her. Soon she had to go to the well to draw her own water, and when she met them they would get out of the way to leave the path to her. Natombi wondered why they did this. At first, she thought that it was because they pitied her so much that they could not look into her eyes. Gradually she realized that theirs was the respect for a leper and not for one in sorrow. Women turned their noses away when they met her, making her feel like one who stinks. From the day when the priest came to the village and the whirlwind ripped off the Chief's roof, no woman brought her food any longer.

'Did Natombi really cut her hair when Dulani died?' asked Simtowe's wife. 'She has so much hair already!'

'Some people say she did,' replied Silwamia's wife, 'but there are also others who say she refused. They say that when Lubinda's wife put the razor-blade under the hair she caught her hand and said that she was not going to have anything of the kind, that she was not of Mpona village, and therefore no one here could cut her hair.'

'And Lubinda's wife, does she confirm this story?' asked Simtowe's wife.

'She doesn't deny it, and there are times when by the manner in which she continues the discussion it can only mean that she agrees that that is what happened. They say that Natombi is not sad about the death of her husband. She refuses to have her hair cut because she has already got other men in mind. If she doesn't mourn then why should she cut her hair? And what about cooking? Those who have seen her house say that she is already cooking, and yet she still hasn't been purified. Also they say that she looks younger and fresher than when Dulani was alive. Where there is smoke there is fire. All those things cannot simply be lies,' concluded Mrs Silwamia.

One evening Natombi was sitting on the veranda of her house, by herself except for Mwape who lay in her lap. She was feeling weak and tired because she had not eaten all day. Now and again at night she would make a quiet fire to cook a little maize, but she could not do this every day lest the people should observe that she was already cooking for herself. Soon she would be back in her hut, because it was not proper for a bereaved woman to appear too much in public. The moon was clear, so clear that she could see the dogs barking on the other side of the village. Mwape suddenly jumped up from his mother's lap, bleating like a sheep. Then he fell back into her arms. He had been dreaming. He had been peering from the bushes at unknown people gathered round his father's grave. The nameless ones were saying: 'Do you know us? Do you know who sent the python, the python which killed you?' The corpse shook its toes because the head was dead. 'No, I don't,' it replied. An old woman, with upturned eyelids as

58

red as pepper, peered into the bushes and spotted him. 'Wahihi, wahihi,' she shouted as the scent grew stronger. That was when Mwape jumped up, trying to run away in terror. But as in many dreams, his feet were bound so that he could not run. He fell back into his mother's lap, fast asleep.

It was then that a man shuffled towards Natombi's hut. In the clear light of the moon she could see his shape clearly. Only Simbeya the leper, her late husband's uncle, walked like that.

'Ou,' intoned the old man, 'my namesake, why does he cry? Ou! is he asleep?'

'I don't know. He is dreaming,' she replied.

'Ou, dreams are not dreams unless they are dreamed,' the old man said. He loved to torture people with mysterious words. He coughed to fill up the awkward silence.

'Greetings, uncle. Are you well?' Natombi said finally, puzzled by the old man's words.

'We are well. How are you?'

'Well, only your namesake is not well,' she replied.

'That is bad,' said Simbeya. 'Mother of the son, I have come to discuss the death.'

Natombi felt uncomfortable. Simbeya poked the fire with his healthy hand. Three fingers on the other had already been eaten away by his disease. The old man placed a burning cinder into his pipe and, covering the mouth of the pipe with his thumb, he pulled hard at it.

'Is the roof of the house well? It will be some time before these rains stop, and there is no dry grass,' he said, looking towards the hut. Natombi knew that these were just preliminaries.

'It will last; there is nothing to do,' she replied. 'But there are too many rats. They even eat your namesake's feet at night.'

'Rats? Ha-ha-ha! The rat has perched itself on the larder, eh?' This was a mystifying question and Natombi did not know whether she had to reply.

'The funeral,' the old man said, after a cough. 'I hear strange things about you, my daughter.' There was silence. 'You are already cooking for yourself?'

'It is true,' she replied.

'And you are wearing new clothes. This is a new cloak, isn't it?' The old man raised his voice. The storm was building up. 'How can you do such things? Your hair and face are well oiled, and every time I pass by the house I smell the smell of meat. Where do you get it from, as a widow?'

'The cloth is an old one, bought by those who have left us,' she said, casting her eyes down.

'You lie! You . . .' he checked himself. 'What about all these other things that we hear?'

Natombi could see the old man's pipe shaking with rage.

'You have hidden all the property of the dead one. All is gone and I can have nothing. I am his uncle,' he said, throwing a piece of burning wood back into the fire. 'And I have nothing except rags. Where is that black cloth he used to wear, and the pipe, and the palm hat, and the helmet he brought from Sinoia? Where is that blanket with the red lines across it, the shovel, and the box? He had money, I know, at least ten shillings.' He clapped his hands together to indicate 'ten'.

'All these things are still here, uncle. They are waiting for you to collect them,' Natombi replied.

'Then there are other things we don't know of which you've hidden. The maize; that bin was full up to here,' he was indicating the level with his hands. 'Now it is there. Where has the maize gone? You've taken it to your mother in Cakuwamba village. Don't deny it.'

'But, uncle, you came to collect the maize for the funeral beer,' Natombi was determined to answer back.

'Don't answer me,' snapped the elderly one. 'These women of today! I told him not to marry such a woman, but he wouldn't listen. Instead he refused his cousin and married you, a woman of ten eyes. We know what we know. Even Lubinda knows.' Simbeya stood up. 'Tomorrow I shall come again to take your clothes. You have given me nothing. If you do not want me to trouble, bring all your clothes to my house. You will find your grandmother there.'

The boy Mwape opened his eyes and got up. Simbeya left. With his eyes he was asking his mother. 'Mama, who is that one?'

Natombi remained silent long after Simbeya had gone. In her heart she was furious with Simbeya, furious with the whole village for what they were doing to her. If they thought that their man left a lot of wealth, why didn't they take it away? Why would they not allow her to leave this village, so that they could take it all? She thought of the difficult times she had shared with Dulani. The time, for example, when he became so ill that everyone thought he would die. How many of these people had ever come to her help then, to help their own man? How many of their women had ever brought food to her house? 'None,' she whispered to herself. 'They were interested only in the animal he had snatched from the lion's mouth, but not in the deep wounds that the lion had left in his neck and on his back. These people would leave my son to be eaten by hyenas,' thought Natombi. 'What did Dulani leave me which I have hidden? These people are cruel; I should never have come here.' Then she thought of Dulani. He had been dead many weeks, and yet it seemed such a short time. He had been so tender and kind to her that she could not believe what was happening to her now. A week before his death Dulani had quarrelled with Simbeya over a goat which he had killed. What strange things Simbeya had said that day! And yet Dulani had said nothing, as if he had known that he would soon be departing.

If Natombi was the woman who was having the most difficult time, she was not the only person that people were talking about. One day, for example, Lubinda set off with his nephew Juma for Cakuwamba village, where some beer had been brewed. Since Dulani's death no beer had been brewed in the village, because to brew ordinary beer before the funeral beer had been drunk would have shown that the people in the village did not mourn Dulani.

'I ask you,' said Lubinda to his nephew Juma, as he held the calabash of beer between his hands. You could see that his hands were trembling as he held it up, his bearded lips ready to drain the beer. 'This beer, who brewed it?'

'Why? It is Tembo's beer. But uncle, why?' asked his nephew.

'Because,' the uncle pulled at the calabash, and then set it down in the centre, 'did you see ordinary beer being brewed at the house of the in-laws before the funeral beer has been drunk?'

'But the funeral was not in this village, and Tembo is not related to Natombi,' replied Juma.

'So you don't know, my nephew. Natombi's mother and Tembo's mother are sisters, because the father of Natombi's mother and the mother of Tembo's mother were related. And yet here we are drinking Tembo's beer in Cakuwamba village. Does the place matter?'

'I don't know, uncle,' replied Juma.

'You young men of today don't understand things. You cannot be sorrowful in the midst of joy. We are fools to drink this beer, I tell you,' said Lubinda, pulling hard at the calabash, as if for the last time. 'You will see what you will see,' he said as he unbent his tall frame from the calabash, to which his lips had been stuck. He set the calabash down and stroked his long beard somewhat absent-mindedly. His small, blood-shot eyes narrowed in his chubby cheeks. Then he brought down his sinewy hands on to his knees, and it seemed for that brief moment that his face, his whole body, was hungry and impatient. When this happened Juma knew that there would be trouble.

'This teacher at our village. You think he is an honest man?' asked Lubinda.

'I hear stories, but I don't know,' replied the nephew.

'Stories!' exclaimed Lubinda, who hated understatements. 'Stories! Things are happening, my young man. Even white men are now involved. Did you see,' he said, drawing Juma towards him, 'how that white missionary held Natombi by the hand, and in public, before all our eyes, as if some of us were not her fathers-in-law? That is to behave like a dog – even for a white one.'

'But my friend,' continued Lubinda, adjusting himself as he sat, 'who led the white one there? Was it not the teacher? That is what the teacher is in our village for, to get the white one black women. And yet Mpona loves the teacher! How long shall we go on giving away our women to white men, to teachers? Even women in sorrow like Natombi whom we should protect? I hear white men are not shy and that in towns they walk hand in hand with any woman in broad daylight. That, my friend, is what Mpona is bringing into this kingdom.'

The wind blew lazily across the face of the tree under which they were sitting. The leaves rustled, and Lubinda whispered, 'I hear the white one now wants to dismiss this teacher of his.'

'Why?' asked Juma.

'Yes, why?' said Lubinda. Then, answering his own question, he continued, 'When thunder rumbles, lightning strikes and the rain falls, you don't ask why it rains. Why? Because rascals cannot cut each other's hair. Each knows the other's tricks. Aphunzitsi thought he could deceive the white one and make him believe that the girl was being kept for him alone. But the white one has now discovered that the teacher himself is not honest. Did you know that until only recently the white one used to travel with a small statue of a woman who looks like Natombi?'

'Is that so?' was all the nephew could say. To him all this was strange, but it seemed to make sense. If not, then why was the teacher losing so much weight, as if he was eating nothing but dried up bed-bugs?

The night was deepening and, although it was the time of year when the rains tailed off, it could become very dark because there was no moon. Lubinda was just about to tell his nephew that they should go back home, when the nephew hissed at him, 'Sssh, ssh,' he said, 'there comes the teacher. What does he want?'

Lubinda immediately jumped up to greet the teacher. 'You have come a long way, like us, to quench your thirst?' asked Lubinda.

'No, not exactly. I came to this village this evening to baptize a sick man,' replied the teacher. 'So when I heard of this beer, and since it is not funeral beer, I thought I would pass here and quench my thirst.'

Lubinda leaned over to his nephew and whispered something. The nephew immediately stood up and said he was going back to Mpona. He had left a sick child.

'Let him go,' said Lubinda in answer to the obvious surprise brooding over the teacher's vague outline in the dark. 'He is wayward, and if he is caught by a lion or beaten up it does not trouble me.' Then Lubinda offered Aphunzitsi the calabash. The latter drank long and deep before finally setting it down.

Soon the teacher was surrounded with people greeting him. This was quite a change from the chilly atmosphere of Mpona, where everyone kept him at a distance. But, in the midst of all this, a voice rose up from behind the hut where the beer was.

'We don't want some people here. What do they want with us? Aren't they satisfied with what they have taken? Aren't they satisfied with having bewitched my brother? Let them know that I am going to inherit my brother – and that includes his wife. Everything!' It was Banda, the brother of Dulani, the dead man. Tembo, the host, was trying to calm him. 'You too!' shouted Banda. 'You're in league with this learned one, eh? Then I'm off. Did you kill my brother together then?'

Several people in the hut whispered to Banda not to say such things in the middle of a funeral beer party.

'What funeral beer? This?' Banda dashed the calabash he was holding to the ground and, going for the teacher, exclaimed, 'This one! I'll beat him now.'

The people held him and Aphunzitsi was advised to leave quietly. At the door of the hut, however, he tripped over the leg of a woman who was sitting spread out as if she owned half the kingdom.

'Whose son are you who breaks my bones?' exclaimed the woman, who turned out to be Banda's wife. 'I die, mother, oh!'

'Who kills my wife?' shouted Banda, with an axe held high. But the teacher had disappeared.

Banda continued drinking, and when he was completely soaked he shouted to his wife, 'And why were you offering that man your leg, you slut?'

The wife, equally drunk, shouted, 'Slut yourself, why didn't you kill him if you are a man?'

'I'll beat you,' he shouted, jumping up. 'Hold me,' he said to the people, 'or I'll beat up this woman. I will beat you,' he shouted again. 'You February!' (Convinced that 'February' was a big insult.)

'And you, you are February too!' retorted the woman. 'Come and beat me if you like!' She was baring her breast to him. He dived at her. She stepped aside. He crashed into the wall behind her. That settled Banda for the time being. But it did not settle the gossip about the teacher.

When you have had a little to drink, even if you are not a religious man like Aphunzitsi, you still feel courage coursing through your veins as you wade through the tall damp grass on your way home. But as you go deeper into the darkness, the significance of what has happened gradually begins to dawn. Aphunzitsi became increasingly worried by what local gossip might say the following morning. What did it matter though? After all, it was not as if he had tried to run away with someone's wife. It was just that the woman was sitting sprawled on the ground and, in his hurry to escape her drunken husband, he had tripped over her. So he walked on, wading through the tall grass like a soldier.

Then . . . what was that? Had he heard something moving? Could it be a hyena? Suddenly something heavy hit him on the head. Another blow, then another, until all he could remember was a succession of hammer blows on his head. Juma stood over his still body and swore, 'You foreigner!'

'Is he dead?' asked Lubinda in a panting whisper.

'No,' replied Juma, 'he is still breathing, but this will teach him a lesson for selling our women to the white ones.'

'Sh-ssh,' whispered Lubinda. 'No more of this. Don't ever tell anyone what has happened. Tomorrow I'll fix everything.' Then Lubinda swore, 'Psh! the Chief and his foreigners!'

Early the following morning, news of the teacher's condition became public knowledge since the high-pitched voice of his wife could be heard accusing him of having been beaten up because he was after someone else's wife. Soon his house was crowded with people ostensibly wishing him a speedy recovery. Lubinda was among the earliest callers, and when he emerged, he was shaking his head. The people walked towards him. Was anything serious the matter? If he, the village's medicine-man, shook his head, could there be any hope?

'It is the spirits who have beaten up our teacher,' he said. 'How could they do that to such a good man? I tell you that the spirits of our forefathers will not rest until we have propitiated the strange death of Dulani. Why the floods? Why the locusts? Why the whirlwind? Why the missionary coming here to insult our manhood? And now why have the ghosts beaten up this man whom we all consider to be a good man? Are the spirits not against what is happening in this village?'

'You people, why do you come to listen to me,' he continued as the numbers grew, 'when you can't tell the Chief what should be done? Who is stopping the coming of the witch-diviner into this village? Isn't it that certain people fear the white ones at the mission and the Boma? Who is allowing this strange thing called the school to continue? Isn't it this that the spirits objected to when they beat up the teacher? Have you seen his head? It's like a huge water-melon. No human being beats up anyone like that!'

When Lubinda stopped talking, the people who had listened

to him felt anger because of what was not being done. They wanted him to say more, but he could see from a distance that the old reptile Simbeya was watching. 'Don't come to me any more to ask for cures if you can't prevent what is happening,' Lubinda said as he slid away.

Chapter 6

'Who can call a witch-diviner?' asked Silwamia scornfully. 'The trouble with you, Simtowe, is you think that people mean what they say. How many people in this village have no witchcraft horns? How many do not ride on the back of hyenas at night, to go and bewitch across the rivers and oceans? Call a kamcape indeed!'

'But Lubinda, he who knows best, says a diviner should come,' replied Simtowe.

'What has he done about it?' Silwamia looked up at Simtowe, whose squint eye gave the impression of knowing all, while the cataract on it gave the impression of blankness. 'Has he even told the Chief about what he feels? Is he not the Chief's adviser?'

Silwamia stood up and shook the dust off his back. He had greased his muzzle-loader and put in the gunpowder. Today if he was lucky he might kill a duiker. For the whole week he had not shared bed with his wife, and he had been anointing himself with the liquid from the roots of a sausage tree steeped in caster oil. So he could not fail to kill an animal, because the bad luck from sharing his wife's bed would not be there to thwart his accuracy and the medicine would ensure that the intended victim did not see or hear him.

'But there are a lot of people talking about this matter,' insisted Simtowe. 'So the Chief will have to listen to them. Have you heard that even other village headmen are worried about what is happening here?'

Silwamia slung his gun across his shoulder and made for the

bush. He would have to walk more than five miles before he could begin to look around stealthily for game. As he hurried on, he thought of what he had just been saying to Simtowe. No one would dare call a witch-diviner, he was sure, not even Lubinda himself. But it suited Lubinda to talk as though it was others that were resisting the move. Silwamia thought of his children at home. Delightful creatures they were, full of questions, full of life. They would be expecting a kill, so he must hurry up. The sun had gone half-way across the afternoon sky. Against the blue he could see the rays of the sun bending towards the horizon, like water from a gourd into a jar. The atmosphere still had the stickiness of a hot rainy-season day even though the last showers had nearly gone.

He was now in the thick forest. Looking around the well which the Kaunga had forgotten about in its hurry to the Luangwa river, he could see some fresh footprints of animals. A kudu maybe? Or was it an antelope? He searched the still, green grass for any further sign. Ah, yes, recent droppings, fresh in fact! As he picked them up he could have made mud with them, they were so new. His hunter's instinct bristled. Already the gun was in his hands. But before settling the finger on the trigger, he picked up dry soil and threw it into the air. The wind was was blowing westwards and so, if he were east of where the animals were, they might smell him. But where were they? He was certain there was more than one. A honey-bird chuckled in the tree above him: chuck-chuck-chuck-chuck. Silwamia stood on his toes, and his grip on the trigger tightened. What was that? He threw himself down. A giraffe craned its neck into the branches of a tree. Elegantly and slowly, it nibbled at the topmost leaf. Silwamia's time had come; it was today or never. Relish at this time of the threatened famine could make a little mealie-meal go very far. He levelled his gun at the giraffe. Now, now, now. The trigger squeezed. There was an explosion, a cloudburst of smoke, and Silwamia's hands and face were spattered with blood. Nothing but the barrel remained of the gun, and the giraffe cantered off gracefully.

It was not for some time that it dawned on Silwamia what had happened. Slowly he felt pain on his face as though it was being stung by bees, and then he felt as if his head, and finally his body, had been held in a roaring bush fire. He ran home, yelling, 'I'm bewitched, I'm bewitched!' He ran on for miles, four, five, six, seven, until it seemed as though he would never arrive. In the meantime, the question kept repeating itself, what had happened, what had happened? So loud was his yelling, 'I've been bewitched!' that it seemed like the answer to his question. Thus two people, within a matter of days, had met with strange fates.

'Whose gun was it?' asked Lubinda after listening to the story of how Silwamia had departed for the forest from Simtowe.

'It was his,' replied Simtowe.

'What about the gunpowder?' asked Lubinda.

'The gunpowder?' asked Simtowe incredulously. He had never liked Lubinda, even though in a discussion with Silwamia he always tried to water down his dislike of Lubinda. 'Gunpowder!' he repeated to himself. Then suddenly he remembered. 'Yes . . .'

'Yes, yes,' said Lubinda, urging him on. 'Whose was it?'

'Aphunzitsi, the teacher. Now I remember. Mawe! Good God!' Lubinda's grin broke through his black dusty beard as he walked away.

'I knew it,' he said, turning back towards Simtowe, 'I knew it.'

When you do not hear things but you suspect them it is more terrible than if somebody says something straight out. If someone can tell you to your face that he thinks you are useless and that your father was the son of a dog, that is better than someone behaving as though you were the son of a dog, but not telling you so. Such was the position of the Chief in the week which passed between these events and the time when there was what Lubinda privately called a 'spontaneous demonstration of the people's anger'. Being a Chief, Mpona could not very well ask, 'What do they say?' unless his Councillor or a delegation of headmen told him what the people said. So far, he had not received an interpretation of the meaning of the events which had taken place in the village from his Councillor and village medicine man. All that he had heard was that the people wanted a witch-diviner because they were convinced that the beating up of the teacher and the explosion of the gun in the hands of Silwamia was due to witchcraft. But how could he act on hearsay? No one among his informants had told him what Lubinda felt about these things. Would it not be undignified for him to act on the basis of rumour? Was it not necessary for him to have the views of the men in the village? And yet, so far, they had not broached the subject, and Lubinda, who had formerly appeared worried whenever he had not been called to the court, now appeared anxious to avoid it.

So the Chief sat on the matter until one day his wife told him that there were people outside wishing to see him.

'I feel you must call in the diviner,' said Juma when the Chief emerged. 'The people are being persecuted.'

The Chief did not reply, but merely waited to hear more.

'I say the people are troubled by what is happening here. There is someone who is a witch and who is causing us all this misfortune. We want you to call a witch-diviner.'

'My son,' replied the Chief, 'a family that calls in a kamcape will no longer remain a family. Even though the diviner may prove that there is no witch, the spear of hatred will have been sharpened. It is the same with us here. We are not only one village but one family . . .'

'One family?' asked Lubinda, who had now crept into the crowd.

'Oh yes, the Chief is right, even foreigners like the teacher are part of our family.' Then he turned to his nephew Juma and brusquely ordered him to stop talking. 'If the Chief does not want to call in a diviner it's none of your business.'

'But what do you say, my Councillor, on this matter?' asked the Chief, turning to Lubinda. The Chief had not liked Lubinda's retort.

'You, Chief, are a good and fair man. If in the interests of the village you do not call in a diviner, there are people among us,' here he deliberately looked back to cast a long look at the house where Simbeya was lying outside sunning his sores, 'who will say that you do so in order to protect yourself. We know that you are not a witch. If you were, would this village, would this kingdom have still been held together? But there will be people who will speak. As for us, people will quickly jump to the conclusion that it is we who stop you from calling the kamcape. It is not these recent events – the beating up by the spirits of this man whom we now find is a member of our family, the bewitching of Silwamia, the floods, the locusts, and many others – which sadden our spirits and make us anxious. It is the death of a man. Since Dulani died, have we done anything to find out who bewitched him? We are a people sitting with a five-month-old corpse in our houses. Until Dulani's death is explained to him he will not sleep in peace. That is why we must have a diviner. That is why we must have him here. Why did Dulani die? Why did he die in the way that he did?'

Dulani's death indeed still had to be accounted for, and atoned for. Up to now there had been speculation, but there was nothing definite. Nothing, no matter how conclusive it might appear, could really be accepted. Only the witch-diviner could say what was the cause. Time was running out, and if those responsible for calling the diviner did not ask him to come they themselves would soon stand in danger of being convicted of being the witches. Already thoughts were turning to Lubinda the village doctor, Mpona the Chief and natural head of the whole family, and Simbeya the uncle of the dead man.

Sufficient evidence could be gathered to incriminate any of these men. Lubinda was the local medicine-man. If he could cure many diseases, it followed that he could also cause many diseases. Judging by his success in curing people, some began to suspect that he might be deliberately causing some of the diseases so that he could cure them and then take the prize. Moreover, Lubinda was virtually the last man to see Dulani alive. The people knew that Lubinda had been told of the black ants by Dulani, and that he had appeared worried about them. Some of the elderly women knew that Lubinda had been sent to Natombi a few years back because Dulani had feared that he was not a full man.

It had all come out at the time Natombi was giving birth. The birth was difficult, and as this showed that she must have been irregular in her ways, the elderly midwife questioned her. First of all Natombi would not own to any dishonesty. 'I know only one man, my husband,' she had said. But after five days, when the labour grew more and more painful, she had admitted that Lubinda had also visited her once.

'Once?' questioned the midwife, 'was it only once? You die if you don't tell the truth.'

Natombi had then admitted that it was twice. But in the gossip of the village, this was magnified to many times. So, was there any good reason to believe that Lubinda had ceased his association with her, even if she had not conceived again afterwards? The woman said that the child, Mwape, looked exactly like Dulani, his father. But this was neither here nor there.

It seemed to people, moreover, that Lubinda's friendship with Dulani was one of blackmail. Dulani was the obsequious mouse who always followed the bidding of his master Lubinda the cat. Lubinda himself had been heard to boast at beer parties about how Dulani had 'employed' him. Lastly, why was it that it was Lubinda who talked most about the teacher and Natombi? The teacher had also given meat to many other people in the village, not just to Dulani. If Lubinda did not get any, the teacher was not to blame. Why should he be expected to continue giving when Lubinda had thrown to the dogs the first meat that the teacher had sent him?

It might have been many years ago, but nevertheless it was

still surprising. What did Ngoza, the young wife of the Chief, who was the cause of his sadness, tell the midwife? How was it that immediately afterwards the midwife fell ill, could not speak, and died a week later? She died just when she was trying to call Lubinda. What had she wanted to say to him? Moreover, Lubinda was her nephew. Could it be that? Lubinda did not seem to be friendly with the Chief. In gatherings he was always whispering things to Yuda. Five years ago he shot into the bush where the Chief was hiding. He must have known where he was. How? And now, even though he was the medicine-man, he did not seem to be in a hurry to find out what killed Dulani. 'This is strange,' said the people to one another.

Then there was the old man Simbeya. People do not contract terrible diseases for nothing. Leprosy is fire sent by the spirits to punish evil-doers. Moreover, the old man was living to a ripe age in spite of his illness. He always seemed well fed and, even though only his wife cultivated, they always seemed to have a lot of food. His eldest son had died mysteriously two years ago. Mysteriously because even though he had been sick for a long time he had died just as he was getting better, and it was immediately after he had drunk beer from the same vessel as the old man. There are some people who kill their own children in order to get the blood to soak the seed in before planting. That red maize which Simbeya planted that year, where did it come from? Red maize had never been heard of, even from the Portuguese across the border where he claimed to have got it. So, what would stop him from bewitching his nephew if the blood of his son was finished?

As for the Chief, there was some doubt about him too. He should have known what his people were doing. Therefore, he must have been in league with either or both of these people. Why was his wife so cruel? Had she forgotten how people had suffered to bring her husband back to his throne? Four of them, and they were all dead! Surely the headman must know these things? When the white one had last been to the village, the Chief had just sat and never raised a voice against him. What was going on between them?

It was against this background that Cumba, the village crier, one evening broadcast a message from the Chief's Councillor in his capacity as the local medicine-man. Being Cumba, he was shouting at the top of his voice and interlacing the awesome message with laughter. A half-idiot can say anything. 'To all of you in this village of Mpona,' shouted out Cumba, 'and to those of you old women who have already set off for the graveyard: the spirits of our ancestors are greatly troubled by what has happened in this village. Some of you are getting fatter and fatter. Where do you find the meat? Tomorrow you will vomit it out even if you push it down into your fattened tummies tonight. The witch-diviner is coming tomorrow. He who escapes from the village tomorrow is a witch, and we know what we shall do to him. You people, why do you like to dance naked at night in other people's houses and at graveyards as if you have no houses of your own? Look at her stick, look at him! In daylight you are blind, but at night you throw your sticks away! Ha, ha, ha. Hehehe!'

Mr Cumba, or rather Cumba of the Forest as he preferred to call himself, was a man for all seasons. Although only twenty-five he had already seen and done much. He had been to Zumba in Mozambique. It was also said that there by feigning death he had narrowly escaped being roasted over a high fire for tax defaulting. The Portuguese authorities, accepting that nature had frustrated the course of justice, had, however, felt bound to whip the corpse, posthumous justice being as important as the correct observation of the Ten Commandments. He had already been to Lusaka, to Her Majesty's Central Prison, for an offence relating again to tax defaulting. Cumba of the Forest was not just the plague of the tax collectors, but also of the people at Mpona and in the valley. Even more people knew him than knew the Chief. To whatever village he had been in the night he left a trail of grief because half its property, even the grass on the roofs, would be gone. Some said he had magic, with which he lulled his victims to sleep. Others thought that he was mad. But none thought that he was just a crook. People swore at him in the morning, but sought his friendship in the afternoon because he had a tongue that made it unbelievable that he would ever steal their goods. Although his name was Cumba – which means 'the impotent one' – there were many women in the valley who could proudly swear to carrying his child.

Cumba had a rectangular head which was slightly curved in at the top so that it was as good as a jar for carrying water. His teeth were bared and rotten from smoking stub ends in town. The jaw was like that of a goat, and his dusty eyes, which were neither red nor white, had perpetual amusement in them. Cumba did not have a dirty beard, because he did not sport one. But his hair was filth itself, and one of his toes was clubbed like a puff-adder's head.

The kamcape did not take long to come. In fact he came from Nyimba within a week of being called. He was a thin, wizened, fellow of uncertain age. He wore a tiny horn which was suspended round his neck by a waxed string. They said that embedded in the horn and right under the dry lump of medicine which was tied in a black cloth, was a small mirror fragment which reflected the witchcraft charms on to one he held in front of him as he ran around stabbing at the invisible witches. His firm, short legs were strongly built, but the right leg was riddled with the ugly lumps of varicose veins. These lumps had their own story to tell, that of a determined effort by one witch to get rid of him. Of course she had failed, but by so trying she had given him the opening dance for his ceremony wherever he went to answer the call of duty.

He was a carefree little man who infected his clients with mirth as he sailed through his dances, skating and twisting, laughing and jumping. He started the first song, the drums reinforced his voice and the people, the witch among them, took it up:

76

Anagonja, Anagonja
Kodi anagonja ndithu?
Anagonja, bwanji tsono?
Mumtukule,
Ai, ai.
Mumtukule,
Anagonja, Anagonja.

The chorus took up every second line. The kamcape asserted
that the witch – more often a she than a he – had failed. The
people asked him if this were true and he asserted that she
really had failed to bewitch him, and asked what he should do
with her. The bloodthirsty crowd returned: 'Kill her!' The
kamcape went round the outside of the ring dancing, and as
he reached each person he tapped him on the head and
shoulders with his fly-whisk. Then he entered the ring and
struck up a new rhythm:

Ndi, ndi, ndi, ndi!
Nyama li le
Mwandituma kuti ndibvine
Nyama li le
Ndikabvina mundipatsenji
Nyama li le
Ndikupatsa mtembo wa munthu
Nyama li le
Ndi ndi
Nyama li le

It was the hyena dance. The hyena asks the people: 'You
have ordered me to dance; if I dance what will you give me?'
The people answer; 'We will give you a dead body.' The hyena
then breaks into lyrical pleasure as he dances.

'There! There!' exclaimed the kamcape, jumping from one
point to the other like fat in a frying-pan. 'There! There! You,
look at that . . . here he comes . . . here he comes . . . stop it,
the child is innocent . . . Ah! you have cut his voice. Cruel
one . . . no, no, no! . . . not his father again . . . the child will

have no voice to ask for water ... think of the speechless one!'

The kamcape ran around as if following someone whom he could see through the mirror which he was holding above his face. Then he shouted frenziedly, 'He has killed the father!' and stabbed into the ground with his fly-switch. His eyes slowly looked up from the feet to the face of the man who was closest to where he had stabbed. 'Witch, you!' he shouted as his eyes met those of the victim. They were the eyes of the teacher, Aphunzitsi.

'Mcape!' called the witch-diviner, jumping to the centre of the circle and indicating with both his hands where the medicine and the victim should be brought. There were exclamations of surprise. But Lubinda jumped into the centre and declared, 'Even he, he is the witch.' The people clapped their gratitude and threw leaves at the teacher, who now stood alone at the far end.

The women taunted him: 'You killed my child, you. You gave us meat, so it was human meat!' Some kicked him with their feet and immediately jumped away lest they should be contaminated.

The men boxed him on the ears. Some lashed his legs with a whip and, the few children who hated school jeered and made all sorts of faces at him. 'Weele! Witch, witch, witch, witch!'

'It's against my practice to let the witch go,' said the kamcape. 'If you want it, it is up to you. But I won't come back again to rid you of the same witch.'

'No, give him mwabvi now,' shouted the people.

'But before he is given mwabvi he must declare that he is not a witch. Will you all ask him now whether he is a witch, so that in telling lies to one he will tell lies to all!' suggested the kamcape.

'Witch!' shouted all of them. 'Are you not a witch?'

The teacher knew that his reply, even though times were changed, could spell disaster. It makes no difference even if you are in the right if you are dead. Indeed, what would be the use of Aphunzitsi denying that he was a witch if he would then have to drink the fatal mwabvi? If he died, both the missionary and the bwana at the Boma would certainly give the village a hard time, because you could not hide the death of such an important man in your tobacco pouch. But, what then? So the teacher looked up, straight into the eyes of the diviner, because he knew he was innocent, and said, 'I am a witch. I am the very witch who bewitched Dulani. If that is what you want me to say, I have said it.'

'What then, brothers?' said the kamcape, facing his audience.

'Give him mwabvi,' shouted Lubinda.

But the villagers could not pay regard to Lubinda's word in this matter. This was a serious affair, and they had to be guided by the Chief, who was also the representative of the white man's rule in the village. So all eyes, including those of the kamcape, turned to Mpona.

Mpona knew that either way there would be trouble. If he hastily reprieved the teacher, people would say in future that he too was a witch and that he had known what the teacher had been up to. After all, it was because of the gossip against him that he had finally been prevailed upon to call the kamcape. Personally, he did not like this business at all. It only served to split the village, even though he did not doubt the findings of the kamcape. They could not be wrong. 'On the other hand,' he reasoned, 'if the teacher drinks the medicine, he will die. The anger of the white man is as great as that of our spirits – sometimes even greater. Where did Kafumu, who killed his wife at Cakuwamba, go? They say he is still in prison awaiting execution. If I decide on this thing the white man will kill me . . . And what about the white missionary? What will he do if he hears that his teacher is dead? If Aphunzitsi is a witch – and the kamcape has said it – did he not do these things hand-in-hand with the white missionary? They say that the white missionary has got axes and winnowing baskets at the mission which he took from the witches. No one can catch a witch except a kamcape unless he is himself a witch. So he must be a witch himself . . .'

They were all still looking at Mpona. What was the matter with him. Would he not speak? They did not want witches in this village. The kamcape had spoken the truth . . .

Suddenly the kamcape found himself helpless. Here he was, the only man whose word in this matter the people accepted without question, and yet he too was waiting on the word of the Chief with fear. If the chief pronounced in favour of what the people wanted, what would happen to him? The white man's messengers, he knew, were on his scent. One of them was a witch whom he had uncovered years back. But he had escaped and joined forces with the white men against him. Everything considered, he concluded, it would be better for him if this man the teacher was reprieved. But he could not very well eat his words and ask the headman to let the man go. He had an idea, a good idea, he thought: 'I will let the headman of Lubinda pour the drink down his throat. Then everybody will see the teacher did not die by my hand.'

The people began to shift uneasily. Then Mpona spoke: 'My people, this matter of witchcraft is a weighty matter. It is proper that I and the elders speak together before anything is done.' Mpona considered the faces hanging on his words and he knew from the looks of expectation on them that they were not satisfied. He would have to speak further. They were waiting for a word of commitment. 'When the discussion is finished, I will tell you. We cannot afford to let witches go without the punishment they deserve,' he offered.

'He has said it,' the crowd murmured. 'It means only one thing. We trust Mpona. He is a good man.' They disappeared into their houses, satisfied that justice would be done. Aphunzitsi was pushed into one of the empty huts and the door was secured from the outside. He was a condemned prisoner . . . Would the axe finally fall?

The axe did not fall that evening. When the elders gathered the meeting immediately became stormy, with Lubinda assuming the role of prosecutor.

'We do not ask him to drink mwabvi because we do not want him here. He came in our midst as a stranger; we wel-

80

comed him as we welcome our own sons and daughters returning from Walale. But look what he has brought to our village. He has brought charms, medicine, and witchcraft. Today you dare not cross any path lest you be bewitched. Were these things so before, I ask you, my friends? This teacher has done unnatural things with Natombi, that foreigner of a woman whom we all accepted as our daughter. No, we ask him to drink mwabvi because justice demands that those who are under suspicion should prove themselves to be good men. If they are not, then we cannot be responsible for what happens to them as we too are instruments of the spirits of our ancestors. Someone might disappear tonight.' He rolled his large eyes round the group. Briefly they met those of the Chief. He could read worry in those eyes, but there was also scorn in them.

'Let me also say a little word on this matter,' said a voice in the dark corner of the hut. It was Simbeya's voice. He coughed a little. 'I have never trusted this man the teacher since he came into our village. And now he is a witch. That is true. In the old days, the days when I was a young man and my body was whole, not this maimed man that I am – I know you young men despise me, yes.' He broke off suddenly. He was choking with anger at the thought of what he had just said. 'I know you despise me!' he said, returning to the charge.

There was silence. He was on his hobby-horse again, and once he was on it he rarely got off. But this time it was different. 'In the old days we would not even be sitting here discussing the obvious. The teacher would have drunk the medicine already and what should happen would have happened already. But here we are discussing. Why? My young men, you are right to discuss. The world has changed. I am an old man and I will soon die. So the world is yours. But discuss properly.'

The Chief was disappointed with the old man. He would have preferred him to have come out in the open against the proposition. But he was a cunning old fox who did not want to tarnish his last days by coming out against the popular feeling of the people. After all, Simbeya was ailing and maimed. He depended, more than anyone else, on the generosity of the people. Mpona also realized that he too had nearly fallen short of the people's expectations, except with his last hastily devised phrase about the culprit getting the punishment he deserved. What did this in fact mean? It would only be meaningful in terms of the discussion that was taking place under his nose, in which he had so far distinguished himself by the temerity of his silence. But his better instinct taught him not to intervene too quickly as the chairman, for the dignity of his position would depend as much on saying nothing as on saying something. So he decided to bide his time.

'Pardon me, Chief. I would also like to speak.' It was Banda, the teacher's greatest enemy if one was to judge by the hard punches that he had treated him to some months back at Cakuwamba's village. 'I am Dulani's brother, and although I am young you should listen to what I have to say. You lost a friend and a relative in his death, but I lost an elder brother. The last thing I would wish to see is that my brother's death should be taken as an opportunity for re-arousing the hate which you and I, Lubinda, have always entertained for each other. But my own brother told me his worry about you, how you, Lubinda, were trying to know my sister-in-law.'

The silence deepened. They had not expected this frank talk about something which they had all heard would ruin the village. Lubinda was a powerful man. How would he take this open challenge to him?

'My brother told me about you, Lubinda, about how you prevailed on him to believe that he was sterile, and how through a series of innuendoes you made my sister-in-law believe this too. You forced his hand by your threats to let him allow you to have free access to his wife. But know, Lubinda, that every meeting you had with his wife was a pain not only to Dulani but to his wife also. Were you not surprised that when it was born the child did not resemble you, in spite of your boast that Dulani, my brother, had employed

82

you? I will go no further with this matter,' he said, looking at the headman, 'but let me say that Lubinda, although he is not a witch, has had good cause for wishing my brother dead.'

He had said it, he had said what the Chief wanted to be said but could not say himself.

'Do you accuse me?' Lubinda was angry. The eyes shot out of his head and he looked fierce. He was a big man, Lubinda. His fists were clenched when he shot up, towering above the humble form of Banda, like an eagle about to sweep away a chicken.

But Banda also jumped up and said: 'No, the teacher is the witch, not you. But you have another idea in your head Lubinda. You are not concerned with avenging my brother's death, but with removing a man you imagine to be in love with Natombi. That is in your mind,' replied Banda quietly but firmly.

'You hyena!' shouted Lubinda, 'how dare you insult me like that, you who can't even stand up to your woman? You are a woman! If you're a man let's go outside and fight. You think I am your teacher, to be easily beaten?'

The others held the two, and removed Lubinda, who was the more troublesome.

'Are there any more to speak?' asked the Chief after settling down again. The Chief, even though he had a lot of power, knew that here he could not use it. This was a family matter rather than an affair of government. It concerned only the village, and they were all related to each other in one way or another.

'Yes, I wish to speak.' It was Cumba. Cumba knew more about the white man than all the rest put together. Moreover, behind that clownish face lay a courageous spirit. So they listened quietly. 'The teacher, let him go unless you all want to be hanged by the white man and the missionary like chickens. But he should go back to his home in Petauke. We do not want an evil one here.' Cumba also had spoken. This time it was not only the Chief who rejoiced, but everybody in the room.

'Yes, we agree, let him go.' And at that they began to troop out of the little hut.

The teacher was free, but not free to stay. No one bade him farewell. He went to the Chief to bid good-bye, but the Chief would not open his door to him. 'Go away, stranger, we do not know you,' shouted the Chief from inside his hut. The teacher and his wife and children left that very night.

Had Mpona carried the people with him, and where did Lubinda stand? Mpona wondered about Lubinda. The manner in which he had left the meeting was not a good one. With so many people depending on his medicines for health, this could be the worst thing ever to happen to the village. It was his fault, he felt. He should have concluded the discussion quickly. He wondered whether, although the people had accepted the reasons against giving Aphunzitsi mwabvi, they had really approved the decision. It was something that the old man Simbeya had advised caution even in the presence of Lubinda. But Banda should not have said such bad things against Lubinda in an open meeting. Moreover he drank too much, and the people would despise anything he said. It was not good to appear too friendly with this man.

Lubinda did not wonder about the Chief. That would have been a waste of time. He was too busy with his own plans: if they had to succeed he would have to work very fast. He cared little for people's company so that when they all deserted him he did not notice it. He had put his hand to the hoe and he did not mean to look back. Lubinda was sharpening the axe of revenge.

Chapter 7

Banda was coming from the bush one afternoon, carrying a bundle of rafters for his mother-in-law's hut, when he heard a voice calling behind him, 'Eti, you!' As the rafters were long and the path narrow, he could not turn with the load. So he stood it up and turned to see who the caller was. It was a Boma messenger, and Banda's insides froze. What could the Boma messengers be after, he thought. Had he heard of the expulsion of the teacher from the village, or was anything wrong he wondered.

'You are from Mpona, eti?' asked the messenger in a crisp tone which indicated exactly where authority lay.

'Yes, bwana,' replied Banda meekly. You had to address these people as bwana if you wanted to avoid trouble.

'Mpona is there, eti?'

'Yes, bwana, he is there,' replied the villager.

'He knows I'm coming, doesn't he, eti?' the messenger asked.

'Maybe he knows, bwana, but I do not know,' replied Banda.

Banda, of course, knew that the Chief did not know. But to have to tell this bwana that the news of his arrival had not preceded him would be insulting, as important people always like to think that their mere presence at one village was news thirty miles away. They reminded one of the short men, perhaps they were pygmies or bushmen, who were found in the valley. They were called the 'How-far-away-did-you-see-me' men, because that was the first question they asked you when you met them in the forest. If you replied, 'When I heard your footsteps near here,' they would shoot you with their poisoned arrows. But if you replied, 'Very far away, beyond those blue hills and the hills after that,' then you would become their greatest friend and they would dance and caper about, saying, 'So I am a tall one, so I am a tall one,' and give you meat and wild berries.

'I am going to Mpona to prepare for the visit next week of Bwana Mkubwa D.C.,' announced the messenger.

'I see, thank you very much, bwana,' replied Banda, at a loss to say something respectful.

'There,' said the messenger, pointing to his bundle of blankets and mealie-meal, 'carry this for me.'

Banda could not object, even if his own load was eating into his shoulders. 'Yes, bwana,' he replied, and proceeded to carry the messenger's load, his own load and the messenger's boots, which he said were pinching him.

The visit of a Boma messenger to any village was not an occasion for joy. Even less so in this case where the village feared for itself. But it was not only the affair of the kamcape and the teacher that bothered them. It was also the fear that the messenger had brought more laws to restrict their freedom, and the fact that any non-observance of these laws, no matter how trivial, could have dire consequences.

When the messenger arrived, the village people gathered round quickly. To a representative of a white man even the Chief was nothing more than part of the flock of sheep, to be gathered at will.

'Mpona!'

'Bwana!'

It was the messenger calling the rolé of all the registered males in the village.

'Simbeya!' There was no answer. The messenger called again. 'Simbeya, where is Simbeya?'

Mpona answered, 'He is not here, he is sick.'

'Sick?' repeated the messenger, 'What sickness?'

86

Should he reveal the sickness to a stranger? wondered Mpona. All the eyes that looked at him were pleading with him not to speak the truth, or at least to avoid the truth.

'He has got wounds, bwana. He burnt himself,' replied Mpona.

'Aha, so he has fits. Bring him out. I must see him,' said the messenger.

'No, bwana, it is not fits. It was just an accident. Hot water,' said Mpona.

'Do you argue with bwana? Bring Simbeya out.' The messenger's tone was final. It would not be well to argue. So two people went to fetch Simbeya.

'Aha!' exclaimed the messenger when Simbeya was brought out, 'so you keep lepers in this village, eti? Ten chickens for not obeying the law.' Then the messenger proceeded with the roll-call.

'Chipwaya.'

'Bwana.'

'Cumba.' There was no reply.

'Friends, let us remind each other,' said the Chief, turning to his colleagues. 'Was Cumba here this morning?' Then he turned to the messenger, 'Bwana, Cumba went to visit at Zumbo.'

'Zumbo? But that is Portuguese land. Why did you allow him to go there?' queried the messenger.

'He did not tell us, bwana, it is the wife who has told us,' replied Mpona.

'Five chickens each of you for helping him to run away. I know you have hidden him. But when the Bwana Mkubwa comes he must be here.'

'Yes, bwana,' replied Chief Mpona promptly, grateful that he had got off so lightly.

'Yuda.'

'Yuda, bwana, has a headache.' The Chief thought that he had answered cleverly by avoiding mention of the swellings on Yuda's face and ears, which were a mass of ugly blobs.

There was a tense silence among the people as they waited to hear the bwana's judgement.

'The head is painful, eh? Hmm, I suppose I had better see him for myself,' said the messenger slowly.

'Why did he not say that Yuda had gone to Walale?' whispered Banda to Lubinda.

'Don't ask me!' said Lubinda with the firmness of a man who was not concerned with stupid answers like the one the Chief had given.

'Bring the baboon out, I say,' shouted the messenger, 'Mpona, do you hear, eti?'

'Yes, bwana, but bwana, he is very sick,' pleaded the Chief. Protests were of no use, and Yuda was called out of his hut and paraded before the crowd. He too had leprosy.

'Now listen, all of you, I have some things to say to you,' the messenger said after checking the roll. 'Number one: when I come back with the Bwana Mkubwa, the D.C., I must have thirty chickens in all. Number two: I must find that you have dug all your latrines. It is not permitted to go into the bush. Number three: You must all have your seven-and-six ready for the tax. Number four: I want to find the village swept. Number five: The two lepers must go to the hospital in Lusaka. The doctor is coming in three days' time to fetch them. Number six: No witchcraft, and no kamcape.'

They listened meekly, but obviously they were worried.

'By the way, where is the teacher?' This was the bombshell that they had hoped to avoid. The Chief fortified himself for the crash. But Banda came to his rescue and replied, 'He went on leave to his home.' The messenger, neither knowing the school calendar nor caring much about the whole business of reading and writing, did not pursue the matter further, and the meeting was ended.

The veil of terror had been lifted for at least another week. But this week would be as long as a month and as short as a day.

As soon as the messenger departed, Cumba emerged from almost nowhere, to the surprise of even those who had supported the lie told to the messenger. He was laughing as usual, and asking about the orders the messenger had issued. But when he was told that his absence would cost each family five fowls and that the Chief had decided that Cumba would have to replace these fowls, he was furious.

'He can give his messengers his own fowls and those of his grandmother and grandmother's mother. Not mine. Was he there when I was sweating it out to rear my chickens? No! If he knew that the messenger would fine the village, why didn't he come to look for me then? If he takes my fowls, that is theft. In the past, when there was justice in this country, the punishment for that was death!' said Cumba.

Cumba was allergic to thieves, who by definition were anyone other than himself who took other people's property without permission, and even the theft of a string would send him yelling to every door, including that of the Chief.

'Taking my fowls without my consent is theft, do you understand, all you people in your houses? Even if you close your doors, you can still hear my voice, the voice of Cumba. Do you understand, you?' It was midnight, but Cumba was still ranting and broadcasting his morality to the village at large. 'If you want,' he continued, 'you can skin me from the nails to the knees, to the stomach, to the chest and the hair on my chest and on my head, including my eyes. We shall see whether your messengers will eat my skin.'

The following morning, when the Chief's child went to let out the chickens, he found that there were none left. Cumba's chickens had also disappeared. And, what was more, the man Cumba had vanished too. If the Chief was worried about his loss it was just too bad, because he must have known – as all the people did – that in owning anything there was always the risk that Cumba might steal it. Besides, there were other more serious matters to worry about. First of all the latrines. The people of Mpona, as indeed the people of the whole valley, were and still are very hard-working. Getting the latrines dug within the fortnight's grace allowed them before the D.C. came was no problem. Most of them dug the equivalent of two latrine pits every day anyway, as they had to bore deep through the sands before they could reach the clay soil to deposit the maize seed for the winter planting. And yet they were worried.

'It is impossible for us to agree to this.' Lubinda was holding forth. 'The white missionary cursed us and brought water to drown our crop, and then, through his teacher, caused the death of Dulani. Now the white bwana comes and we must dig latrines. How far shall we go in obeying these people without skins? The time has come for us to tell them to kill us, if that is what they want.' There was a murmur of approval.

He continued: 'How can we go to the same hole as our mothers-in-law when we cannot even eat in each other's sight? Are we mfungo?' They all laughed, but uneasily, because the greater the objections the more worried they became at the thought of obeying the white man.

'Does he want us to stink like mfungo?' asked Lubinda. 'That is the animal the latrine should be dug for, because it always excretes in one place. Are we mfungo, or does the Chief think that we are?'

They debated the matter as each worked on his basket, axe handle, or pig trap. More and more reasons were advanced against latrine pits, such as that children would fall into them. If that happened, then they could not be taken out and they would have to be buried there and then. This would be the end of the village, as it would now become a graveyard.

'Think of me standing up from a beer party and going into this house,' said Banda. 'Everyone, including my children and my in-laws, will know what I am doing in there. Who is going to respect me after that?'

'It's a dirty habit, this habit of the white man. We don't want it here. If we agree to this, he will soon be asking us to bury all our dead in one hole and maybe – who knows – we shall soon be blowing our noses in one hole too.' Lubinda's imagination was at work. They had a good laugh. But what would they do?

'I think I know what to do, friends,' said the Chief. 'Let's build the houses the white man wants. But no one should dig the holes. The white man cannot go into where the black one goes to excrete. He will be satisfied if he sees the small houses.'

'But why should we take all this trouble?' objected Lubinda. 'Let us tell him that it is against our custom to build such things and dig such holes. If we don't refuse now, he will think that he has won, and tomorrow we will have to do other things. I have got medicine that can make him forget to ask for the latrines.'

'It's not safe,' replied Simbeya, who had been carried there to participate in the debate. 'Your medicines can't work against the white man, and, if they do, you won't know in what way they will work. We shall be in trouble.' As usual, Simbeya had not committed himself to any course of action except to warn against the use of medicine. 'My days are numbered,' he continued. 'In our times these things could not be talked of. The white man is disgracing us. It is as though my daughter-in-law goes to the bush in my house.'

The debate finally ended, and all set to building the small huts in the trees behind their living quarters. They did not dig more than a foot deep. But from outside, the huts looked like real latrines and even from inside, unless you lifted the grass cover, you would not have noticed that the pit was shallow. They did, however, dig a real latrine pit for the D.C., and another for his messengers. But this was far away from the village at the camp where the white man and his messengers would quarter.

A week later the D.C. duly arrived. He was preceded by a long procession of carriers, too many certainly to count on one's fingers and toes. Each of them carried a large box, a basket or bucket of something or other. The big bwana himself finally arrived: he must have been about six foot tall; his arms were large and, although his legs were hidden behind the khaki trousers, they too were obviously very big. As for his face, it was fiercely red and puffed up, looking very much like an underdone piece of baboon steak.

His nostrils, which were narrow slits in his breathing apparatus, looked as though they were suspended from the bridge of the nose, which ran horizontal, and parallel to his feet. Consequently, his upper lip barely covered his upper teeth, and it was as thin and stretched as the skin of an inflated balloon. His chin, which fell down perpendicularly to his neck for the first part of its course, ended in an ominous confusion with the lower part of the neck, so that it was impossible to say where the chin ended and the neck proper started. Then his unbuttoned chest was covered in a mass of black hair. He breathed heavily and noisily. All in all he was very strange looking. It was not surprising that such an owlish individual could conceive of such terrible schemes as latrine pits, thought Lubinda, in which to dispose of the children as quickly as possible.

His title was Bwana Mkubwa the D.C., but the people called him Bwana Mandimu, which means lemon. Bwana Mandimu always carried a bottle of gin, which he drank with a slice of lemon and a drop or two of water.

On the afternoon of his arrival, the slow beat of the drum was heard, the beat which summoned the village to gather for war. But everyone knew that it was not a war-call. They were all required at the D.C.'s camp. When all the people had assembled, the senior messenger called on the women to form a circle. It was as though they were being lined up for a slave march. Then the D.C. himself appeared and sat in the middle of the circle with his messengers and kapasos. Drums struck; the women took up the song. It was the ndendeule dance. The main fascination of this dance is that at fixed intervals in the drumming and singing, the women wheel, set and click. As their dress consists of nothing but a simple cloth wrapped around their waists, when they set they exposed part of their thighs. This delighted the big bwana enormously. He threw halfpenny after halfpenny into the dancing ring. In the meantime, the senior messenger surveyed the thighs and breasts of the nearly naked dancing women. His trained and roving eye fell on one – a young and lithe girl. He said: 'Stop!' raising his arms. 'You are not doing the dance properly.' Then he demonstrated how it should be done. Everyone laughed including the D.C. It was good to laugh with such a fierce-looking man. The senior messenger, in the split second of goodwill, darted a glance at the D.C. as if to say 'there is your kill for tonight'. So the dance resumed and the women gyrated in circles.

'You,' said the messenger, pointing to the pretty girl, 'come here!' He brought the coy creature into the centre of the circle, so close to the big bwana that his ferreting nose was almost touching her bare tummy. His eyes ogled her smooth body with glee.

'Drums. Start the drums. I want only her to dance this time,' said the messenger.

The young girl looked back at her newly-wed husband to seek approval. But how could she expect him to approve, as if he had told the messenger to pick on her, or to disapprove, as though it was not for the white man that these things were being done? She was, for the brief moment, her village's ambassador of goodwill to the white man. All other eyes urged her to show the white man how well the beautiful girls of the village danced.

So the girl danced. She turned her cloth this way and that, she wriggled her body and shook her bare breasts, loosening her whole body in a dance of crazy abandon. The white man, beside himself with joy, lifted up one edge of her cloth and chuckled massively. The drummers played on until their hands and the skins of the drums were covered in sweat. Their muscles glistened in the setting twilight. Then the messenger lifted his hand to indicate 'stop', and the Bwana Mkubwa handed the dancer one shilling, and the drummers sixpence between the five of them.

That evening after draining a full bottle of gin, the D.C. made the following entry in his Tour Report Book: 'Visited Mpona village 24 July. Treated to a primitive and uncivilized pagan dance called *Dedeule* – a culturally barren dance in which the indolent native revels. The stench exuding from the unwashed bodies of the dancers and drummers is enough to knock out even an Italian.'

The following day the D.C. collected taxes. Cumba, of course, was missing. At the end of the proceedings, a large number of chickens were presented to him. He inquired about the latrines, but when the headman pointed them out, he ticked off the item and was satisfied.

'What about the lepers, have they gone?' asked the messenger, by way of showing the D.C. that the preparation for his trip had been thorough.

'No, Bwana, the doctor has not come yet. We hear that he will come next week,' replied Mpona.

The whole thing was over and done with, and this time an even heavier cloud lifted from the shoulders of the village as they sang and clapped the Bwana Mkubwa away. But the messenger said to them all in a parting shot, 'The lepers, I don't want to find them when I come again. Next week they must go, the two of them.'

Many of the people were surprised at how much kinder the big bwana appeared to be than his messengers. This was in spite of the fact that the D.C. had remarked about the poor quality of chickens that the village had offered him, and had exhorted them to do better next time. The messenger, the one with the very fat stomach, had felt it necessary to elaborate on this theme and had paraphrased the D.C.'s remarks as follows:

'Bwana Mkubwa says that the chickens you have given him are as thin as your grandmothers. Next time, they must be as fat as himself. Right, eti?'

The Chief did not say anything, but simply stood up with all his kapasos and the Councillor to accompany the D.C. But Lubinda, before departing and when the messenger was out of earshot said, 'You pig!'

The women cheered, and Lubinda took his leave with more ceremony than the Chief.

·   ·   ·   ·   ·

Two days later, Mpona returned and found that the bubble of calm which had followed the visit of the D.C. had been pricked. A more serious issue had now to be considered. It concerned the deportation from the village of the two lepers.

'He comes tomorrow, the doctor?' Simbeya stirred up from his bed.

'Yes,' said his wife, wiping a tear from her eyes. 'But I will go with you.'

'You can't go with me, mother of Msonda, you must remain to look after the grandchildren. Who will look after them with their father away?' replied Simbeya.

'But you cannot go alone to a strange land which no one knows. You are a sick man.'

'Things have changed, mother of Msonda. It was not so bad in the old days when they set you apart at the end of the village if you were a leper. The people still knew where you were and they threw you some food. But this journey – I'll never see these children again, my grandchildren and you.' Then Simbeya thought for a moment and asked, 'Is it true, my wife, what they say about the white man, that he removes your inside before you die?'

'It must be true. He is a cruel one though he may not show it,' replied his wife.

'In that case, in that case, well . . .' Simbeya stopped. It was womanish, even at his age, to show self-pity. This woman needed to be comforted because she would suffer as much.

An entirely different scene was being enacted in the house farther down the village.

'Naome, do you know I go tomorrow?' rasped Yuda.

'Yes, I know,' replied the woman.

'Then, why don't you prepare my food for the journey? Don't you know I'll never come back again?' asked Yuda.

'So you want to go, do you? Can't you think of the children? Who will look after the children?' asked the wife in anger.

'Do I want to go? You heard the messenger, didn't you? The white man has said so, not I.' He stopped for a moment and he began to feel anger that this woman was accusing him of wanting to go. 'Don't sit there like a pumpkin. Prepare me the food. Do you want to eat all the chickens when I am gone?'

'But you can't leave me alone with the children. I must go with you. We shall build a house near where the white man will take you,' pleaded Naome.

'Shut up, you . . .' he checked himself. But, why not torture her? 'It will give you the chance you have been waiting for. You want to marry a young man who has no sores on his face, hands, or feet, don't you?'

'You lie and you know it,' Naome was crying.

'Then why do you always chase flies away from you as if they have come from a rotting corpse? Why don't you eat from the same dish as me? I am treated like a rotting leper in this house.' He stood up. 'I can't even touch my own children. Never! So what's the use of staying, tell me!'

'But you yourself stopped me and the children from eating with you,' replied Naome.

'Yes, because when you ate with me you looked as if you were eating a frog. Didn't you?' Yuda was really angry. The woman sobbed, but Yuda went on. 'Shut up, you harlot,' he yelled, 'you arranged it all with the senior messenger who came here. You think I didn't know, eh?'

'You are a liar. You know I do not want to leave you,' moaned the woman.

'Ha, ha! Then why did you give the messenger six fowls when all the other people only gave four? And you chose my fattest fowls. Why did you take the food to the tent late at night when all the other women took it there while it was still light? At the dance I hear that you danced very hard, always in the direction of this messenger. What were you showing him? You'll go to your fat messenger when I leave this house, I know it. I know the fat pig with the fat fingers is waiting for you.'

A voice outside said, 'Odi.' It was the Chief.

'You come early,' said Yuda when Mpona entered the hut.

'Yes, my son,' replied the Chief.

'Is it well at the house?' asked Yuda.

'It is well. What about here; are you well, my son?'

'I am well. A maimed man cannot expect to be as well as those who are lucky enough to have health,' replied Yuda. 'You come to ask after my health, eh? It is as good as can be expected after being paraded round like rotten meat full of maggots which no one will touch.'

'But, my son, it was the white man's wish,' said the Chief.

'I know a thing or two, all the same. Lubinda has told me how much you did to protect me. You are a wonderful father of the village, aren't you! Naome!' he roared, 'give the Chief some of that kacasu I have left.' The Chief thanked him, but protested that he did not drink such strong liquor, and in any case, it was too early.

'All right, do not say then that I did not give you some drink. You are all the same, you people in this village. I give you drink, and you refuse because you do not want to share a bottle with a leper. Then, when you leave here, you say, "Yuda is selfish, he doesn't give." I don't care for you, you kind people!' Yuda's voice built up to a deafening crescendo.

The Chief had not expected this. But with Yuda everything and anything was possible; lepers are short-tempered.

'I have come about the visit of the Bwana Mkubwa,' said Mpona.

'Yes, when are you casting me away? Tomorrow, isn't it?' Yuda was not co-operating. 'Are you going to say "no" to the white man then? "No" for the first time in your life since you came out of your mother?' This was rude talk to an elder. You don't state the origins of an elder as crudely as that. But what could Mpona do?

'How can I say no to the white man's orders?' said Mpona. 'My nephew,' he continued, 'we have thought long and hard about this matter. It is useless to refuse. We shall all go to the white man's prison, the whole village, if we refuse, and probably we shall all be killed. Think of the village. Your mother, who will look after her if we all go to prison?'

'Who will look after my children and my wife if I go? Oh, I

forgot. You will give her to your fat messenger for a third wife, won't you?' Yuda was rubbing it in.

Mpona pitied his nephew very much. He had grown so sour-mouthed since his illness. He thought of the days when this boy would climb his knees in joy, and then of the time he returned from town. How many things he had brought for him, so that even his father was jealous of the uncle. Was it right to obey the white man in a matter such as this? If so, once again, where would the white man stop? Why did the white man not allow them to separate the lepers at the end of the village? Then they could see their children, and food could be taken to them every day. But this thing of going to Lusaka, eighteen days' journey on foot, was too much. How would they know what was happening to them? It was a cruel thing, this thing that they were doing to these lepers.

A voice said, 'Odi' outside.

'Mpona!' said the new arrival, 'the men want to talk of this matter of the white man. It has not pleased them.' It was Lubinda.

'Lubinda,' said the Chief, 'what else can we do? The white man has guns, which can see you from afar. He can see what we do here from Lusaka.' Mpona was speaking more to himself than to Lubinda.

'You and your guns,' said Lubinda contemptuously. 'Why did he fail to shoot us all when we went on strike at the mines? The white man failed to kill us, even though he had guns and we had nothing except our hands and our words. Here you have everything. We have guns, knives and spears. When shall we use them? Why are you afraid of doing what is right?'

When they reached the meeting place at the big tree which stood in the centre of the village, Mpona could sense greater anger in the people's faces than ever before.

'It's too much now,' said Lubinda. 'Our customs are being despised by the missionary, and our children have been made to turn against the breast that fed them. We can't mourn our dead without the missionary breaking up our ceremony. We

98

must not go to the bush as we like, but we must dig a pit. Then we must dig long trenches in our fields to protect the crop against water. Where is the rain in this country, and when it comes doesn't it form a river? How many rivers shall we dig to protect our crop? From when we stopped praying for rain, how much rain has come, except as floods?'

People murmured approval.

He continued: 'Now,' he said, heaving his chest, 'this new thing. We must bury our lepers alive. Will the white man soon decide our wives? Why was he looking at their thighs like that, even in the presence of their husbands and fathers-in-law?'

Yet another murmur of approval, which broke into, 'It's true, it's true.' Lubinda had scored.

'And now,' resumed Lubinda, 'we must resist. The time has come to . . .' They heard the cackling of hens from the hut behind them. They all looked and there was Cumba, carrying two large crates of chickens! For the moment there was astonishment and the people remained silent. Cumba walked straight up to Mpona and deposited the fowls at his feet. He whispered, 'I have returned your fowls. I didn't want the white man to eat them.'

'This is a man,' whispered several voices, and then there was loud cheering for Cumba and shouts of, 'you have done well, we would have lost our chickens.'

It was quite clear to the Chief that the white man's law had to be defied. Mpona said: 'Friends, it is the stranger who travels with a sharp razor blade,' meaning that the stranger may have wise counsel. 'Let us talk this matter over again.' Then he recounted the situation to Cumba, from the arrival of the Bwana's messenger to the present debate. Cumba kept nodding his head significantly and knitting his brows. His plans were forming.

'I don't agree with this way of doing things,' Cumba said after listening to him. They were all surprised that Cumba did not approve of their resistance.

'No, comrades,' continued Cumba, 'if you offend the white man, then you are finished. I don't mind annoying him myself.

But the whole village? No.' Then came his judgement: 'Let Yuda go. Wherever they will send him, I will follow and be near him. You know that I can go anywhere I want. But Simbeya, no, he is an old one. You must tell the doctor when he comes tomorrow that he is too old and would die if he travelled. He will understand.'

It was clear. They all trusted Cumba in matters concerning the white man. Lubinda wanted to speak, but the other people said that Cumba knew the white man better. If he promised to be near Yuda, then he would be. Had he not come back, and with all Mpona's chickens, because he wanted to help the village?

The following day, in the evening, the health orderly came from Lusaka. This was the 'doctor' the messenger had referred to. He came when the sun had almost set. All the people had gathered to bid good-bye to Yuda, or Yuda and Simbeya; the only absentee was Cumba, whose practice it was not to meet anyone from the Boma. The orderly intended to travel the thirty miles to the bridge that night, as it was hot during the day and the sores of the lepers would stink, as he put it. The question of Simbeya was easily disposed of, as the orderly was not interested in anyone who was too old and could not walk the distance in a reasonable time. So, after the orderly had eaten at Mpona's house, the Chief and the other people gathered outside Yuda's house, waiting for him to come out.

'Yuda! Leper! are you ready to travel now?' called out the orderly who, with a full stomach, now thought it proper to appear impatient. 'Come and join your fellow lepers, they are waiting for you on the outskirts of the village.'

'I'm coming,' said a rough voice from within. 'You can take me.'

To the orderly these lepers were just names, names to be matched against the numbers just as you brand cattle. It was not for him to share in the tragedy of parting from friends and loved ones. He did his job better if he ignored these things. After all, this fellow Yuda, who sounded rather rough from his voice, was only one of several lepers he had to drive to the bridge. He too, if his hands were not covered with wounds, would have to take his turn at carrying his luggage.

'Come out, leper!' the orderly roared. 'Do you want me to tie you to a rope like a goat?'

'I'm coming,' said a voice within, 'my blanket, ah, here!' The Chief pricked up his ears. Something seemed strange.

'Leper! You goat, come out!' yelled the orderly. The leper emerged. He wore a hood which just allowed enough of an opening for his face to jut out. His hands and feet were bound in black pieces of cloth, with the rope bound over and over. The man walked with a painful gait and his head was cast down so that no one could see his face. Mpona bent sideways to look at the leper closely. The leper pressed his hand with meaning as he passed him and silently hobbled away with the blanket slung over his back. Cumba, and not Yuda, was on his way to Lusaka.

The travellers reached Luangwa Bridge early in the morning when it was still dark, the time when you begin to see the shape of objects if you look long enough. They were in luck. They had hardly sat down by the roadside to rest when a lorry came by. It was carrying pigs from Chipata.

'These men go to Lusaka, driver. They are Government passengers and here is the warrant for all the six,' said the orderly.

'But the lorry is full of pigs. I have no room for people,' replied the driver.

'Don't worry,' said the orderly, 'they are only lepers, all of them. You see, I am the Government doctor from Lusaka and I have been collecting these things from the villages around here.'

'But there is no room for you in front, sir,' replied the driver. When the orderly said that he himself did not have to go, as he could spend the time fishing out some more lepers, the driver, who was afraid to carry lepers, said, 'But sir, I cannot carry lepers in the same truck as pigs which are going to be eaten by white men in Lusaka.'

Even the orderly became annoyed. 'You stupid driver, are pigs better than people?' he exclaimed. 'These are your fellow black men.'

'But, sir, if they are my fellow black men, why should I carry them with pigs, like pigs? Do you want me to leave the pigs then?' asked the driver.

The orderly, too much of a realist not to appreciate the dire consequences of leaving the pigs behind, gave way, saying, 'I will see you in Lusaka. You understand driver!' And the pigs sped on their way to slaughter.

But he had to give vent to his feelings of frustration. 'You!' he said to Cumba, 'take those dirty bandages off your hands.' Cumba did not reply, but simply offered his hands to the orderly. Cumba had taken care to oil the clothes thoroughly so that it would appear that the wounds were oozing pus. If he unties my bandages, Cumba thought, then I will hit him. Why should he expect these lepers to ride with pigs?

'Take away your paws,' the orderly rasped. 'I don't touch diseases.' So that ended the first test.

Soon another lorry came. By this time the sun was just rising. Fortunately, the orderly knew the driver. Within moments they were off. This was no joy-ride. Perhaps they would never return.

The first hundred miles or so went slowly and in silence. But then you have to share your loss with someone, even though you know that he has lost as much as you or even more. Thus conversation started. Cumba soon learnt a lot about these strange fellow-travellers and about the stage of their illnesses.

'I have five children,' said one. 'The youngest is only one year old and the mother died last month. My father hanged himself when I was young. Now I don't know who will look after them.'

'That was a strange thing to do,' said Cumba after some silence. 'Why did he hang himself, as if there were no witches to bewitch him?' They all laughed, but uneasily. You could laugh at what happened so many years ago, especially if you were too young even to remember your father.

'He quarrelled with my mother because she accused him of giving all the things that he had brought from Walale to his mother, my grandmother,' the narrator replied.

Cumba did not speak further. But he wondered that some people could kill themselves because of a woman. Personally, he would far sooner find a quarrel to separate him from his wife than live with her. He had tried several forms of provocation. But his wife had a thick skin and had never taken offence. On the contrary, every time he sent her to her mother she came back. He was thoroughly fed up with her. To quarrel because you give your wealth to your mother! Who else can you give it to? The woman is not your relation. And then to hang yourself! 'Ha, ha,' Cumba laughed aloud. They all looked at him in surprise.

'I, too, I will miss my wife,' stated Cumba, 'and children too.' Cumba, of course, had no children. 'My maize field will lie fallow.' (It had lain so ever since the Chief had given it to him.) 'And I will miss the Sunday hymns at prayers.' (The first and last time that he had attended mass it had never been completed because at the Offertory the priest had suddenly discovered that the two bottles of wine had gone.)

'I have large wounds, my friends, especially on the fingers,' continued Cumba.

'Are they as terrible as these?' asked one leper, showing his mutilated hand.

'Don't show such ugly hands,' interrupted Cumba, sniffing with disgust. 'Why do you have to show your wounds like that? Do you think we like them?'

All the others agreed with Cumba and the enthusiastic one

felt bashful. You could not share your sufferings even with these men.

The lorry stopped at Chongwe. The driver, who did not need to tell the passengers why and for how long they had stopped, slammed his door as he walked away. He had social responsibilities to fulfil.

'Ah, it's you, you naughty one,' said a mosquito voice from within a house.

'Why, aren't you happy to see me?' replied a deep voice.

'Why didn't you stop here last time? You stopped at Luangwa Bridge, I know that. When I meet her we will fight,' replied the coquettish one.

'Ha, ha, ha,' laughed the deep voice. 'Come, what have you cooked for me?'

And so hours passed and the driver did not appear. When he finally mounted the lorry to start off, he heard someone thumping the roof of his cabin.

'What is it?' he asked.

'Cumba has not returned yet,' replied a voice in the back of the lorry.

'Where is he, then?' asked the driver.

'He said he knew the woman you had gone to visit and he wanted to make sure she gave you food,' replied the voice again.

'What? So he is there now? I am going to skin that woman.' So saying, he leapt down and ran back to the house.

'Where is the leper, woman?' he asked.

'Which leper? I don't know any leper,' replied the woman.

'You know him, and you are hiding him in your bed,' protested the man.

'Mr Lungu, would I sleep with a leper, me?' the woman inquired scornfully of the driver.

'Yes, you street women sleep with anything. Show me your bed,' insisted Mr Lungu. 'I know the stinking idiot is there. You women are animals, monkeys!'

Saying that, he rushed towards the door. She ran to bar his way, but he smacked her and, jumping over her fallen body, pushed the door open and threw the mat and blanket off the bed of sticks. A blow struck him on the neck. He looked back: 'You leper!' he exclaimed. Then another, and then another, and the driver passed out. Cumba fled with his mistress. It was, after all, only thirty miles to Lusaka.

Chapter 8

The village of Mpona should have gone back to normal. The witch had been disposed of in a manner that appeared to have satisfied the people and, up to now, there had been no official reaction from either the missionary or the D.C. The village had successfully evaded digging the white man's latrines and, what was more important, using them. Through the good offices of Cumba, the village had not given up even one of their lepers, not even his sores!

But the village of Mpona did not return to normal. No person dies from one blow unless he is drunk. In the case of the late Dulani it could not have been just one man, the teacher, who had bewitched him. So the gossip that had started before Dulani was buried increased.

'That woman,' said Lubinda confidentially to his nephew: 'Do you believe that she didn't help the teacher?'

'To do what?' asked the nephew.

'You know what I mean.' He kept quiet. 'I will tell you something I haven't told anybody else.' The nephew was the fifth man he was telling. This means that he was the fourteenth person, making allowance for the higher velocity of circulation of rumours among women.

'Natombi,' he confided. 'I caught her with the teacher in the maize.'

'But why didn't you speak out when Banda was saying those bad things against you?' asked the nephew.

'My boy,' replied Lubinda, 'I know many things which would ruin this village of yours. This village floats on the river. It won't be long before it will sink.' He stopped to watch the effect. 'Mpona, do you think he is as upright as he looks? There are many children, and many women in this village. But the fathers, they are few.'

'I see.'

'That woman, she doesn't like me. Why?' asked Lubinda. Then he answered his own question. 'She knows I know what I know. She and the teacher bewitched Dulani. Don't doubt it.'

'But uncle, the teacher, he ne —'

'My boy, I see what I see. But I don't talk like other people do. Do you know why the Chief didn't like to call the witch-diviner?' asked Lubinda. 'Don't speak to anyone else about these things,' he said, pressing his nephew's hand.

Lubinda also took care to keep his old first wife well-supplied with similar hints.

'Why don't you marry your concubine now that the man is dead?' said the woman irritated by his sitting down as though he had been worn out by moving mountains. But Lubinda knew how to handle this woman. She was old, but easily the best cook of all his three wives. Moreover, he even loved her.

'Ha, ha, ha,' he laughed, 'you too! Ha, ha, ha! Lubinda going around with your daughters, eh? Ha, ha, ha! That small chicken, you cooked it well yesterday. Bring the pot, you know they say that the remains of the pot are for the husband.'

'Your other women, they will cook for you tonight,' said the woman, already feeling rather proud of herself and hoping that he would spend the night with her.

'Them? Ha, ha, ha! They are just for hoeing the garden. Especially the mother of Mwai – her mother did not teach her how to cook. These women do not understand that it is eating that makes a man. You should look at his stomach.' He paused, and his wife asked him:

'What about Namayele, isn't she pretty?' He knew she was teasing him, so he pursued the matter to the real issue.

'Some little old men!' he clapped his hands together in a gesture of bafflement. 'Is it true about the widow and the teacher?'

'What happened?' the woman was all ears.

'Oh well, it's an old story. But now I hear the Chief of the village throws a leg there. Listening to too much hearsay destroyed the squirrel's marriage,' he concluded.

'Ha, the people of this village!' exclaimed his wife, hoping for more information. Lubinda was too clever to go any further.

Thus it was that the women of the village avoided Natombi's company. Whenever they were gathered, and if she went to join them, they would disperse one by one until she too had to leave. It felt awkward to sit outside the house when other people were pounding maize. So she went to help, as was often done. She offered her services to one woman. The woman said, 'No, there is just a little left, I will finish it.' Then to another, who exclaimed, 'Oh no, poor me, no one ever helps me. Why should they now?' And to a third, who shouted to her friends in Natombi's full hearing. 'Beware hungry vixens who pound their way to your husbands' hearts.' They all laughed and deserted the place, leaving her alone with the mortars and the pounding sticks.

Several men had been watching this from the verandas of their huts, as it was noon. As she passed one hut on her way back, one man shouted to another across her path, 'The meat of a hyena!'

The other answered, 'Only witches eat it.'

And then the first man shouted back, 'The meat which never finishes.'

The other replied, 'It is human meat.' They both laughed and whistled. Natombi understood what these conundrums meant. She was a witch.

When Natombi crossed the path of any of the women as they went to draw water, they would go into the grass, leaving the whole way for her, even if it was they who had filled jars.

Some would say to the others as they passed her, 'She who drinks with the one of the night must have a charm to protect her.'

But these gestures of animosity did not seem to be making an impression on Natombi as far as they were concerned, even though she and the dumb child Mwape were becoming thinner and thinner.

'It's the meat of her husband which is turning against her now,' said one woman.

'Have you seen the marks on her face?' asked another. 'These strange things she does at night will snare you young girls!'

So some three women, including Lubinda's senior wife, decided on a confrontation. Natombi was carrying a jar full of water from the well when she met these women. As usual they gave her a wide berth. But when she was abreast of them, they jostled her.

'Why do you knock me over like this?' said one.

'What have I done to you, you slut?' asked another.

'Ha, you want to kill my friends,' exclaimed the third.

Then they fell on her, clawing her face and arms and beating her up. The jar crashed to the ground.

'You witch, you ate your husband and now you want to take ours. Take this, take that.' Then they ran away. Natombi got up and walked back to her hut without any water.

So she began to avoid meeting people. She drew her water after sunset or in the dark, around dawn. By daybreak she and the child had already left for the garden – not that there was any maize to look after, but it was a way of spending time in a sheltered place. If she walked during daylight, she took the most lonely paths and sometimes went through the bush. There was a small path to the fields which no one took because it had a bad reputation. It was said that some years ago the witch-diviner had petrified a procession of witches there as they were crossing the path at night. In the morning the whole village had gone there and found ten or so people riveted to the ground carrying meali-meal and human flesh from the grave. But now Natombi had to use paths like this one, and people talked.

'Why does she walk at night?' asked Banda, whose hatred for her had grown intense at the thought that she had been the real cause of his brother's death, even though he knew that what he had said about Lubinda at that other meeting when the teacher was to die was true.

'You think she sleeps at night?' queried his wife. 'I tell you, she gets up to things at night. If you go to her garden during the day, you will find her asleep.'

It was on one of these evening visits to the well by this secret and frightening path that she heard a voice whisper from behind her, so near that she jumped forward before she could turn round.

'Natombi,' whispered the voice in clear tones. 'Natombi!' Her heart beat hard against her frail chest and the body squirmed with fear as though a snake was crawling into her head from the stomach.

'Natombi, I want you, you, and only you,' whispered the hoarse voice, panting with emotion.

She stood there perplexed and trembling with fear. A snake-like hand crept on to her body. She had not realized in the dark that the owner of the voice was so near. She jumped with a scream and began to run, running farther into the bush, not knowing where to run. The voice caught up with her and soon it was in front of her, barring her way.

'Natombi,' it whispered, 'I don't want to harm you. But, if you don't agree, I will . . .' Saying that, the voice lunged forward. She felt hands close upon her, cold, slippery, but firm hands. She struggled and yelled. It was Lubinda. He clamped her mouth with one hand and pinned her to the ground with the other, so that she fell with her back to the ground. She kicked him hard in the belly with her feet. He fell back and, as he made to rush on her like a wounded leopard, she ran. He too ran after her in the dark. Her hands fell on a stick. She flung it back without turning round. The stick crashed into Lubinda's face. Before he could recover his balance, she was gone.

No one saw her pant into her hut, as all the villagers had already gone into their houses. Lubinda told his wife that he had fallen down while coming home from setting the traps for the wild pigs. He was sure that she would believe him, and after the hints he had given about the Chief and Natombi, who could ever think that it was he and not Mpona who was trying to put his leg there?

The gossip about Natombi did not decrease with the greater difficulties that fell upon the village; on the contrary, it increased.

The floods that took Dulani had not made complete havoc of the crop. But when the locusts had come they had chewed up every blade of maize. Now the people were waiting for the winter crop. All their hopes were pinned on it. Would it grow, and would the grain be given time to form, time to ripen?

Mpona rose early one morning to go to his garden. The night had been cold. His wife, who had been awakened by the bustle of his departure, heard a shrill cry from the direction of the gardens. She rushed out of the hut, sure that it was her husband's voice.

'My husband, the lion has killed him, the lion has killed him.' She was running up and down the village shouting in a frenzy. The men jumped out of their beds and, grabbing axes and spears, ran in the direction he had taken. Then they heard the shrill cry for themselves and saw Mpona running towards them.

'Where has the lion gone?' shouted one excitedly. 'Some of you go back to the village. It may have run that way.'

The Chief was panting.

'What is it, Chief?' asked another.

'The . . . the maize. All g. . . gone,' panted Mpona.

'What? Who has stolen it?' asked several voices.

'F . . . frost. It's all burnt out,' he replied.

The men ran to their gardens, and soon cries of distress were heard. Hunger had come again.

Have you ever experienced real hunger? Not the hunger of one day or one week, but the hunger that knows no end because there is no food? It is not the hunger that they call malnutrition. For while this kills you in the long run, you will die still smiling because your stomach is full. There is a hunger that gnaws at your stomach and then intestines until you can no longer feel them because they have become so light. You can cry if you want to, but even tears have an end; tears after all come from the food you eat. Even as I speak, there are stomachs in this country of ours whose skins part from the spine only once a week. This is hunger. So you know it now.

When there is enough for everybody, then to give is not necessary, though it helps social contacts. Look at the people of Lusaka – they stand drinks in turn either at the old men's pub, or at Saigar, or in their houses. They call friends to drink at their houses because tomorrow they will also drink in their friends' houses. It is a good thing. But to give when you have little is a different thing to do, and more so to give when you have little to people who have even less than you.

Here in town it is easier not to give in these circumstances because a man can close his door and eat alone with his family, and if his chewing is noisy, he can drown it with the noise of the radiogram. But in the village, where people eat outside – usually the men together and the women together – how can you stand up and close your door and eat inside your house? What will other people say? And will the lump of food not stick in your throat?

So the people of Mpona had no choice but to help each other. Soon the communal eating ceased, but small plates of mealie-meal continued to pass between houses and families. Then fewer fires began to appear outside each house, and people entered their houses early because it was good to smell the little food as it cooked in their own house. But small parcels of mealie-meal and sometimes some meat continued to pass. They say that the citizens of a village are like roots: they meet underground.

But the roots of one person did not meet underground with those of the other people. This person was Natombi. Why, they asked, should we help her when it was she and her teacher, with the help of the white missionary, who caused the flood that killed her husband? The flood that ate the crop, and the snake that was still swallowing them? When the men came back from searching for food from other villages far away, it was as if the dying plant had received water. The village came to life again, drums beat and children played. But what is not of your home does not multiply. It finishes quickly.

So the hunger would return with more force and soon people began to finish off their chickens, then goats, and then they began to forget that their dogs were not goats.

It was against this background that Natombi set off one day early at dawn with her faithful Mwape, in search of food. Where, it did not matter, so long as she went to where people did not know her. They had laughed at her enough, she thought.

'Now,' said Lubinda to his nephew and newly found ally, Yuda, 'we have got rid of the second witch without even so much as a kamcape. Now for the third and biggest witch.' The very night of Natombi's departure, her house was partly gutted by flames.

Natombi left Mpona in the crisp hours of early dawn alone with her child, Mwape. Who was there to bid good-bye to? Hunger can put many miles of sand between people who once cared for each other. She had never cared for Lubinda, in fact she despised him. To her Lubinda was unrelieved evil. It was because she had refused him that she had become ostracized. The Chief should not be friendly with him. And yet now they were so close. It was strange, she said in her heart, how hunger could bring a snake and a lamb so close together. Her heart leapt into her mouth at the thought of a snake. It was the snake that had killed her husband. Who could have sent it? There was only one person. 'But they all think he is the saviour of the village,' she muttered aloud as anger and contempt for the people of Mpona welled up in her heart. 'A saviour of the village against me, me; when I've lost my husband, now I am treated like the soil on the footpath.' Blood raced through her veins at the thought of the way in which even Simbeya had betrayed her. Simbeya, the man who had always smiled at her when her husband was alive, had now become a tiger. How unbecoming, she thought, for such a good old man to show evil in his last days.

She looked at Mwape slouching at her side, and he looked up at her as if for an explanation. She sobbed quietly. But she had to walk on. Every pace towards where she knew not, but where she might get food, mattered much. Would the boy make it? Would she have to carry him on her back? The boy felt the mother's sorrows coursing through his heart. As if to reassure her, he quickened his pace. 'I am strong, mother,' it seemed the boy was saying. 'If you stumble, I will carry you on my back.' Now, at nine, the boy was tall but thin. Even in the dark of the dawn you could see his bones shining out of the wrinkled skin like the white teeth of a skeleton. 'You will walk, my son,' whispered Natombi to herself. 'You will walk, and when we find food you will eat, eat.'

By the break of day they had covered a long distance and were almost on top of the hill which marks the boundary between the valley and the unknown land on the eastern side. Mwape stopped and looked back into the valley. The mother's gaze followed him. There was the Kaunga valley spread out before them, serene and calm as though it was a peaceful valley full of love. The massed foliage, the other hills firmly marking its boundaries, the Kaunga river in the faint misty background; they all looked like jealous guards of the peace and love of the valley. Yet for her it was a pit inhabited by scorpions and poisonous snakes. As she looked into the misty valley below, she tried to close her eyes firmly to forget the indignity, shame, and deprivation she had suffered. But in closing her eyes the little mound of earth, the tall trees surrounding it, the gravediggers, the large reed coffin covering

114

the swollen body, all these memories crowded into her head. A strong clear voice rang out in her mind: 'You cannot turn your back on the valley for ever. She who turns her back upon this valley of peace turns her back upon her own. Do you wish to turn your back upon Dulani's bones?'

Mwape took in the scene. For him this journey was just an adventure, even though he was hungry; after all, he had been hungry for many weeks now. For him the valley only held happy memories, memories of the excited cries of his friends, memories of the happy faces and the green maize.

For once in her struggle since Dulani died, Natombi felt really alone. In anger she turned away from the scene, marching into the unknown. Mwape followed.

Back at home, within a few moments of discovering Natombi's disappearance, her house was set on fire by an unknown person. Simbeya was furious as he looked on helplessly from his house at the wild flames lapping up the grass-thatched hut. Lubinda and the other men stood laughing at the sight and threw dried wood into the furnace that was the house. Immediately after the fire had died down and the excitement of the village had somewhat subsided, Simbeya summoned Lubinda and the other men to his hut and urged that the house be rebuilt right away.

'If that is what your Chief wants,' said Lubinda, shaking his fist at Simbeya, 'you can build it yourself, and we shall see how a leper with clubbed hands and a cunning mouth builds a house.'

Simbeya was quick-tempered, like most lepers. 'How dare you insult me like that? Did I say the house should be rebuilt? I merely told you what the Chief said. It is for you to tell him of your disagreement and not for me. I can fight you if you want.' Simbeya wriggled like a listless worm in his bed. He looked furtively around for a weapon to snatch at.

Lubinda grimaced and spat on the ground in front of Simbeya. 'You are a fool, Simbeya, a fool. Only yesterday Mpona would have sacrificed you to the white men so that you could go and die like a speared porcupine. Alone, alone in the bush of unknown white faces. Today you dare carry orders from him to me, his Councillor. Who saved you from deportation? Who put his foot down and said, this ends here? Who rid the village of the witch who posed as your children's teacher? Who made it difficult for this woman, whose house you now ask me to rebuild, to stay here any longer? Was it not Lubinda?' asked Lubinda rhetorically. 'Who has suffered more for Dulani than myself?'

'But if you loved Dulani, why should you allow his remains to be burnt up like that?' persisted Simbeya.

'Did I set the house on fire? Was it not I who stopped the fire from swallowing up the whole of it? Was it not I who stopped it from spreading to this house of yours? If only I had let it roast you to death! The fire was sent by the spirits to blot out the last remains of a witch. Natombi was a witch, just like the teacher she did strange things with.' Lubinda paused to regain his breath. Then he continued: 'This house should have been razed to the ground when Dulani died and not left standing like this. That is the custom of our country. Everything that the dead man left should have been burnt and his wife given to someone else. Have any of these things been done? And here you are telling me what your Chief thinks I should do. If a Chief does not follow our laws, is Lubinda still bound to obey him? To obey him even when he hasn't got the courage to tell his own Councillor what it is he wants, but must go through festering minions like yourself?'

Meanwhile Natombi and her child continued their journey. They had been walking for a very long time through the thick bush when suddenly they heard a voice: 'Are you alone?' Who was the woman and where had she come from? Was there a village near by? Natombi simply stood, and it was a long time before she said, 'Yes, with my child.'

'You must have come from far away. There are no villages between here and Kaunga,' said the woman, regarding them with suspicion.

'Yes,' said Natombi.

'And you, my grandson,' said the woman, bending down to

116

touch Mwape's head, 'you are tired, aren't you?' The boy looked up at her.

'Why won't you speak to your grandmother?' asked the woman in an encouraging way.

'He is dumb,' replied Natombi.

'Ou!' exclaimed the woman. She quickly withdrew her hand from his head. No child becomes dumb unless he is bewitched.

'You go far?' asked the woman. 'The village is just behind those trees.'

How could you tell such a one that you cannot go any farther, that you have come to beg for food here, that you may have to stay here for even as long as two weeks to regain your strength? Will she not ask if you have relatives in the village? Will she not tell you, at that house they pay you in maize if you draw water for the men to knead the mud for the new house?

So there was no alternative but to tell the woman confidently, 'Oh no, we go to the village after this one. My father lives there and I am taking this child there.'

'Which village?' asked the woman. 'The next village is one full day from here, if it is Mwanjawanthu you mean. Between this village and the next there are many lions, and you cannot walk this distance at night. Only last week a man was eaten by a lion, and those drums you hear are being beaten because the kamcape is here to find out who bewitched him or who turned into a lion to eat the man.'

Natombi was silent. How could she stay in a village where there was a kamcape, maybe the same man who had accused Aphunzitsi? She turned and without even saying good-bye she walked on, leaving the village on one side so that no one would notice them.

For two days they walked on without meeting anybody or coming across a village. Could the woman have been wrong about the next village being one full day away, or had they missed it? By this time the little boy was so tired and weak that Natombi had to carry him on her back. There Mwape lay limp and folded up. Towards the evening of the second day, and after boring through the thick bush, they suddenly came upon an open and cleared space, and then a field of corn. They knew a village was near. A man straightened his back to look as he heard footsteps coming his way. He blinked his eyes and knit his massive brows. He stood waiting to see who the strangers were. Mwape, who had gone ahead of his mother, saw the man. He bleated some noise and turned back to the mother, running.

'What is it, my son?' asked the woman.

Mwape pointed in the direction of the man. It was Aphunzitsi, the village teacher. He, too, had recognized her, and he came towards her in his slow, thoughtful way. He was still tall, but very thin, and his shaven head showed how the flesh had deserted even the bones of his head. His cheeks were hollow and his adam's apple kept bobbing up and down as if he were experiencing great difficulty in swallowing. He has become so thin, she thought to herself. Could it be that here too there was starvation?

When he focused his distant eyes fully on her, he was shocked beyond measure. She looked so small, frail, and dry. Her legs were as thin as those of a white stalk, and you could see where the arms joined the trunk. How much the death of her husband had changed her! Then, then, he remembered. He was supposed to have bewitched him. Did she believe it? His lips burned to ask her there and then: did she believe it, believe that he was a witch? But how could he confront a stranger with such a question?

'You have come from far away, my daughter,' he said in a distant voice. Through her he saw his own daughter, who had died many years ago, and this reminded him of his wife. 'Let me take you home,' he said, 'you must be tired and hungry.'

She did not move. She, too, was dreaming, dreaming of a village in which people were people, and good men like this man were not cast away to die a living death. But doubts were crossing her mind. Could it be that the whole village did this man injustice, or was it true, true that he had bewitched her husband? She, too, was burning to ask him that question.

'No, no, I can't. I can't come with you.' She laid emphasis on the 'you'.

The man was stunned. The question that he had wanted to ask bolted through his lips, and as he uttered it his mouth shivered and his throat went up and down with the rapidity of a piston.

'Natombi, do you believe what the people said about me then?' he asked.

It was too much for Natombi. She broke down and wept. Mwape looked on in surprise. But soon he too was weeping.

'Why did I come here?' wept Natombi. 'Oh, if only I had known he would be here!'

When her weeping had subsided, the teacher approached her and, taking her by the hand, he said: 'My child, your mother, my wife, died last week. It was too much for her, poor woman.'

'No!' she screamed and threw herself down weeping all the louder. 'Forgive us, forgive me, teacher, we did you wrong,' she wept. He too wept. He wept for this frail creature, for his wife, and for all mankind. In his sorrow his heart extended to all those who wept.

In the morning, Aphunzitsi's sister brought them water to wash, and then some nsima and chicken for relish. When, later on in the day, the teacher came to see them, he recounted to Natombi what had happened since he had left the village. The teacher was worried about his rosary, which someone in the crowd around the kamcape had taken from his neck. Had Natombi heard of anyone finding a rosary?

'But don't let me waste time telling you all the things that happened to me and the wife who has just left us. You yourself, have you just come to visit?

By this time Natombi was more composed. She had realized that she could not go on and on from one village to another, never saying what she had come for. Besides, she knew the teacher, he was a kind and understanding man. So she decided to tell all. It did her good to be able to tell someone about her problems, and at the end of it her heart felt lighter. 'Poor me!

Do you realize you are the first person that I have ever talked to about my difficulties for a long time now?'

The teacher nodded. He told her she could either stay with them permanently, or go whenever she wanted to. There would be enough food for her to carry home.

In Mpona's village the debate was still raging. By now the disagreement that threatened to rend the village into two hostile camps had moved to the Chief's court. Those who insisted with Lubinda that the house should not be rebuilt were now clearly in a respectable majority, respectable because even neutrals like Silwamia and Simtowe had come out in support of them.

'It is against our tradition,' said Lubinda for the seventh time, 'to rebuild a house which we should have destroyed in the first instance because he that lived in it had died. We did not destroy it and yet we should have done so. That is why the spirits were annoyed with us and took it upon themselves to do that which we had neither the religion nor the foresight to do.' Lubinda stood up before the Chief to emphasize his point. 'Now that the deed has been done we hear some people yapping like wolves, shouting their heads off, and commanding us to oppose the spirits.'

'Who is a wolf here?' asked Simbeya. He was trembling with anger. 'Is that what you call me, I who nursed you when you were nothing more than a foetus?'

'Foetus yourself,' barked Lubinda at Simbeya. Lubinda threw his cloth on to his shoulder. His biceps firmed as he closed his hands into fists. 'I will beat you up, Simbeya!' he yelled, jumping towards the prostrate man.

'My friends,' said the Chief after calming them, 'what you say, Lubinda, is true. Anything else is against our tradition, our culture.' Lubinda looked impassively at the Chief. In the past the Chief had raised his hopes only to disappoint him later. Where Simbeya was concerned, it seemed to him, wrong was always right. 'What you say, Lubinda, is right,' he repeated, somewhat irritated by Lubinda's impassivity, 'but there is another side to the matter.' Lubinda, who had now sat down, shifted impatiently, but the Chief proceeded steadily. 'According to our tradition the dead man's house must be demolished, and this must be done in a proper manner. A sacrifice must be made before the demolition so that the spirits will be pleased to receive his belongings. But this is no sacrifice.' The Chief's tone became urgent. 'It is mere thuggery. If he who has burnt this house gets away with it, whose house in this village, in this kingdom, is safe?

'Thugs have frustrated the working-out of our tradition, our ritual. But our responsibility to the dead still remains. We must rebuild the burnt-down house immediately. Every part of it must be as it was before. Then, when that is done and his character has returned into it, we can discuss the demolition of the house.'

Lubinda rose in anger. He was fed up. He was going to speak up against the Chief. The Chief too rose abruptly, and throwing his kalimadole cloth back on to his shoulder he said decisively, 'I have spoken,' and strode off to his house.

'Who does he think he is?' said Lubinda to the others. Then he turned to Simbeya, and brandishing his fists shouted, 'You and your Chief can build the house yourselves! As for Natombi if she comes back we shall burn her alive.'

When there is food in the village, even if it is at night and everybody is asleep, the village still feels warm. If you arrive hungry at night you know that tomorrow you will eat because there is food. But when there is hunger you can smell it even before entering the village, because hunger is death and death stinks. Not even the dogs will bark at you as you come in because they too get their strength to bark from the food which their masters throw at them. When daylight broke, Natombi, who had arrived back the previous night from the search for food, found that it was just the same. Except for an occasional lazy yawn of a dog, all was stillness itself. When the sun rose, she saw Mpona emerge from his hut and then slouch off in the direction of the gardens. These weeks of her absence had changed him. He too had lost a lot of weight.

Then she heard a voice outside saying, 'I heard the sound of voices around this house last night. Did Natombi come?' It was Lubinda.

The other man replied, 'Maybe they came. You wouldn't expect them to show up if they had brought some food, would you?'

The voices faded away, and Natombi went back to soothe Mwape's blisters. The child was hungry, but you could not make a fire in your house in daylight because then other people would know that you were cooking something and that you were eating it alone. So they ate yesterday's cooked nsima, which they had been given along the way. Natombi was sure that by now the people knew that she had returned. But up to now no one had called to greet her or even to ask how she had travelled. The position had not changed; whatever else she might be, she was a witch.

But even if you are a witch, you are still a human being. Even if the meat that you have is human flesh, you feel better if you can share it with another witch, especially when they all know that you have got it. So, when it was dark, Natombi took a small basketful of the mealie-meal she had brought with her, and asked Mwape to take it to the Chief of the village, so that if he did not know before, he might know now that she had returned. Mwape was pleased to take the mealie-meal because he had been missing his friends, the Chief's children, and the other children of the village. Being short of memory, he only remembered the good days that he had had with them, and forgot the last days when even they threw stones at him.

'Mama,' called one of Mpona's children when he saw Mwape walking towards their hut, 'Mwape has come back.'

The mother did not show any interest, but simply continued smoking as she sat sprawled outside her hut. Mwape walked straight to the Chief's wife and deposited the mealie-meal beside her, indicating with gestures that it was from his mother. The woman jumped up and, taking the basket, threw it into the boy's face.

'Who eats bewitched mealie-meal?' she shouted. 'Take it away. Did I tell you that I had no food?' Then she grabbed a stick and began to beat the boy as he ran to his home. The mother heard feet stamping and the boy bleating as he ran towards her. She rushed out, only to collide in the doorway with Mpona's wife. The stick poised for a bigger swipe. Swish! went the stick, missing Natombi and breaking in two as it hit the veranda pole. Natombi grabbed a cooking stick. Then they rushed at each other and were soon wrestling. Mwape picked up a clay pot and threw it at Mpona's wife. But it missed and smashed. People rushed out of their huts and separated the two women, or rather caught Natombi.

'Shut up, you silly woman,' bellowed Lubinda, locking her in his powerful hand.

'She wanted to bewitch me!' yelled Mrs Mpona. 'She is a dangerous one.'

'You lie. You beat my child,' said Natombi.

A great deal of shouting followed from Mrs Mpona and the other women, who were now ranged against Natombi. Amidst the insults she withdrew into her hut. There was no door to close. A pursued mouse had withdrawn into its lair.

After her return Natombi did not speak to anyone for a long time. No one, apart from those who had come to quarrel with her, had ever said a kind word to her, asked her how she had travelled, or if she needed hot water to rinse her sore feet. Instead they had insulted her, turned away the food that she had given them, even spat into it. They were a proud and hating people, the people of this village. And yet this was where the bones of her husband were. This was where her son belonged. Besides, how could she leave before she had been purified? She would continue to refuse to be handed over to Banda. Do not judge people until you are weak enough to be exploited, she kept repeating to herself. That was the lesson she had learnt from all that had happened. People who respected her and even cared for her when Dulani was alive, had not merely deserted her, but were spitting on her. 'Banda, my husband's own brother!' She shook her head.

The food she had brought with her was getting low. From two meals a day when she first arrived they were now down to a meal every two days. Soon it would be every three days and then, and then . . . What was the point of knowing every step to your death, to your child's death? Help would not come from that village, from the kingdom which was also under the scourge of hunger and which had been turned against her as the woman who had struck down a member of the royal family, Dulani. She thought of the young men who had left the village of Cakuwamba and gone to work in town. Yes, her cousin Yelesani was working at Mufulira. He might be able to help her. So she went early one morning to the mission, not daring to leave her son behind. There she found a letter-writer.

'My dear Yelesani,' spoke Natombi, and the letter-writer pencilled her words with great concentration. The letter-writer was taking his time. He had to translate the Nsenga of her speech into Nyanja. 'If you are well, I and Mwape are well too and I am very happy.' The writer asked her to stop for a while until he had finished. After about five minutes he looked up, and she continued, 'I have come to the mission with my child to write you this letter because not one of the educated children at our village will write a letter for Natombi.'

'Na-tom-bi,' the writer muttered, giving her the cue that he had come to the end of the sentence.

'I do not know if you know it,' she continued, 'but your brother-in-law, my husband, died many months ago.'

The writer looked up, 'Your husband died? I am sorry about that?' He continued writing.

'They say I and the teacher bewitched him. So no one gives me food. Your son Mwape is starving, cousin: we are dying of hunger here. There are no fowls, no goats, everything has been killed and even the children, they are now dying. If you do not send any money you will hear that I and Mwape have died. If you are not interested in saving your cousin, do not

124

send anything.' She paused and wiped tears from her eyes. Then she concluded, 'I am your cousin, Natombi.'

The letter-writer dated the letter 24 October. He read it over again and addressed it.

Then followed the period of waiting, waiting for something, or nothing, to happen. If only the nothing would happen quickly. It was like casting a hook into the river. You did not know if the fish would bite, or when. You just had to wait, wait for something to happen. At the slightest pull of the string by the moving current your muscles would tense. Have I got it, should I pull, or is it too early?

Every piece of paper that she saw the children tearing up she thought: that must be my letter. They must have read it to know that it is worth tearing up like that. But, when you cannot read, what is the use of going up there, gathering up all the pieces, and piecing them together into the original letter?

Sometimes a man came from Cakuwamba, which was on the main route to the mission, bearing a letter in a cleft stick. She saw him through the small hole in the hut which she used at night. She came out of the hut. She felt sure it was her letter. Should she shout to him as he passed by? 'I am here! I am Natombi, the woman whose letter you have brought from Yelesani, Yelesani who stays in Mufulira. My cousin who works in the mines of the white man.' But she steadied herself: 'This is not the way to do things, Natombi. The whole village would laugh at you and write to Yelesani to tell him that you are a witch.'

So the long days passed and there was no letter. One day the mail runner himself came to the village. This caused great excitement among the children. 'What is Luangwa Bridge like?' asked one. 'Is it true that you can see it a very, very long way away? Then why don't we see it here? Koko, please, is it true that you are older than my grandfather? Is it true that there is a lot of money on the road at the bridge and that the white man travels in a thing with two white eyes?'

Koko made straight for the Chief's hut and delivered his

letter there. The people, knowing that Koko never delivered letters personally unless they contained money, knew that either the Chief himself or someone else had received money. They waited to see who, and Natombi waited, but with mounting anxiety.

After the mail man's visit things suddenly began to brighten up at the Chief's house. Small plates of something again began to pass to the other people, and the Chief visited distant villages more, returning every time with a sizeable parcel. But these plates of something did not reach Natombi's house, and she kept waiting for the reply to her letter. To know the limits of friendship in a crisis, that would be something. But this waiting, how could she go on living the future while the present rotted away under her feet? Someone had remembered Mpona in his hour of necessity. Why not her? 'Natombi,' said a voice within her, 'you are a witch, an adulteress in the eyes of these people. Can it be that they have not told everybody that you are a bad woman?'

A few weeks after Koko had left, Natombi received a letter. It read:

> My dear cousin Natombi,
>
> If you are well, I am well too. I sent you £2 through the Chief. Have you received it? Why have you not replied? Cordial greetings for every day.
>
> Stay well,
>
> > I am yours,
> > Yelesani.

Chapter 9

When it becomes hot in the valley you can smell the sun. Look around you and you will see the distant sands dancing in the big frying-pan. Above the sands and soil you see a hazy movement of heat disappearing into the day. When the day is like this, do not venture out of your hut without something to cover your feet and head. Your soles will burn and your brain will roast: how much more so then will the plants, which have no feet to run away from the heat, the plants which drink up the sun in the same way as they drink water, and transmit it to the leaves.

The hot sun scorched all the vegetable relish on which the people had now come to depend. It dried up the well so that only crusts of black earth remained where once water had stood. So the women everywhere dug deeper every day in search of water. The valley was like one huge sheet of iron quivering with heat. Thus it was that the hunger, instead of easing towards the rains, became more tormenting. Only when you are confronted with this situation do you realize what a suicide already knows, that it takes a long time to kill human life. Those skeletons that roamed the paths to the well were surely dead. But they were not. Even Chief Mpona's house had now yielded to the onslaught, and though it had had a temporary reprieve, no one in that house could now remember when they had last eaten a meal, even a modest one.

During real hunger we are all like chickens, my brother and sister; you pick up a morsel there, a fried grain of dried maize here, and then you drink cupfuls of water to wash down any particle that may have lost its way to the stomach in the maze of hungry teeth.

The people prayed the spirits for rain. But how could you ask for rain when there was not even a cloud in the sky? People said that their dogs had died of hunger. At the back of each house could be found the bones of animals which had never been eaten or seen before. The great hunger was taking over the village, and lean jaws jutted out of every face in search of food.

It was in the midst of this conquest of the body that one evening in the moonlight strangers arrived in the village. Hardly a voice spoke welcome or greetings to them as they set their loads down outside the Chief's hut. It was like walking into a deserted village. The buildings were there, but even they looked starved and neglected. The roof of Mpona's house, for example, looked dilapidated, with large chunks of grass gone. Even at night you could see the bare rafters.

After a long silence from within the hut, the Chief cleared his throat and called out in a weak voice, 'Are you people outside?' It could, of course, have been anything and anyone. How was one to tell whether voices whispering in the dark were those of real human beings? Then he drew back the door. A thin, tall figure, he stood in the way wondering for a moment whether to venture farther into the dark. He could discern some six or seven people, and several bundles on the ground.

'We are strangers,' said one of them, in an effort to reassure the old man.

'Strangers,' said the Chief, walking forward like a mechanical toy. 'What is your journey, friends?' Then he whispered, 'There is no food in this village, here is only hunger. We cannot help you, friends.'

'We have come a long way, far beyond the hills and even further,' replied one of them.

'So you need food,' said the old man, more to himself than to them. 'I say, strangers, go on your way. Die somewhere else, even outside this village. But do not die here. You will leave us more misfortune.'

'We heard of your hunger,' said the spokesman, 'and our women determined to help, so we have brought you food.'

By then several village elders, including Lubinda, had crept up to the gathering and stood there in silence, listening listlessly to Mpona and the strangers.

'Food!' exclaimed Mpona, 'do you mean "food"? You mean . . .'

'Yes, we have brought you food, and in the name of Our Lord Jesus Christ we ask you to take it. We have brought ten and one parcels between us, enough for each household in the village,' replied the spokesman.

'Stranger!' exclaimed Mpona, enthusiasm suddenly falling away. Something about the stranger was worrying him. Had he not heard that voice before somewhere, or even in a dream? 'Stranger,' he repeated, 'I should know you, stranger. Your voice, haven't I heard it before?'

Lubinda leaned forward, sheltering his eyes against the bright light of the moon. He peered hard at the spokesman of the party and suddenly he cried, 'The witch, it is the witch.'

'The teacher!' exclaimed the Chief, 'yes, you're the teacher, aren't you?'

There was a hushed silence. Mpona stood there with his chin stabbed into his chest as if in a trance. For each one of the people of the village the world was going round in a senseless gyration. It could not be true. How could a condemned man dare come back to confront them with this insult? How had he known that they were starving? What also had the witch come to take now? Would he not content himself with waiting until hunger had killed them all? Terror struck into the numbed bones of these helpless people. But they would resist.

'Stranger,' said the Chief finally, 'you are a witch. My people would not accept your food.'

'But the people are starving,' protested the teacher, his heart knocking at the walls of his chest. 'The people are starving, Chief, soon they will die. Without food you can't live much longer.'

'Strange one, the people would rather die according to the wishes of the spirits than be bewitched by you.' It was Lubinda. Even in these moments of great suffering his voice rang clear. Now his eyes shone out like balls of red fire in the light of the moon. He had told the Chief, he was saying aloud to himself, that it was wrong to trust a witch. And now the witch had come to complete his work.

Mpona was saying: 'You are a witch, the village will not accept your food.' The words were burning his throat. He knew that the teacher was a good man. But who was he to undo the judgement of the kamcape? He was, after all, only a chief, and who could still be a chief if the spirits of the village's ancestors did not consent?

'There is a killer, a witch, an eater of human flesh in our midst,' Lubinda paused. 'Where he has come from we don't know. Why he has come to our village, all the way from beyond the hills and beyond, we don't know. Who his companions are, or whether indeed they are real men, or the people who issue out of charms at night, we don't know.' He was warming up to his indictment. Now he had to fight the battle against the teacher fully, and destroy Mpona. For it was his lack of decisiveness which had brought about this state of affairs. 'But we know one thing, that in our midst now is a man whom the kamcape condemned for witchcraft and whom, through lack of fire in our bellies, through the timidity of our leadership in this village, we let go – as if he had not killed Dulani, our own flesh and blood, as if he had not killed our own children before; as if to kill him would have brought death on the whole village.'

Lubinda looked at Mpona briefly. He would stifle this silly old man. But to kill so directly would not do. 'Now this witch, seeing that we are women in this village, daughters of the vixen, has come to mock our manhood further. This mealie-meal, do we know who prepared it? No. Do we even know that it is real mealie-meal?' Then, quickly, he wound up: 'The spirits have brought this man back to us because last time we did not do the job properly. We let a witch go. If you, Chief, are still the Chief of this village and this valley, you will do what the spirits have told you to do by this act. I won't say any more. Don't spread the smallpox. Nip it in the bud while you can. If you do not, then, Mpona, in the name of the spirit of my grandmother who lies below this earth,' he stamped furiously with his foot, 'there in Mundo the burial place, you are certainly not fit to be our . . .' he stopped.

It was a clear challenge, and Mpona knew it. Lubinda cured people. He could also kill them. The mealie-meal must be rejected. But Lubinda had gone further. Were these strangers to be returned home, or lynched? It was, once again, too big a matter for him alone to decide. Lubinda's word was not the word of the whole village. He would hear from those who were there and those who were asleep. In the meantime the visitors were shepherded off to the dilapidated hut which once belonged to the school-teacher, to await the judgement of the people.

Early in the dawn, at the time when the darkness begins to lift and you can just see the form of the object but not the thing itself, the strangers set off. They had waited the whole night after the sentence had been passed against accepting the mealie-meal in the hope that these starving people would change their minds. Lubinda had been sent to break the news. 'We do not need your food,' he had said, 'not even if you bring meat and honey with you.' Just that and no more. At any slight noise, such as the fall of ants, the teacher had sat up listening for the footsteps of hope which he was sure would come. He was sure that a people's pride and superstition could not go beyond the needs of the body. But they did, and with every passing moment the teacher felt as though he was a prisoner. For the torture of frustration when one is prevented from doing a good deed is even greater than that of imprisonment when one has done ill.

Silently they marched away, their shoulders still weighed down by the parcels of hope that they had brought with them.

As they walked away in the crisp dawn an owl hooted. That bird only hooted to signal death or the departure of witches. Aphunzitsi wondered about Natombi. What had happened to her? Was she still alive?

He was too deep in thought to realize what was happening when the young man at the head of the procession suddenly crouched down, whispering, 'S-sh . . .' At that very moment they were walking through a thicket, and on the left was the path that led to the graveyard. They all threw themselves down, shivering with terror.

'Did you see that?' whispered the young man to the teacher. The teacher had also seen the light in front of them flick on and off. All of them had seen it. Then another flicker of white light behind them, and in a moment there were lights all around them, rushing towards them.

'Witches!' whispered one of them, and they stood there like a cluster of statues. The lights swooped down on them, together with a jabber of human voices. Then shouts of, 'Uyo, uyo!' and sounds like the roaring of lions. The strangers threw down their loads and ran for dear life in the direction of the village. One of the pursuers groaned, 'I die, I die,' as the knobkerry which the tall man in the group threw at them found its target.

'It was the ghosts,' said the Chief, as he listened to their panting explanation on their return. 'I told you that the spirits are angry with your deeds.'

'It wasn't ghosts!' protested the teacher. 'They were human voices. I heard them.'

'They were ghosts!' shouted Mpona, whose lack of sleep had not improved his temper. 'Witches! Get away from here.'

'No, I tell you, Chief, they were not ghosts. I know one of my people injured one of them. And I tell you, we are not moving from here until we know who has done this thing to us. The mission is near,' threatened the teacher, 'I will go and tell the white missionary about this. There is evil in this village of yours, Chief.'

By now the sun had begun to appear. Attracted by the noisy argument, people came out of their houses. The story had spread that the witches, who had wished to bewitch the village with their mealie-meal, had been turned back in their journey by the ghosts.

'This is taboo,' said Lubinda's nephew. 'It shows the spirits do not want these witches to depart until we have done something to them. Lubinda was right.'

'Lubinda!' exclaimed the Chief. 'Where is Lubinda? Go and call him. We must speak on this new matter.'

The nephew went to Lubinda's house, and returned saying that Lubinda's message was that he had said all that he had to say. 'How many times does your foolish Chief want me to say the same thing?' Lubinda had retorted to the intruder.

'Chief,' said Banda, 'this matter is too big for you alone. Lubinda must come. Only he can tell us the wishes of the spirits.'

So the Chief himself went to call him out.

'Lubinda!' called Mpona, as he stood outside the hut. 'You are still asleep, and you are a man?'

'What business of yours is it if I sleep?' Lubinda was truculent in his lair. 'I have told you everything, but you just want to talk and talk. When will you act?'

'We acted and sent them away, but the ghosts have chased them back to us,' replied the Chief, raising his voice. 'If you don't come out then I will pull you out.'

'If you want to see what you have never seen, come,' called Lubinda from within. 'This is my house. No one can pull me out of my bed.'

Two men burst into the hut and pulled Lubinda out. Running down his forehead was a nasty cut, and his hair was covered in mealie-meal!

'So!' exclaimed the Chief. Turning to the teacher, he said, 'Teacher, stay with us. We thank you for the mealie-meal.' But the mealie-meal had vanished.

Chapter 10

Nothing had been heard about Cumba for many months now, but nobody, least of all his wife, really bothered. They knew that Cumba was certain to take care of himself. Why worry about a person who was bound to be doing better than yourself? There were more important matters to occupy the village. The rains had started two months after the Lubinda episode. During this time the teacher had organized another food mission and life was returning to the village, so that the people went about their work of sowing their seeds with greater strength. Natombi too shared in the renewed life, and her relations with the village were now greatly improved, though by no means cordial.

But the village was still torn by internal dissensions. The tumour of hatred grew thicker in Lubinda's heart. He considered that he had been disgraced by Mpona and betrayed by those he had gone with on that fateful night. The list of enemies, which now included his nephew, had grown, and it troubled him much that his original strategy would no longer be viable.

Outwardly Mpona's village was doing well, and Aphunzitsi also blossomed in this new air. His face and legs were becoming well filled out and the exaggerated stoop was disappearing. As he stood there before the class of expectant young boys his eyes glinted with the perfect joy of a man who has been tested. For him every day in the class was a full justification for the rigours of his return. These children, they were made to be moulded into anything that he pleased. He prayed God day and night that he might mould, not according to his own wishes, but in accordance with His wishes. They were young, supple plants. A little light here and a little water there and their whole spiritual posture would be changed. He loved most the way these children hung upon his voice as he told them a story. There was the story of the little boy, for example, who would not cross the stream alone but who, on being borne on the shoulders of St Christopher, was found to be heavier than a grown-up man. And this in mid-stream. Then there was the story of the hare who challenged Mr Elephant and Mr Hippo separately to a tug-of-war against him. They realized too late, when their skulls collided, that they had been tricked.

'Who is this one?' the teacher was singing.
'It is A, the Big One, A the Big One.
His name is A, his name is A.
A the big one, his name is A.'

It was not music, but the cries were spontaneous and they warmed the heart.

'Who created you?' asked the teacher, straining his voice to overcome the enthusiastic chatter unleashed by the song.

'Father,' replied one boy.

There was a howl from the others. 'Weele! God, God.' The boy sat down, his enthusiasm completely flattened.

'Excuse me, teacher,' said the boy, who would not be intimidated into silence, 'but why has he stopped now?'

'Stopped?' replied the teacher a little puzzled. 'But he has not. For example, he has created your baby sister too.'

'You lie, teacher,' said the boy, 'my sister was made by my father. That's what my mother said.'

The others lost interest in this boy who stood between them and their next story, and all eyes were peering outside. Then whispers of 'Father Chiphwanya' ran through the room.

'Mwendo!' called out the teacher.

'It's not only me that's looking outside at the Father coming,' Mwendo replied.

The teacher's heart missed a beat. 'Father?' he exclaimed to himself, trying not to have heard the boy. As he was saying, 'Where is F . . .' the priest walked in, and even before he could finish his question, the pupils, who had been rehearsed in how to greet a priest, shouted at the tops of their voices, 'May the Lord be adored!'

'Forever and ever,' answered the priest.

'Amen,' piped up the young voices in a discordant crescendo.

The teacher had cause to thank the Lord, because Father Chiphwanya was particularly quick of temper if any mistake was made in the matter of greeting. Moreover, the visit passed without incident. The priest was happy with the progress of the pupils in their catechism. In the course of going round the class, however, Father Chiphwanya had come across a dumb boy, Mwape. He had a look into the boy's mouth and, from his past experience, saw at once that the boy would need an operation before he could speak.

'Teacher,' said the priest, 'I want this child to come along with me to the mission.'

'But Father, unless you will it, it cannot be done. The people will not agree,' replied the teacher.

'He must come, because he will need an operation.' The priest's words were final and, judging from the twitches in the right-hand corner of his mouth, Aphunzitsi knew that he would not brook argument.

'Why don't the people want the boy to speak?' continued the priest.

'That isn't the point,' the teacher replied, wondering whether the white man would lose his temper. 'Dulani, the father of the boy, was killed by a python here in this village, and this happened, as you know, shortly before your first visit.'

'So what?' the priest cut in. 'You too are still a pagan, eh?'

'It isn't I who believe, it's these people. These are strange things. Unless you yourself speak to the Chief, they will close this school again,' replied the teacher.

'Close the school? Who can close the school here if I don't?'

The white man's face turned as red as a tomato. 'Tell your Chief, if the school closes he goes to jail. I'll fix these pagans,' he added aloud to himself.

We have tried all manner of medicines,' said Mpona when he was summoned, 'but they have not worked. This child is bewitched. I can tell you that. Are the spirits of our fathers not free to do what they want with our own children? Must this white man stand in our way always?'

'You, priest . . .' Lubinda was pointing at him. 'You are the cause of all this. You white man, you have planted a witch in our midst.'

The priest cut through the air with his hand in a gesture of great anger. 'You are the son of Beelzebub himself, you pagan. The child must go.'

'Your own child, not ours,' shouted back Lubinda. 'Enough is enough. We have no use for your religion here. Why don't you leave us alone?' Lubinda shouted at the teacher.

It was more infuriating to the priest that a black man should talk in this way to a white man than it was alarming that the black man's soul had been irretrievably lost. One could tolerate the arguing with heretics in the refined surroundings of the University of Cracow. It could even be stimulating. But these creatures, what right had they even to think for themselves?

'You are a pagan, you,' were the only words Father Chiphwanya could find. 'The Lord will punish you.'

'You are a foreigner!' screamed Lubinda.

All efforts to restrain him failed; Lubinda was becoming wild. The missionary turned away in anger, muttering that the village would hear next from the D.C. at the Boma.

'Let him come!' shouted Lubinda. But the other people and Mpona were afraid, because while you could talk in this way to the missionary even though he was a white man, you could not to the D.C., the terror of whose office was real.

'No, don't call the D.C. The child goes with you today,' pleaded Mpona.

'Then let the child's mother accompany the child,' said the

priest, forcing a faint smile to break through the clouds of his anger. He did not realize that he had again stirred up a hornets' nest.

'No!' said Lubinda, who had an undeclared vested interest. 'The white one has no woman. Can we trust him to travel alone with the woman and a child who cannot speak?'

'The priest knows no woman,' replied the teacher, shaking his head with the shock of sacrilege.

'Is he not a man then?' retorted Lubinda. 'You were married,' he said to the teacher, 'are you not of the same religion, then?'

The priest's contempt rose. How could such people say such things about him? He had left many beautiful white women at home in order to follow Christ. One of them had even tried to commit suicide, and now she was in a mental hospital.

'What about the D.C.? Where do all the pink children at the Boma come from? The white man won't eat with us, but he will share our women if we don't look out,' said Lubinda.

The other people cast their eyes down. It was not proper to speak in such a manner to a white missionary.

Many weeks passed after the priest's visit. But there was no news of the boy Mwape. Natombi became more and more anxious about him until, finally, she could stand it no longer. She went to the teacher to find out if he had any news. The teacher had not heard anything, but he assured her that so long as the boy was with the white man he was safe.

'But the hospital?' said Natombi. 'If he has gone to Lusaka already, is he safe there too, away from the priest?'

To the teacher every white man was like the priest, but he understood the anxieties of the woman. Only a visit to the mission, far away though it was, would satisfy her. So he arranged with the Chief for the two of them to accompany her to the mission.

They rose at dawn two days later to go to the mission. As soon as Mpona and the other two had departed, Lubinda said 'Odi' at Yuda's house. Yuda was not there: he had hobbled off early to the fields with his wife. Lubinda hurried there too.

'You start early today, my friend. How are you?' asked Lubinda, trying to start a conversation.

'My young maize is coming on, isn't it? And you say I am a leper! Ha, ha, ha!'

But Lubinda did not give Yuda time to enlarge on his sorrows. 'My friend,' he proceeded, clasping Yuda's sore hand. 'That Chief of yours, he has gone off with the witch and Natombi to the mission.' Yuda did not appreciate the significance of this, and waited for Lubinda to continue.

'You don't understand,' said Lubinda. 'Don't you see that this is the beginning of the end, that Mpona has gone to turn the white man at the mission against us?'

'But what is the real purpose of the journey?' asked Yuda, certain that Lubinda did not sincerely mean what he was saying.

'My friend, you don't understand. Ostensibly it is to see the child, but you and I know what we know,' replied Lubinda, kneading Yuda's hand.

'You really mean?' exclaimed Yuda, light dawning.

'Ehe!' Lubinda was increasing the pressure on the hand. 'Exactly. Haatongo, Banda, Simbeya, even that silly nephew of mine, Juma, and all of us, we need your support, my friend. We must stop Mpona turning the world against us.'

'Then you have spoken to these men? What is your plan?' asked Yuda.

Lubinda coughed a little. 'It's this. The Chief is not the proper nephew of Mpona-mkulu, the one he succeeded as Chief.'

'What?' asked Yuda in surprise. 'Wasn't he the eldest son of his father?'

'Yes, but also no,' Lubinda said. He really loved the world of words. Was he not, after all, the village philosopher? 'For this young Mpona, while he was the son of his father, was not the son of his mother.'

'You mean?' Yuda was knitting his brows and wrinkling

his forehead. A combination of these two produced the best thinking posture, especially when you did not really understand and you knew that the problem would always be beyond you.

'Yes,' replied Lubinda. 'It is as you understand. But – and here is the real trouble – his mother, that is the mother who bore him, was . . . have you ever heard of an old woman who was chased away from this village at spear-point many years ago?'

'You mean the one who was a witch? Nyalutila you mean?' asked Yuda, who was becoming extremely captivated by the way the pieces were falling into place.

'Aha! Well, now you know the real mother of Mpona.' Then Lubinda whispered, 'My friend, your Chief is the son of a witch. Therefore . . .'

'Therefore he too must be a witch,' said Yuda, searching for agreement in Lubinda's eyes.

'What you say, you say. I did not say it,' replied Lubinda. 'We will speak further. Good-bye.'

Before Yuda could protest at his sudden departure, Lubinda had disappeared into the maize plants and all was as quiet as before.

'Father of the boy!' called out Yuda's wife. 'Was that Lubinda you were talking to?'

'Shut up, woman,' shouted back Yuda, 'even if it was a hyena, its no business of yours.'

At the mission itself things had remained very much the same as before. But the last few months had been hectic months, especially for Father Chiphwanya and Brother Aruppe. Villagers from all over the district had been flocking to the mission in search of food. Father Chiphwanya had worked very hard, writing letters of appeal to all his friends, to the Monseigneur in Lusaka, to the D.C. at Feira Boma, and to all kinds of people. When now and again the appeal was answered and a bag of maize had landed at Luangwa Bridge thirty-five miles away, Father Chiphwanya had personally jumped into the risky canoe, paddling through difficult waters all the way up to the bridge, and on the way back he had stopped at every village to share out the maize.

To the D.C. at Feira he had written only one letter, and that letter had been replied to in such unkind terms that even he who cared little for 'kind' words was furious. The reply had read:

Reverend Sir,

With reference to your unreferenced and undated minute, presumably of this century, I have the honour to advise you that the government is unable to accept that there is famine in this area and cannot therefore countenance your appeal for assistance in the form of corn. I wish also to take the opportunity of emphasizing to your Reverend good self the fact that the physical welfare of the natives in N. Rhodesia is the responsibility of His Majesty's Government and that your action in appealing for assistance on behalf of these natives constitutes grave and unwarranted interference and is calculated to cause dissension and disaffection among these primitive people who, by the way, appear to have managed quite well ever since Creation. Finally one may be tempted to reflect on the sobriety of Malthusian alarmists who paint such a gloomy picture of a people who are living much happier lives than before we, the British, came on to the scene. In this particular case I will not because, notwithstanding your Polish background, I am informed that you are reasonably educated. It is not all of us that can afford an Oxford education.

I have the honour to be, Reverend Sir,
    Your most obedient servant,
        James Coates,
        District Commissioner, Feira District.

James Coates, or Lemon as was his nickname, had smiled as he passed his tongue across the envelope. He had not minded the old priest at the mission, but this uncouth young man of a Father Oliver who seemed to have an unfailing knack of annoying everyone, including the natives, was the last straw.

For his part, when he had received it Father Chiphwanya had set a match to the letter and, running to Father Superior and pointing to the flame, had shouted: 'That rubbish is all your D.C. cares for the people here, and yet you want me to agree with all the government stands for. Oppression! Slavery! Savagery!'

The strain of the operation was telling badly on Father Chiphwanya. He was more peppery than ever before, and the whole presbytery was permeated by the atmosphere of crisis. But the old man, the Father Superior, understood, and he was grateful that Father Chiphwanya was there. He continued to pray for him, for the success of his work and that of Brother Aruppe. He prayed that he might be a better anchor of peace to which these hard-working men could return every evening. That, however, was not to be.

It all started with the discovery by Father Gonzago after five weeks that Father Chiphwanya had taken a dumb child from Mpona village against the wishes of the people there.

'It doesn't matter what our good motives are. It is important that the people must agree,' the Superior was saying to Chiphwanya. As usual he was lifting up his helmet now and again as he sat in the dining-room talking to Father Chiphwanya after Brother Aruppe had gone ahead to tune in the radio for the eight o'clock BBC news.

It was a clear August evening. The air was hot, and in the room where they were talking the hurricane lamp was smoking very badly. Maybe it needed a new wick. But that would have to be ordered from Lusaka. It gave enough light, and provided one kept cleaning the glass it was all right.

'The only time these natives will agree with you is if you ask them to agree to being fed. Otherwise they won't do anything positive. Did you want me to leave the child, so that in years to come he will be the laughing-stock of the whole village?' fumed Father Chiphwanya, who felt insulted by this little man who did nothing but doze over his breviary all day. 'You believe the story that the boy is bewitched, don't you? And that therefore nothing should be done to make him speak.'

It was not a serious accusation. But Father Gonzago, in his small, monotonous singsong, replied, 'It is possible, is it not?'

'You shock me, Father!' replied Father Chiphwanya.

'Have you not read of people who were possessed in the Bible?'

'That's not the same thing, and anyway someone had to come and remove the devil in them so they might be free again,' replied Chiphwanya, raising his voice.

'That is true,' replied the old man. 'But only prayer could do it. Prayer will remove more than the dumbness of this boy you have sent to Lusaka. Prayer will remove the devil that is among the people in Mpona village. Sometimes, Father, there is more understanding among the speechless than among those who talk.'

Father Superior stood up. It was news time. Father Chiphwanya also had to stand up and go and listen to the news. That was the way of the Order. You may argue, but you must follow the leader. After news time the procession of three trooped to the church for vespers.

'*In manus tuos Domine*,' began the Superior.

'*Commendo spiritus meus*,' joined in the other two. '*Redemisti nos Domine, Deus veritatis. In manus tuos Domine commendo spiritus meus*.'

As the Father Superior rose from his pew, Brother Aruppe's thoughts turned to the noise that was coming through the open church window from the fowl-run.

'Oh God,' he whispered, hastily concluding his prayer, 'into Thy hands I commend my spirit.' Then he made the sign of the cross with the crucifix of his rosary and put it away into his pocket. 'It must be a snake,' he thought. 'The last python that went in there swallowed a lot of chickens. The Africans have some plant which frightens away snakes.' If he could only use that he would be able to sleep at night.

'Did you hear the noise at the fowl-run?' asked Father Chiphwanya, standing in the doorway to Brother Aruppe's room. You did not have to knock at the door to enter a brother's room.

'I'm going out there, Father, but I think it's a snake,' replied the brother.

'Hurry up, then,' said the priest, 'or I'll go.'

That was an order and Brother Aruppe scrambled out of his white cassock, picked up his rifle and hurricane lamp, and went down to investigate.

Father Chiphwanya heard the crunch of boots on the cobblestones and he was satisfied that the order was being obeyed. Slowly he closed his door and unlaced his shoes. He was angry with the Superior for not reproving Aruppe at news time. The little brother had grunted a 'No' to an item announcing the introduction of capital punishment for witchcraft in the Cameroun. He was still annoyed with Father Superior for suggesting disapproval of his sending the boy Mwape to hospital. But his lips mechanically uttered the 'Our Father' as he paced up and down his room in bare feet, thinking.

Brother Aruppe descended to the chicken-run below. The light was flickering in the sudden gust of air. He did not fear anything and he had done this trip over and over before, even in pitch dark as the skies flashed lightning and the heavens rained water. To him the fowls were pets, and while he dressed them for the table he would never eat them. But this night he was frightened, and every step among the stones seemed like a step into deeper darkness. He was shivering and a chill was creeping over his body and head.

'Pray for us sinners now and at the hour of our death,' he was mumbling. But his mind was not on the words.

The chickens were getting more and more restless and he could hear them flapping their wings. He stepped up his pace and then raised his lamp into the fowl-run as he paused at the door. The fowls knew Brother Aruppe. They knew the sweaty smell of his greasy little body. So they all rushed to the door,

144

clucking and cackling a welcome in their own way. A weight lifted from him: the chickens were safe. So he put his lamp down, laid his gun aside, took some grain from his pocket and started to scatter it to the chickens. Then came a rush, a roar, a heavy crash, and Brother Aruppe was dead. Nyakacala, the clawless lion, had caught him.

Father Superior at the presbytery heard the heavy thud. The air filled with furious roars of the lion. The people knew that the clawless one was in the mission. They bolted their doors tightly and went to bed. Father Chiphwanya had already fallen asleep.

'Don't go out,' said Father Superior at Father Chiphwanya's door. 'There's a lion outside.' He heard the loud snores of God's ordained. He repeated the same message at Brother Aruppe's door. Hearing nothing, he assumed that he too was asleep. He had not known of Brother Aruppe's errand that evening.

The people gathered from all the villages near the mission the following morning. They came to mourn the simple white man who had come to be their main link with the mission. They owed it to him that they were fed. Always dressed in his shabby khaki shirt and patched trousers, the little brother had comforted the sick that came to the mission. He had always been in trouble with Father Chiphwanya, the father minister, for the way in which chickens failed to turn up at the table, and bananas in the hot-house seemed to walk away. But Father Chiphwanya did not know until now where these things had been going.

'Last night,' began the old priest as Brother Aruppe's body was laid before the altar, 'I prayed here in this church with Brother Aruppe. Last night also my Lord and Creator called for him. Now Brother Aruppe lies before you. As he begged your blessings even as he gave of what he had to you, today he is a greater beggar who has nothing to give you but further pleas for your prayers. The day of anger, the day of judgement, has come for him. Among you he came as a refugee seeking shelter from the ravages of war in his own country. He stayed because you welcomed him as one of you . . .'

Father Superior wiped his eyes. His chest began to heave with suppressed emotion. 'Brother Aruppe!' he broke out in a sob, 'not mine but the Lord's will be . . .' It was too much for the little old man and for the people too. The women cried openly, the men sobbed, and Father Superior buried his face in his black cassock and crouched over the coffin in a prayer of tears. Father Chiphwanya stood sternly upright, holding the holy water before him.

Natombi and her party, who had come to the mission the very night of the tragedy, saw all this. They too shared in the grief for the man they did not know. When the headmaster struck up the hymn 'Salve Regina', even the school-children could not sing it clearly. The old priest's voice trembled as he accompanied the sobbing children. '*Mater misericordia, vita dulcedo et spes nostra salve*. Then came the appeal to the Blessed Virgin to turn her eyes of mercy towards them, the children who mourned and wept in that valley of tears.

As the coffin left the church, borne by four strong men, the mission teacher started the hymn; *What shall we do* . . . The crowd took it up:

> . . . *with all the things of this world?*
> *Shall we take them with us when we are dying?*
> *We shall leave them as we die, never taking anything*
> *But the cloth with which to wrap our corpse.*

And so to the last stanza:

> *Is there wisdom in despising God*
> *And in forgetting that we all shall die?*
> *Yesterday it struck our fellow man*
> *It awaits all of us truly*
> *Today we are here, tomorrow we too are not here.*

Mpona too was sobbing. It had never occurred to him that the white man could also be touched by these things. He

146

thought back to the death of Dulani and how he had treated Natombi. These people were saying that death would come to all of us. Who had sent the Clawless One to kill a European, a man of God? If these people prayed so much for the dead one to be received well by the spirits, did this not show that the white man was also a man with a heart like a real human being?

That day the mission was overcast, not only with sorrow, but with fear also, fear that the Clawless One might return to strike another victim. She had killed a white man; what could stop her killing a black man? Father Chiphwanya had wounded the lion in the search for the body early that morning. A wounded lion was worse than a whole one.

'You think the big white one will tell us what has happened to Mwape?' asked Mpona of Aphunzitsi.

'Not today or tomorrow,' replied Aphunzitsi. 'But my friend Gasi here assures me that the boy was sent to Lusaka and is safe.'

There was a common bond between Aphunzitsi and this teacher at the mission. They were both educated men, and had some affinity with the white man. It was for this reason that when Aphunzitsi had arrived at the mission on that fateful night he had gone straight away to Gasi's house. Natombi listened to the conversation, as did the Chief too. Not only for Natombi but also for the Chief it was a matter of life and death that the boy should be well. Mpona suspected that there was much happening at his village in his absence. He knew Lubinda was busy influencing people against him, telling them that it was he who had offered the boy to the white one to kill him. 'If it is the Chieftainship that he wants, why doesn't he simply take it? – even though everyone knows he is an orphan, and my nephew only because my grandfather kept him alive?' Such were Mpona's thoughts.

As the two teachers talked, they heard the voices of people singing in the distance. The voices were coming from the direction of the mission compound. The two teachers suddenly stopped their conversation, struck with horror. They were pagan songs that these people were singing. How would the priests – Father Chiphwanya especially – react to one of their number being mourned in a pagan manner?

The people at the mission had felt the need to mourn their man and so in the evening they had set up a big fire in the compound and begun to sing funeral songs. Now and then a muzzle-loader would be fired into the air and the women would start wailing all over again. They sang:

> *Knock, knock at the door,*
> *Knock, knock at the door.*
> *O witch, what do you want?*
> *The child has gone already.*
> *You have seen the airplane,*
> *Haven't you seen the airplane?*
> *You have seen the airplane,*
> *That airplane you have seen,*
> *You have seen the airplane.*

Beer passed round and people sang. But it was not the song of drunken people, or of people rejoicing. It was the song of people sorrowing and people who sipped at the calabash to lighten their hearts.

Right out of the blue the figure of Father Chiphwanya loomed ominously before the crowd of chanting mourners. The light from the fire fell across part of the huge white cassock, slicing him in half. Standing there he looked like a ghost. He adjusted the wide belt of his cassock as if to prepare for a fight, but stood still. The singing ceased. You could hear the crackle of the fire.

'This is the man who has bewitched our brother,'whispered one.

'Don't you see that he does not sorrow with us?' whispered another. 'Did you see how he nailed down the coffin?'

Father Chiphwanya was gazing straight before him into the fire, and beyond. Then he turned away abruptly and they knew that he was angry with them. But he was angry with the Superior too. It was his softness which has led to this, he said to himself as he stumped back to the residence fuming with anger.

'Father,' called Father Chiphwanya to the old priest who sat outside his room, reading from a sacred book by the light of a hurricane lamp. 'I want to talk to you.'

The old man hastily inserted a marker in his holy book, lifted his helmet, and looked up at Father Chiphwanya. 'Yes, Father?' he said.

'You allowed the people to mourn Brother Aruppe in a pagan way.' It was an accusation, not a question.

'Why, what have they done? Do they want to kill a child to accompany Brother Aruppe then?' asked the old man with great alarm.

'You and your social anthropology,' said Father Chiphwanya, pointing a finger at the old man, 'that's all you think of at this mission. You don't care what paganism they bring to the altar so long as they don't kill anyone. These men are savages, and unless you stop them the work of the Church will come to nought. Nought, do you understand?' Father Chiphwanya had now bent down and was shouting into the old priest's ear.

'But they can't do anything like that. These men are good people, Father,' replied Father Superior, emphasizing the word 'good', his eyes shining with holy joy at this word.

'Do you know what they are saying now? They think I am a witch, that I bewitched Brother Aruppe. You must have heard the guns they are shooting into the air. Haven't you heard the pagan songs?' asked Father Chiphwanya. 'It's always the same with you and your Christians.' He said the word 'Christians' with a grinding irony in his voice.

'These are good people, I tell you, Father,' replied the old man quietly, but enthusiastically. 'They may not be white, but they are human beings. They are even better than some of our own people, we the carriers of Christianity. Father' – the old man stood up. He had touched on a matter about which he felt very strongly. 'Do you realize that your words may be uncharitable?' He was pacing up and down. Now he did not care what Father Chiphwanya might say or do. He was an old and infirm man, but he was still the Superior. Father Chiphwanya would not be deterred, however.

'Yes,' he cut in, 'call it lack of charity when I speak the truth. This is what's wrong with you. You have been too long in Africa, Father Superior. Anything that I do is wrong, but anything that a native does is right, is good, is Christian and is charitable.' He paused for breath. He too was pacing up and down. If it came to a showdown, he knew that might was on his side. He continued: 'The D.C. was here the other day. How did you treat him? You walked away from him because an African had come to see you. Do you realize that the D.C. represents the Governor in this area, that without him you would have no protection against these Africans, these savages, these cannibals?' Father Chiphwanya was conveniently forgetting his own former fury against the D.C.

'I don't care about the D.C. He can look after himself. These people can't. And even the D.C., with all his power, can have no security except through the confidence and trust of these people,' replied the old man. 'I have known them for a long time, longer than any white man here. I suppose you would call me a native, but I don't care. They are my people and it is these people who will bury me, and, I trust, pray for me when I die.' The old man paused. He was out of breath again. These white men infuriated him more than the natives.

He might as well have been speaking to a statue, for immediately he paused Father Chiphwanya hit back.

'About these marriages of yours,' he charged.

'They are not my marriages, they are God's marriages,' retorted Father Superior. This was a familiar argument from Father Chiphwanya and the old man was sensitive about any suggestion that he was doing anything against Mother Church.

'You allow bereaved husbands to marry their wives' sisters. At what point does a pagan custom become a Christian practice? Are your actions not heretical? And here you are posing as a little god before these illiterate people.'

'You are wrong, Father, and you know that is not the point. There is more love between man and wife among these people than in our own country. In our country we kiss our women in public, in the streets, in order to sjambok them better in the homes. The holy love that these people have for their wives extends to the woman's family. Isn't it only fair that Christianity should provide for the ultimate consummation of this love in Christian marriage?' The old man paused again, but this time Father Chiphwanya was not taking over. 'I would remind you, Father, that the only impediment to a proper marriage in this case is consanguinity, of which there is none.'

'You know this is not true teaching. You know it, don't you?' stormed Father Chiphwanya. 'You just want to please these pagans. You don't understand these natives, Gonzago. You don't. You just sit in that little shell of yours, going round the mission counting the number of ripe avocados. What do you know about these people? What do you care for their souls?'

'Chief Mpona is here right now, in trouble because of you, of you, Father. You have made him obey your orders like a faithful spaniel before his own people and you have reduced him to the status of a coward. Now his people are going to rise against him.' Father Superior swallowed hard. 'Tell me, Father, when you went to Mpona and found the people weeping after one of their number had died, did you even so much as sympathize with them?'

'Don't ask me foolish questions, Gonzago. I did,' replied Father Chiphwanya.

'Yes,' said the little man slowly, 'after the white man's fashion. Yes, I just sit in this little shell of mine. When you have lived long in Africa you will learn that it is not the child that looks for food from house to house that is fed, but the one that stays at home.'

The old man cleared his throat again and tilted his helmet. Something was worrying him about what he was saying. He had started by defending what he knew to be the truth, but now he was defending himself against the smarting accusations of Father Chiphwanya. He only had the right to defend the truth, to defend Christ, but never to defend himself. If father Chiphwanya accused him of incompetence, why did he have to sear him with abuse, right into his heart? But he had started it and it was impossible to stop. For the sake of the Faith Father Chiphwanya had to be forcefully shocked into understanding these people.

'Father,' he said again, after swallowing even harder, 'let me be frank with you. These pagans loved Brother Aruppe as one of them. What did you do for Brother Aruppe? You treated him worse than a leper. You goaded him at table, at prayer, even in his sleep. Now he is dead. Only yesterday you emptied a jug of dirty soapy water on his head. All in the name of Christianity, no doubt. Have these pagans done any such thing against you?'

This was the last straw. Father Chiphwanya shot off, shouting, 'You'll see, you'll see!'

The old priest sat down, re-adjusted the light, replaced his helmet, and resumed his reading. He read on in the *Confessions of St Augustine*:

> And I resolved in Thyne sight, not tumultuously to tear, but gently to withdraw, the service of my tongue from the service of lip-labour; that the young, no students in Thy law, nor in Thy peace, but in lying dotages and law-skirmishes, should no longer buy at my mouth for their madness . . .

The funeral vigil went on. The fire rose higher and higher and the singing grew louder and louder as more people gathered there. Neither Natombi nor Mpona could understand why the white men did not come to disperse the gathering, as the teacher never attended such unchristian meetings back at their own village.

In the middle of the following morning, a delegation came to Father Chiphwanya. They told him that the lion had been killed that morning. They asked for permission to bury the head separately lest the terrible lion should rise from the dead.

'Go see your Father Superior yourselves,' replied Father Chiphwanya curtly.

When they saw him the old priest replied, 'My children, only Our Lord Jesus Christ could rise from the dead. But, if this is your wish, do as you please. Sergio our cook will give you the tools.'

'May Jesus Christ be honoured,' said the people in chorus. Father Superior replied, 'For ever and ever, Amen,' and entered his room.

Father Chiphwanya had not been to the dining-room since the previous night. Now at supper the old priest sat all by himself looking at the basket of oranges in the centre of the table, the oranges that were always Brother Aruppe's pride. Brother Aruppe would have been sitting in this chair, thought the priest. A stray tear rolled down his cheek. He looked at the other vacant chair. This one was Father Chiphwanya's. He thought, 'He is an unbending one.' Just then the door opened abruptly and Father Chiphwanya swept in. Before the old priest could say 'Good evening' Father Chiphwanya was gone, having swept away the basket of oranges.

'Throw these oranges away!' Father Superior heard him order the servant outside.

Father Superior listened further, but Father Chiphwanya had gone. The servant stood in the doorway with the oranges, looking at Father Superior.

'Shall I throw these oranges away?' The old man looked at him, and through clouded eyes he said, 'Take them to your children.' He stood up, gave thanks, and left to go to the church. Then again he heard Father Chiphwanya shout down to the servant, 'Sergio, bring my two bicycles to my room and deflate them.'

'But Father Superior is going to the village tomorrow,' said Sergio, convinced that Father Chiphwanya had forgotten.

'Do what I tell you. He can walk. That's what he did before I came here,' said Father Chiphwanya.

The old priest walked away silently. He remained in the church for a long time praying for Brother Aruppe, praying for the mission, that it would be preserved through the clouds of despair that enveloped it. He prayed too for Father Chiphwanya, and for himself, that he might accept God's yoke more readily. He had no right, he confessed, to lose his temper with Father Chiphwanya. Without him and his wide net of friends abroad, where would the mission have been? There would have been no quinine, which had saved the lives of many Africans around the mission. Above all there would have been little money and, therefore, no bandages. These were the things that mattered – the saving of people's lives and their souls. So why deny Father Chiphwanya the credit for all this? Without his bicycles would he have reached Alozhio in good time to administer Baptism and the Last Sacrament? There was a need, thought Father Superior as he slowly made his way back to his own room, to be reminded that, remote from the Monseigneur's authority in Lusaka though one was, one was not free to amend the doctrine of the Church. Father Chiphwanya might be too inflexible, but he might still be right.

'O Lord,' he sighed, 'have I exceeded my brief? Have I sought to please men instead of doing your work? Then Lord, cast me away, tear me apart and scatter my remains to the winds, for You have given me the great honour of assisting at your Table, but I have failed You.' Why, he thought to himself, did I have to dispute with Father Chiphwanya about the Church's doctrine? Only sophists and pharisees talk as though they know everything. Proud Lucifer, you did not like a junior to correct you . . .

As the little old man passed Father Chiphwanya's room he heard the typewriter clacking away furiously. It was 2.00 a.m. but Father Chiphwanya was still working. What could he have been doing? The old man slipped into his room and, after saying his rosary, fell asleep. Not so Father Chiphwanya, who was still typing at 3.00 a.m. By 4.00 a.m. he was reading through his forty-page, closely-typed document to his

154

Superior, with a copy to the Monseigneur in Lusaka, and a spare copy, perhaps for onward transmission to the Apostolic Delegate in Mombasa.

The document read:

Reverend Fr. Superior, Katondwe Mission, we were ordained in Holy Orders to continue the fight which Our Lord Himself started against Beelzebub as He stood poised on the precipice, dared by Satan to dash Himself to the bottom. Now and again, being human, we fall into the trap of preferring the glitter of Satan's illusory city to the tortuousness of the narrow and thorny path. At this time, if those colleagues in Holy Orders whom we call our friends do not summon us anew to our pledge to serve Our Lord with all our might, then truly Beelzebub will go back and call seven others worse than himself to inhabit the festering city.

I am a friend of yours, who will not allow you to perish in this manner. *You know I am the true beginning and you know also that I could be the sad end of this mission if I chose to act for today and not for eternity.* You, Father, are acting for today and not for eternity. You have twisted the law of God into an instrument of pleasure, lascivious pleasure.

You have taught that the law against eating meat on Friday was made for the white man, who can eat meat every other day, and not for the black man, who can only find meat to eat at a funeral. You have, therefore, unknown to Lusaka, to Rome, waived this rule, and now people eat as much meat on Friday as on feast days ... That is very good so long as you continue pretending that you are the god of this primitive little mission, and so long as you continue to think that I will continue as your slavish instrument.

Many are the doctrines of Mother Church which you have prostituted for your own convenience . . .

You talk often of the necessity for flexibility in the Church, but you must know that nothing that is wrong can be right even with the maximum of flexibility. There are many natives today living in sin who owe it to you that they are living in this manner. It is permitted, and indeed expected by native custom, that when the wife dies the husband should inherit the dead woman's sister. But it is not permitted by Mother Church to extend a blessing to such a union. To do so is to bring the couple within the pale of God's censure. For, while certain unions contracted as pagans may be tolerated because the people concerned do not know any better, such unions cannot be contracted by Catholics . . .

Father Chiphwanya dealt at length with his Superior's doctrinal transgressions. He attacked the manner in which in a Sunday sermon the Superior had failed to emphasize the centrality of priestly celibacy by references to the possible but rare contingency of a dispensation from the Pope. He also attacked the encouragement that he had given to the people to receive Holy Communion as often as possible.

He continued:

Some weeks back you preached a sermon which made me wonder whether you were still for Christ or against Him. You talked of priestly celibacy as though it were something not completely necessary. You chose to make undue use of the precedent set by old Father Schultz in Germany, who was given dispensation to live with his wife after his ordination. You know that the circumstances were exceptional – an unusually late vocation – and yet you went on to mislead the people. These natives are not refined. What thinking they do is of necessity crude. They cannot understand subtle exceptions to the rule.

He cancelled 'rule' and wrote in 'law'.

'And now,' wrote Father Chiphwanya towards the last ten pages of his thesis, 'comes this last straw.'

It makes me weep for you, Father, that a man so devoted, a man who has spent all his life in the House of God, should act in the manner that you are acting. You know that I did not send Brother Aruppe to his death, that his time had come. And yet you have behaved to the people as though I had killed him – or, to use the language you understand best – as though I had bewitched him. You and your natives, you both believe in witchcraft. How else could you have approved the people's dramatic display of mourning, the kind of mourning that is only possible among people who do not share our belief in eternity? If you had gone there, as I did, you would have heard the utter desecration of the image of our departed Brother. It was not the *Kyrie* nor indeed the *Pange Lingua* which these people sang; their prayers were magical incantations to the spirits of their ancestors to avenge the death. You loved our brother in Jesus, as much as I did. In fact, you taught me to overcome my dislike for him. Yet it is you who allowed his death to be mourned by pagans, as if our prayers were not enough. . . .

'For all these reasons and many more,' concluded the letter, after further discourse on the Father Superior's liturgical transgressions, 'I must give you notice of my intention to depart this mission. I leave tomorrow morning, whether with your blessing or not. Do not fear, I will praise your good deeds towards the natives before the Monseigneur.'

Father Chiphwanya looked at his watch. Lord! It was already morning – 4.30. He slumped into his chair and fell fast asleep . . .

By that time Father Superior had left on foot for the village to say Mass.

Later that morning Aphunzitsi asked the teacher at the mission to take his party to Father Chiphwanya, so that Natombi and the chief could hear with their own ears how the boy Mwape was getting on.

'What do you want to know?' asked Father Chiphwanya,

after the teacher at the mission had introduced the party of Chief Mpona, Natombi, and Aphunzitsi to him. 'Weren't they among the people who were saying that I was a witch last night?' he asked, turning to the mission teacher. Then he recognized Aphunzitsi. It was clear that his eyes were awaiting the salutation from him.

'May Jesus Christ be honoured,' said Aphunzitsi after clearing his throat.

'For ever and ever,' replied the priest.

'Amen,' concluded the teacher from Mpona. 'It's about the child,' said Aphunzitsi uneasily.

'What about him? Do these people think I bewitched him too?' Then he said to himself, 'Good heavens! These natives really are terrible! They always want help, help. Never do anything on their own. Huggins is right.' He turned to the party. 'Get out of here, all of you. Go and see your pigmy of a superior.' He stormed away, shouting 'Malnutrition, malnutrition! Kwashiorkor!'

How could they possibly go without hearing about the child? How would the mother feel? Would not Lubinda revile them, even openly, if they left without any news of the boy? Father Superior was not there, so they decided to wait for him. He eventually came back to the mission in the evening, having walked close on twenty miles that day. The party was waiting outside his room.

'This is Chief Mpona, Father,' said Aphunzitsi. 'We came to find out about . . .'

'Ah, Mpona my friend!' exclaimed the little old priest, embracing the chief. 'I did not know that you were here. You have found us in difficulties.'

'It is true, this is sad news,' replied Mpona, who did not know how to react to a white man's warmth or how to express the sorrow that the black one feels for the sorrows of the white one.

The priest suddenly stopped. Tears coursed down his small face. He cast his eyes aside. They fell on the door of Brother

Aruppe's room. The key was still there as Brother Aruppe had left it on that fateful night.

'Ah!' exclaimed the little man at last, after a long silence, 'the boy, I remember. We have received a letter from Lusaka. He will have to be operated upon but he is still too weak now. He was not eating well at the village, so he suffers from malnutrition.'

'Not eating well?' repeated Natombi incredulously. 'But the boy always ate well. He always filled his stomach and was satisfied. Please teacher, tell the white one it is not true, it is not true that my boy was hungry. Oh! they want to cut his tongue! My son, my only . . .' She burst into tears. They came on fast until she was wailing like one mourning a dead person.

Father Superior blinked. 'Don't be afraid, woman,' he said. 'I understand what you feel, but the boy will be well.'

After further assurances, the mother became more cheerful. She asked about the living conditions at the hospital. Did her son sleep in one bed with all the other children or did he sleep on the floor? What did they give him to wear, or to cover himself at night? Father Superior patiently answered her questions. He explained how it was that a child could eat a lot and fill his stomach and yet still suffer from the disease that comes because you do not eat enough of the proper food. He asked about the village and the kingdom. Was it well?

'We are your people, Chief,' he said to Mpona, 'look after us well.' Here too Mpona did not know what to say.

The following morning the party left for Mpona.

As they approached the village in the evening, Natombi, being the only woman in the group, began to mourn. This is the manner of announcing bad news. Immediately the women in the village heard the wailing, they too began to mourn aloud even before she was in sight. They knew it was Natombi's voice and, even if they all disliked her, they had to cry, because someone had died.

'Is it her child?' asked Lubinda coming out of his hut. 'I

told Mpona not to agree to giving the child to the white man. It was witchcraft, what he did.'

The party trooped into the village, and immediately a crowd of curious children, yelling women, and silent men gathered around them. After the preliminaries of greeting, Lubinda led the charge.

'You travelled well, Chief?' he asked.

'Yes, except that the teacher's friend was killed by a lion two days ago,' replied Mpona.

Lubinda looked at Yuda as if to say, 'You see! I told you so.'

'Which one?' he asked. 'We do not know his friends. Only those who eat with him know his friends. He does not look upon us as human beings.'

'A white man at the mission,' replied the Chief.

'A white one!' exclaimed Lubinda. 'What have we got to do with a white one even if he died like a leper?' He checked himself. Yuda would not be happy with that. 'Like a lizard.' Then he growled at the women, 'Stop mourning! It is not yours that has died.'

'Why does Natombi cry as though a man had died? These white men, we do not know where they come from nor what happens to them when they die! Do we even know if they really die? How could this lion kill a white man?'

'Natombi cries because this dead white man was very kind to Mwape,' replied the teacher.

'Mwape? Yes, of course, you went to see Mwape, all three of you, didn't you?' Lubinda was at his cynical best. 'Does the boy speak now? You are always seeking to disgrace us,' he said, pointing to himself and the kamcape. 'We told you that that child was bewitched and that nothing would ever make him speak. Why do you pretend to have gone to the mission for his sake, when we all know what you went for? You went to speak to your fellow witch-missionary, didn't you?'

The Chief wondered at Lubinda's direct manner. He knew that Lubinda was busy organizing the village against him. He had even begun to get in touch with the headmen of the other villages. But he had never been so direct and aggressive with him before. What was it that had suddenly made him so bold? Mpona looked around the gathered crowd. He thought there was one man he could not recognize, but then it was dark and he put it down to his bad eyesight. Should he, a Chief of the Kaunga Kingdom, reply to this insulting charge from a menial who had become what he was today because of the goodness of his grandfather? Did he think that because he was the Councillor at the court he could not be removed? What had happened in his brief absence, wondered Mpona.

The teacher and Natombi, who had now stopped wailing, simply stood still.

'It is not true, and you know it,' was all Mpona would say. There was a glint of defiant but stately anger in his otherwise flat voice. The people crowded closer to the two men confronting each other.

'What has been happening here in my absence?' asked Mpona.

'You know,' replied Lubinda.

Yes, by now Mpona knew what was happening. According to custom, Lubinda could not challenge the Chief in that way unless he knew that Mpona was a witch, and thus accused him. At this point Mpona would be defenceless because the mantle of authority would fall away. A Chief does not remain a Chief until he can prove in the face of accusation that he is innocent. This was why Lubinda had become bold. But what witchcraft was he accusing Mpona of?

'Mpona!' said Lubinda, 'you are not the son of your mother. Your real mother is that witch Nyalutila who was chased out of this village many years ago. You were born in the bush.' Lubinda paused for breath. The kamcape looked at him as though to urge him on. He continued.

'We, the real people of this village, we have brought the kamcape to show us the truth. You have cheated us too much, Mpona, you have tried to alienate me from my own people. Do I not speak truly, my people?' The villagers shouted agreement. 'If he is a witch he must die. It was he who made it possible for the teacher to escape death. They must both die!'

There were some among the crowd who would not speak but simply cast down their eyes. They knew Mpona too well to think so ill of him. Yet they would have to exile him if the kamcape said that he was a witch.

The integrity of the village, of the whole fabric of society, was at stake. The village had survived the strange laws of the white man at the Boma, it had even managed to evade some of them. It had told the white man where he got off. So long as it continued to be united from within, the village would continue to succeed, and all that the white man would get from it would be the chickens and eggs and tax money which he so cruelly wrenched from the labour-bruised hands of its people. But to preserve this unity it would be necessary to purge the village of all revisionist elements, and this included the teacher, Natombi, and the Chief himself. Natombi, the one who had offered her son to the white man so that he could cut his tongue, the Chief, and the teacher, had they not conspired with the white missionary against the other European who died at the mission? How else could the Chief's timely departure for the mission be explained? Had he not gone to attend the funeral even before the white one was killed? His witchcraft could be countered. But this association with the white man was sabotage. Would the village survive? Such were the thoughts running through the people's minds as they shouted, 'If he is a witch, he must die.'

The kamcape stood up; they all stood up as one. Only Mpona and his party remained seated.

'Mpona, you witch', said the kamcape, 'I'm returning home today; I'll be back in a month's time. I give you time,' he continued, his voice rising to a passionate crescendo, 'to clean up your stinking house, to do away with your trickery. Destroy all charms and the horns stuffed with the tails of lizards. That dead man's hair which you carry in the charm on your arm, burn it now.'

Then he turned to the people, cutting through the air with

his fly-switch: 'Don't touch him, I warn you. His charms are too strong for you. Even I must go back to fortify myself before I dare touch him.'

The people shouted, 'Mfiti, mfiti!' (meaning 'witch!') and none dared touch him. The kamcape turned sharply to go, Lubinda followed, and all the villagers dispersed to their houses and gardens. There was fear in their hearts. Within a month anything could happen. A person could die and you could forget all about him. It was such a long time to wait to be rid of a dangerous witch.

Mpona, standing there and feeling alone, looked around him. The teacher and Natombi were still there, too surprised to understand.

'Stay with me,' whispered Mpona to the teacher and Natombi, 'you will stay with me, won't you?'

Mosquitoes buzzed around the three people as the thick blanket of night descended upon them. Somewhere not far off stood Mrs Mpona fuming with rage. She was angry with Lubinda for what he had done against the Chief, but she was even more angry with the Chief himself for having hidden this 'fact' from her all his life. Had she not been through much with him? Hadn't he nearly hacked her to pieces when he went mad? Why had he gone mad anyway? Not because of her, but because of Ngoza, that impish little wretch of a woman who had disgraced not only Mpona but herself too. And now he was a witch. The presence of the kamcape confirmed that he really was a witch. Everything after this would be mere formality. If Mpona was a witch she could have no dealings with him. Was that why she had lost two children since her marriage to him? If he had been so dishonest as to conceal his true nature, he was probably hiding his real relationship with Natombi too. She adjusted her fat belly by shaking it down with both hands. She was waiting for Mpona to retire to his house, and there she would . . . she would . . .

Chapter 11

News of the happenings at Mpona, the village of the Chief, was bound to get out to the rest of the villages of the kingdom. Gossip had started many years back about the goings on in that village. What the Chief did or what happened to him was not really the business of the rest of the kingdom, but he was not only Chief of Kaunga; he was also head of his village and the royal family. Strictly speaking, although the other villages would continue to be interested in the power game at the court, they would not reject anyone the royal family put up as the successor.

However, the village headmen were important. If Mpona was replaced as head of the royal family, they would go to the court and one by one pledge their loyalty to the new man. If the cause of the removal of the present Mpona was witchcraft, then it would be a foregone conclusion that they would, without exception, all pledge their loyalty to the new man.

One month passed and the kamcape did not return. Tension in the village increased. Lubinda kept telling the people that the kamcape would return, but he did not. In the meantime, the maize in the fields had ripened but there was no ceremony to mark the new crop, for there was no Chief of the village to whom they could take a little of the green maize and say: 'Here, lord of the village, the spirits of our fathers have blessed us with a good crop, we are offering this to you as the representative of our spirits.'

For Lubinda the first critical test of whether he would be regarded as the head of the royal family was already at hand.

If he could persuade the people in the village to make the thanksgiving to him so that he could send it on to the spirits, then this in itself would be a sign of loyalty to himself. Would the people agree to this? So far he had been surprised by the quick support that he had been given. He knew that his charge against the Chief did not make sense. But then this was a charge of witchcraft, which did not need to be fully explicit. Everyone in the village appeared to back him, except Simbeya. 'He is too old,' said Lubinda to himself, 'and anyway he can be made to disappear. No one would ask about how an old leper like that had disappeared.'

Lubinda need not have worried. When the news went round that there would be a Thanksgiving, people from many villages flocked into the headquarters, and Lubinda found himself presiding over the ceremony. The occasion was always a popular one.

Nevertheless there was talk, spread as widely as the alleged witchcraft of Mpona, about Lubinda himself. Long ago, when Ngoza, the Chief's young wife, was found to have had a child by another man, Mpona had become deranged. The woman and child afterwards disappeared, and had never been heard of again. The Chief, as Chief, could dispose of anyone, especially one who had crossed his path in this manner, but the Chief would have disposed of the man who had caused the pregnancy rather than his young wife. So far no one in the kingdom had disappeared. Moreover, the Chief, having become mad immediately after hearing the news, could not have been responsible for the disappearance of Ngoza and the child.

'About these things that are happening at the court,' said village headman Mkando to headman Ciwera. 'Is it true they are saying the Chief is a witch?'

Ciwera set the calabash of beer down. He was a slow man who liked to think over every answer he gave. To him time did not mean much, in fact, it meant nothing. He looked at the clear sky, and at the solitary bird flitting across it. He sniffed the heat of the air which was blowing into the veranda of the hut where they were drinking beer. The heat was as strong as the smell of raw blood.

'Tomorrow it will be cold,' he said finally, 'but it doesn't matter because the maize is almost ready. If the cold had come at the time it did last year, with the young maize coming up, then there could have been real trouble.'

'Yes,' replied Mkando, who was of a slightly impatient disposition. 'But what about these stories going round, what do you think?' he asked again.

'Well,' replied Ciwera, 'it was strange, wasn't it?'

'What?' asked Mkando.

'Aren't you talking about the disappearance of that woman so many years ago?'

Mkando nodded his head. He did not want to reply again because this would lead to more waiting for Ciwera to compose his thoughts.

'They say that Lubinda had her and the child drowned in the river and then buried in a hidden place.' Ciwera stopped.

'Really!' exclaimed Mkando. He too had heard something to that effect, but not quite in that way.

'You didn't ask why, my friend,' said Ciwera, eyeing Mkando somewhat suspiciously.

'Why?'

'Well, that is the question. Who do you think was responsible for that child?' asked Ciwera.

'I don't know,' replied Mkando, 'but I think I can see now.'

'The Thanksgiving for the new crop will be soon. Let us wait and see, when we go to the Chief's village, who will be doing what,' said Ciwera in a confidential tone. 'If I were you I would wait and see. Mpona hasn't called us to his beer for a long time now. In the past, before you became headman, your uncle and I were always given a lot of the crops that the people offered to the Chief at Thanksgiving. No, no, not since this young Mpona took over.' He searched Mkando's face for assurance, and quickly put in, 'That is what the people are saying, not I.'

The Thanksgiving was an annual affair. Every year, round

about the second month when the maize was getting ripe, the people would, on an appointed day, gather together with their baskets of produce – maize, pumpkins, cucumbers – at the Chief's court. These were the offerings to the spirits in thanksgiving for the crop of that year. Before this was done, no one was allowed to eat the new maize; not until the Chief had tasted of the fruit, no one else, not even a child, could eat it. Offerings came not only from Mpona's village but from the whole kingdom. There were long processions of women carrying large baskets of food from all over the valley.

There were certain beliefs and stories about this ceremony. If you tasted of the new crop before Thanksgiving, you would die. So to prevent people from dying you were expected to tie a knot of medicine to one mealie stalk in the garden. If anyone tried to get a cob of maize he would be stuck to the maize until the owner came to undo the charm of the medicine. This charm was also useful in keeping thieves out since they too would get stuck if they tried to steal the maize.

This time Lubinda was conducting the ritual. He prayed aloud:

'To the spirits of our fathers and ancestors, this beer we consecrate. We have not been able until now, oh spirits, to offer you the first maize of our gardens. Through your kindness you have shown to us the crocodile who we took to be our Chief. Now we ask your forgiveness for never having turned to you, our spirits, for counsel.' Then he poured out a jar of beer under the big tree and continued: 'With this sacrifice you will truly forgive and allow us to pay you the debt that is yours. For, without giving you our first crop, how shall we provide for the next one? Will you not, in anger, scorch the fields and make us pay twice, as you did last year, for our sins of omission, and the sins of this snake that we thought to be the head of our village?'

The people found themselves automatically kneeling and clapping at every sentence.

'Now,' he continued, 'with this beer we ask you to re-open the river of mercy and forgiveness so that our gifts for this year may flow into your sacred quarters, which are wherever you wish them to be.'

Lubinda's wife brought a basketful of green maize, cucumbers, and pumpkins and set them before the gathering. Ceremonially, Lubinda lit the pile, and the people watched the consecrated fumes of smoke rise up into the clouds.

'It is done, it is done,' said Lubinda to himself, simmering with excitement.

Very early the following morning the people began emptying their baskets of maize on Lubinda's doorstep. The procession continued into the afternoon, since each kind of crop had to be brought on a separate journey. By the end of the morning the pile was already higher than his house. But the kamcape did not return. What was worse, the victory of the Thanksgiving appeared illusory in retrospect. Mpona, to many of the people, was still the Chief; he had simply delegated the ceremony to his Councillor.

Chapter 12

When Luangwa river quarrels with Zambezi river the reeds know that they are not safe. When the elephant fights the lion it is the grass that suffers. Again, when the pestle pounds the wooden mortar it is the grain that suffers. So how could the teacher expect to escape the anger that had grown between Lubinda and Mpona? Already within the last few days the teacher had become an outcast again. The days of bitterness had returned.

When a man lives on his own in a village, the women of the village know that it is their duty to cook for him. It does not matter whether he stays alone in the village for one day, one month, one year or the whole of his lifetime. For a man to draw his own water and cook for himself is the greatest humiliation that he can suffer. Only lepers who are thrown out of the village can be treated like dogs in this manner. But this was what was happening to the teacher.

Of all the women who had formerly taken turns to cook for him there was now only Mpona's wife left, and it was clear to the teacher that she too resented doing this for a man whom she held responsible for her husband's misfortunes. So he began to avoid her food, to go out on long walks when he knew that the food was nearly ready, and to go to the well to draw his own water. It was on one of these trips from the well that, bowed down with the sudden age that comes from not eating, he was surprised by an intruder.

The sun was shining brightly. The blades of grass were dancing in its beams and there was a hum from the cicadas hidden in the grass. In the distance, as he set his jar of water down under the sausage tree and stretched his back to regain his strength, he could see the hazy outline of the distant hill. His thoughts were fixing on that haze. Somewhere under the hill was the mysterious cave which the people of the valley talked about so rarely and yet with so much fear. That was the cave from which no one who entered it ever returned. His memory went back to the day which had, until now, appeared so far away, the day when he had stood on trial for his life in that same village. Someone had then mentioned the possibility of sending him to the cave. Why had he come back to this village after all that had happened to him?

Then he remembered his child, his only son now buried in the valley at Mundo. His thoughts leapt into the past. They pierced the darkness of forgetfulness with a shaft of pain. There was his child, romping away and jumping up and down. His mother had just slaughtered a chicken for supper. But when the nsima and relish had been prepared and set on the floor for them all to eat, the child had simply curled up in his mother's lap. The mother had scolded him and slapped him for not eating. With pleading eyes, the child had said: 'Tonight I am ill.' Then he had started to squirm like an eel that has swallowed a spear and, within a short time, he was dead.

Lost in his little world of robbed love, he lifted up the jar of water and set it on his head. He had to live on for the sake of his dead child, for the sake of his wife buried many miles away in Nyimba, for the sake of himself.

A gruff voice called suddenly from nowhere: 'Stop, you!' it commanded. The jar of water cascaded and shattered, thudding on to the damp earth.

'I see you are now a woman also, as well as being a teacher.' It was Yuda. 'Isn't it funny the way some people are always torturing themselves?'

His little world was also shattered as he saw the mocking smile of Yuda, twiddling the two remaining fingers on his hands with great satisfaction. Two months ago Yuda would not have dared challenge this man. But now here he was, a bundle of scraped bones, a lanky goat for the slaughter.

'Ho! The famous teacher and lover of white things carrying water on his head!' He was taunting him. 'I always knew you were a woman. You are saying to yourself, "This dirty leper!". I am much stronger than you,' yelled Yuda, striking Aphunzitsi with his clubbed hand. Then the pain seemed to upset Yuda and he threw his walking-stick at him. The old teacher remained motionless, neither challenging Yuda with his eyes nor saying anything. His thoughts had turned again to his boy, to his wife. He could see the tender skull of the young boy upturned to him.

'You scorpion!' said Yuda, beside himself with rage at the teacher's indifference. 'Do you hear me?'

'What, my friend?' said Aphunzitsi, returning to the world.

'Lubinda, the Chief, would like to speak to you. He wants to protect you against this witch Mpona. Mpona is not only a witch but a murderer.' The denunciation rose to a frenzy. 'Who made me into that thing which I am now? Who made me into a leper who must wear a bell to warn all you clean people of the approach of death? Yes, you clean people!' Yuda was stumping around like a wounded buffalo, his feet bleeding as he burst a blood vessel.

'Friend, it is not possible for me to see Lubinda,' replied the teacher.

'Why?' snapped Yuda.

'He is not the Chief. He is just a cheat, a corrupt son of the devil, and may the Lord help him!' Aphunzitsi was shaking with anger as he made the sign of the cross.

'It is you and your fellow witch who are corrupt,' challenged Yuda. Aphunzitsi did not answer.

'You don't answer,' resumed Yuda, 'because you think that what I am saying is rubbish. But you will see what you have never seen.' He paused. 'Do you know that Mpona has been to Lubinda to ask him to get rid of you, so that you can disappear, disappear?' He paddled his open palms sideways in a gesture of complete annihilation. 'But Lubinda the good one has refused,' he said, shaking his head vigorously. 'Lubinda will not destroy a good man like yourself for a bad man like Mpona.'

Yuda could see through the corner of his squinting eye that Aphunzitsi was listening. Honest men are simple men, he was thinking.

'To get rid of me?' asked the teacher, with a stupid, glazed look on his furrowed face. 'But why?'

'That, my friend, is the question: why? Why? Lubinda asks himself, we will ask ourselves,' replied Yuda. 'But, of course, only those who do not know him can ask why Mpona should want to do this to you. But, know this, my friend, that evil comes more naturally to Mpona than good.' Yuda's voice was low and confidential as he crept up to Aphunzitsi until he was talking right into his face, knitting his brows like a porcupine that has been shorn of its eyelids. 'My friend, have you ever seen where a snake urinates?' asked Yuda.

'No,' replied Aphunzitsi.

'Or do you know why a rabbit has a skin like a goat and not like an elephant?'

'No,' replied the mystified teacher.

'So, then you do not know why a snake does not piss. But you know it eats, don't you?'

'Yes, it does,' replied the teacher.

'So then you know that when you stand between Mpona the snake, and his food he will eat you up first? You are a clever one, I can see,' concluded Yuda, turning away. 'But I see you still don't understand,' he went on. 'You may speak the same language as Mpona, but you are not of his tribe. Stranger, you come from far across the Luangwa, from the country of the unknown. "Stranger",' intoned Yuda in a mysterious whisper, 'do you remember that? Was it Lubinda who said it?'

The teacher remembered, he remembered everything, and the realization was as though lightning had split his head open. He remembered the night when he and his friends had sat waiting for the judgement of those people. Then Mpona had said: 'Stranger, go away, we do not trust you; stranger, leave us alone.' The way Mpona had uttered that word, how it had seared his heart!

'You mean,' stammered the old man, 'Mpona regards me as a foreigner?'

'How can *I* say such things?' said Yuda. 'Only Mpona can speak in this way.'

'But why, why him of all people, and now when I need every help?' the teacher asked himself. Tears began to force themselves into his eyes. 'My own friend, the Chief!' The old man's body shook.

'Don't let it worry you: this Chief of yours has done the same to all of us. Do you know he's been telling everybody that I eat frogs? No, obviously you don't,' replied Yuda in mock consolation.

'But Yuda,' said Aphunzitsi, cupping his hands in earnest appeal, 'I don't believe you. I just can't believe you.' He was almost shouting. 'Do you understand?' He lowered his voice. He was after all still the teacher and a Christian.

'There is only one thing for you to do,' said Yuda, 'follow the way of righteousness. Then you can't go wrong. You are the teacher of justice, of a religion that is right even though we may not believe it. Aphunzitsi,' he said, turning to face him in a dramatic gesture, 'do you know that even though we may all appear to be against you . . . I will say no more. Enough is enough even for a fool.' He broke off.

Aphunzitsi began to walk away. Yuda hobbled behind him. Then the teacher stopped abruptly. 'So the Chief wants to get rid of me?'

'Eh?' muttered Yuda, catching up. 'If you say so, but you haven't heard the full story, my friend. It is said that Mpona wanted something and that you were in the way.

'What?' asked the teacher.

'If you must know – but how can I speak so to an upright and God-fearing man? It is Natombi,' he whispered confidentially, flapping his once-large ears.

'Natombi! But I don't know her – I mean, I haven't had

173

anything to do with her,' said Aphunzitsi, his heart filling with rage.

'My friend,' said Yuda, 'I must be off.' He cast his eyes towards the broken jar. 'And you must go back and draw your water. But be careful, Mpona is on the warpath.'

'It's a lie!' yelled the teacher above the confused drums pounding in his brain. 'I know it, it's a lie. You are corrupt people, all of you.'

'Who is not corrupt then? Mpona? E-he!' exclaimed Yuda.

'You and Lubinda, you have been giving the people all kinds of things so that they will support you. Lubinda wants to become the Chief of this kingdom, and even Mpona knows it.' Aphunzitsi was now shouting with anger.

'Oh, that? As if there is anybody in the village who doesn't know that Lubinda is the Chief! But we buy favours, the people's favours, with our good. What's wrong with buying the highest commodity, the favour and support of your own people, with the little wealth that you have?' Yuda turned to face the teacher. 'You too buy your needs with the dirty money of the white man. But you buy goods which are worthless things to people of good nature. We buy favours, the people's favours. Is yours not the bribery of the pig?' He stopped, then went on passionately, 'You must believe what I say about this Chief of yours. He is dangerous.'

Aphunzitsi did not reply. He stood there like a pricked balloon; his anger had evaporated. A hawk fluttered towards the village and the sounds of harassed chickens floated to his ears. He realized that Lubinda's claws were sinking into his neck even as the hawk was enjoying its kill . . .

That evening, Mpona waited for Aphunzitsi to come to eat until it began to get dark. But the teacher did not come and the food began to get cold. As he sat in his doorway mopping up the last of his soup with his nsima, he heard the hurried footsteps of someone coming from the direction of the gardens. The man strode away past Mpona, not turning to nod a good evening, or even to acknowledge his presence. In the obscure light of the sinking sun, Mpona could distinguish the stoop.

'It's Aphunzitsi!' he muttered under his breath. 'What's the matter, my wife?' he asked. 'The teacher seems to be angry. Have we annoyed him?'

'Let him alone,' rasped the wife in anger. 'I cook for him every day like his slave, and this is what I get! Haven't I told you before, father of my son, that these foreigners are no good? But you continue to alienate all my people from me because you will not tell them the truth that it is he who is the witch.'

Mpona did not speak. He returned the lump of nsima which he was about to swallow to the plate and washed his hands. Then he buried his head on his knees and remained in this huddled position for a long time.

The teacher too lay awake for a long time, fretting with anger and disillusionment. This was what these people were, he thought to himself, dogs, absolute dogs. You gave them so many years of your life, but you were still a foreigner. For that they would neither trust nor forgive you. 'Dogs!' His lips trembled. He could put up with everything else and anyone else. But the Chief, the man by whom he had stood firmly to risk all, the only man through whom God was surely working out the salvation of the village! 'Lubinda!' His body shivered at the sound of the name. My time may be at hand, he said to himself. He pulled his new rosary from the wall; mechanically he passed the beads through his hands like a miser counting his change.

The following morning, long after the sun had risen, the Chief and his wife, huddled in their house, heard voices down at the other end of the village, where a drinking party was going on. Before now, no one would have brewed beer without sending a jar to the court before the people began to drink. But now it was different.

A voice was saying:

'Two months ago, nay, only a few weeks ago, never a week passed without a white visitor. Who invited them here? Who called them to come and laugh at us, mock our traditions, and chase away our beloved sick people? The skinless people were here almost every day, like flies visiting a rotten carcass.'

The crowd was roaring: 'Mpona, Mpona!'

'Do you know to whom Mpona gave the maize, the beer, and all the things that you used to offer through him to the spirits of our ancestors? If you do not,' Lubinda continued after a pause, 'can you tell me how that missionary came by the winnowing basket which I hear is at the mission? From today, my people,' he continued, 'no one will offer anything to anyone. Everything that you produce is yours. We shall offer to the spirits collectively and together, and not through one man who may, once again, exploit our goodness.'

The applause was deafening.

'I am angry with you, my people, for allowing Mpona to exploit you for so long. I am angry with myself for not having strangled him before now.' The crowd swayed with anger. 'Where is Mwape today, the young boy whom Mpona, the stupid teacher, and that harlot of a woman Natombi, offered to the white man? Do you see, my people, how Mpona has not only been bewitching you but also selling you into slavery?'

'Kill him, kill her, kill them all!' It was Banda, the brother of Dulani, who had never forgiven Natombi for his death.

'Shut up, all of you!' shouted Yuda. 'You are all women, women only! If you were like me and I had your hands you would have already seen that which you would have seen. Kill them!' he shouted with epileptic frenzy.

'Not all of them,' shouted Lubinda above the din. 'The teacher has repented. Maybe he whom you once called "Chief" will also repent.' Lubinda said 'Chief' in such a way that the tense crowd broke into derisory laughter.

The Chief and his wife listened to the noise from the other end of the village. Even though neither spoke to the other, it was clear that they were getting more and more restive. For some weeks now Mpona's wife had become waspish, and the Chief had learnt to dread her taunts more than the jeers and isolation of the village.

'What do you think they are laughing at now?' challenged his wife.

'People laugh when they drink. Don't they?' replied Mpona.

'You baboon, do you even dare answer me when you know that I am what I am today because of your stupidity? They are talking about you, the greatest idiot and witch that has ever lived in this village. Why don't you accept everything and let them leave you in peace?'

'But I'm not a witch,' said the Chief firmly.

'What does it matter even though you may not be? I was the wife of the Chief before – are you any longer a Chief here? Don't you see how all these simple women no longer respect me, and instead they respect Lubinda's wives? Where is your power, you . . .' the wife broke off despairingly.

'I still have my authority. I am the Chief here, not Lubinda,' replied Mpona.

'Then why do I have to live like a slave? Why can't you do something about Lubinda?' she asked.

'Such as?' asked Mpona, whose impotent anger was rising.

'Do I have to tell you what to do? If Natombi told you to do something for her, you would do it. I know that when Natombi asks for salt, even if I haven't got any, you want me to go out into the village begging for salt for her. Why do you disgrace me like this?' she asked, growing more and more vehement.

'Natombi has no one to look after her, my wife. The whole village is against her and she is only a woman. Don't you see?' replied Mpona.

'So I, your wife, I am not a woman? So, it is true what I have been hearing about you and Natombi, that there is something going on between you two, eh?' asked the wife.

'I am just helping her because she is in difficulties. We are all in difficulties,' he added.

'Don't include me in your difficulties with Natombi. These

are difficulties of your own making, and if you want, even if you have forgotten all that I have done for you, you can bring her into the house – and we shall see whether she will satisfy you. How are some people made?' she asked rhetorically. 'Old enough to be grandfathers, and yet they cast their eyes on mere children.'

'You annoy me, woman,' said Mpona abruptly.

'I annoy you? I wish I could bewitch you, you creature. But you are too deep in your witchcraft, and I am sure by tomorrow it is I who will be dead.' Then she began to sob, saying, 'When I die wrap me in the cloth my father gave me when he returned.'

> *I die tonight or tomorrow,*
> *Wrap me not in your cloth with which you wrap your women,*
> *But in that black one my father left to me,*
> *To me the only daughter whom he loved,*
> *Whom he loved more than her husband loves her,*
> *The husband who hates her for a pullet,*
> *Whose mucous has hardly dried from her lips,*
> *Oh, what are men made of that they do not know what to keep?*
> *Let them find what love they want to find.*
> *Tomorrow I die. You, husband, bury me well.*

Mpona left the place where she was weeping and disappeared into the bush with his dog. This woman was getting on his nerves more and more every day. But he understood and, besides, old people had to stick to each other. There was nothing else for it.

In her anger Mrs Mpona had forgotten all about the drunken party at the other end of the village which had caused it. Now she could hear the loud shouting and laughter. They were at it again, she thought to herself. These people, what did they want to do with her husband? Did they think that he minded if they snatched his throne away from him? He had a lot of wealth, more goats than any of them would ever have in their lives even if they bewitched all their grandmothers and lived longer than the spirits themselves. Which of these pigs could ever make a good Chief? Lubinda! She spat at the ground before her at the thought of the name.

Suddenly, the noise from the other end of the village became more excited. Before she knew what was happening, a crowd carrying sticks, knobkerries, and stones was rushing towards her house. 'We told you,' the crowd was shouting. 'Even this bird of witchcraft knows. Destroy him! Kill him! Kill his fat ugly wife!'

'Me ugly, fat?' Mrs Mpona swore. 'If they come here, they will see what they have never seen. They think I am Mpona whom they treat like a child!'

The crowd was now running towards her house. She stood up. She was going to swear grandly at the whole lot of them. She was, after all, the Chief's wife, the most important woman in the kingdom. A large stone whizzed close to her ear. She ducked, ran into the house and closed the door firmly.

Outside she could hear the walls and the roof being pelted. Stones were showering the roof and already some were dropping into the house. A spear found its mark in the muddy wall only a short distance from where she was standing. Should she jump into the jar in the corner? A large stone shattered the jar. There were people pushing the door open. 'Kill him! Kill him!' they were shouting from outside . . .

Mpona had been uneasy about the way in which he had left his wife. The hunting was a mere excuse, but he had wanted to get away from it all, from her taunts and everything else. After covering only a short distance, he saw a procession of black ants. Something puzzled him about the way they moved, and they were all so large and fat.

'This is taboo,' he said at last, after watching them for some time. 'Something is the matter somewhere.' Then he stopped to think. 'Could it be at home?' he whispered to himself. Then he remembered what it was that had caused the quarrel with his wife. Could it be that these people had now bewitched his wife?

He turned back abruptly and hurried towards home. As he approached he heard excited and angry voices. Someone was mentioning an owl. What had happened in the village during his very brief absence?

'We don't want your owl in our village. Tell your master to build somewhere else.' The voice was clear. It had Lubinda's deep bullying note.

He hurried back. Then as he reached the village he saw that there was a large crowd of people, vehement and rowdy, throwing stones and spears at his house. Where was his wife? His heart pounded with fear. Should he rush upon the crowd? He looked up at the roof and there, perched with serene composure, was an owl. He was speechless. 'An owl!' he gasped at last.

Then he heard a voice say, 'Get on with it. You miss the owl like women and you miss Mpona like cowards. To kill the lice you must kill the mother!' It was Yuda, the director of operations, issuing instructions from the safety of his hut.

Mpona ran forward into the crowd. 'Stop this, you people. You have killed my wife.' He grabbed Lubinda.

'So he had run away,' said Lubinda's nephew. 'Leave Lubinda alone, you witch.'

'Don't touch me,' said Lubinda, shaking himself free. 'It's not I but the village that does not want you. Don't you see that the owl is waiting for you? What did you plan with it?'

'Do anything to me that you please, but don't kill my wife,' pleaded Mpona.

'His wife? Ha, ha, ha, which one?' laughed Banda.

The stoning, however, ceased as everyone crowded around Lubinda to hear what the witch had to say. Immediately the owl, which had dodged all the stones and spears, hooted three times and took off slowly in the direction of the graveyard. Its wings flapped majestically.

It was no use Mpona arguing that the owl only sits on the roof of the one to be bewitched, and not on the roof of its master. One and all the people were convinced that it had come to him to take instructions for the next operation.

'I have done nothing to deserve all this,' said Mpona, looking at the ruins that had been his home only a few moments ago.

His wife looked at him like a toad about to explode with anger as he mumbled around the house. It was all his fault that she had nearly been assassinated. For his information, did he know that if Lubinda had not taken her away to his house just after the stoning started, she would have been a dead woman? Even then, did he see how that big stone lying there had missed her by the skin of her teeth? Mpona instinctively looked at her toothless gums. 'And,' said the woman, stumping about, 'you would have brought Natombi into this house tomorrow, even before you threw my body away!'

The teacher, barricaded in his lair since the interview with Yuda, had heard the noise of the scuffle, and when he had peeped out he had seen the owl perched on top of Mpona's roof. What more evidence was needed to prove that Mpona really was a witch? He would have liked to have been out there to batter his head to pieces. But he checked himself: even so was St Stephen battered to death. And, besides, how many of these people, except Yuda and Lubinda, realized just what Mpona had been about to do to him? 'Mpona!' he whispered to himself. There seemed to be no hate in that name. 'Mpona, he wants to kill me!' he whispered again as if to convince himself. Instinctively he picked up a stone to rush out. But he remembered suddenly that those people out there did not know what Mpona had wanted to do to him. Would they not mistake him for an attacker and batter him to pieces instead?

So there he stood in his own doorway, neither daring to go out nor forgiving enough to remain within. Not all the pictures of a dying Jesus Christ along his wall could shake him out of his stupor of hate. They had become meaningless masks mocking his irresolution.

'I will do whatever you want,' he heard Mpona's voice above the din of mockery outside, 'but please leave my wife alone.'

The teacher dashed the stone to the ground in a stupendous fling of energy, muttering, 'Forgive me, forgive me, Lord,' as

Yuda was shouting, 'Kill him, kill him!' Then he sank back on to his reed mat out of sheer exhaustion. Not having eaten for three days, he fell fast asleep. Lubinda withdrew his army, leaving the Chief and his wife badly shaken.

As the night settled upon the tumult-torn headquarters of the Kaunga Kingdom, the teacher was sinking into the third degree of his sleep, dreaming about birds with large beaks but no wings. Every time he tried to get at one of them they quickly formed a cloud and lifted into the air . . .

Lubinda, for his part, was conferring with Yuda deep into the night. The events of the last few days had brought these two closer and closer together. The people had dispersed unwillingly to their houses as the night had deepened. It had been a strange September evening for them all. The moon was supposed to be shining fully upon the little village, but somehow or other there was no moon that night. Instead, the clouds had raced towards it, strangling the last fighting ray of light and consuming the rabbit which rides triumphant on it. More strange, in the middle of the hot dry weather, when no rain could be expected for many more months to come, there was a gentle drizzle whispering outside. Lubinda and Yuda went on discussing matters.

It was about 4.00 a.m. Mpona jumped out of bed. 'My hair! My hair! It's burning!' he shouted. He was dreaming.

His wife rolled her fat body over in the bed and, rolling her eyes in his direction, swore at him. 'I wish it was your legs, you son of a hyena.' Then she shouted, 'Get back to bed, you . . .'

Mpona, still in a trance, collapsed back into bed and started to snore.

'The witch!' snorted his wife again, 'the human flesh that he eats is beginning to stir him in his sleep.' She pulled her cloth up to her head, and she too fell asleep among the debris that was their house.

Early that morning Mpona's wife was awakened by pounding and incessant thuds at the door. 'What's that?' she exclaimed, shaking his sleepy head by the hair. 'What's that, you . . . ? Can't you hear? The door's being pushed. Someone's outside. Help, help!' she screamed into his ears.

The Chief jumped up. 'Eh! What is it? Who are you? Who do you want?' Then he realized what was happening. Someone was pushing hard at the door and hammering at it.

'Open, you witch!' called out a gruff voice from outside. 'Open or I will burn you alive.' It was Lubinda's voice.

'Help!' screamed Mpona's wife from within. 'My mother, you left me in misfortune. You could not know that you were marrying me to a witch, a hyena. I'm dying with no one to help me. Mother, mother!'

The door, being already a wreck, was easily pushed open and Lubinda and Banda rushed in.

'My husband is a witch!' she shouted, dashing for the door. 'I saw it all last night.'

'What do you want with me?' asked Mpona.

'You know very well,' replied Lubinda.

'What have I done?' pleaded the Chief as his hands were pinned behind his back. 'Please, I plead with you, leave me alone.'

'Even your wife now knows you are a witch,' said Lubinda.

'She lies, she is a liar,' pleaded Mpona.

'Who is a liar?' said the wife. 'Weren't you talking about a burning head in your sleep last night?'

'So, he is the one!' shouted Banda. 'He knows he has done it.'

'Lubinda does not make a mistake,' said Lubinda matter-of-factly.

'What have I done, Lubinda? I plead with you. Please tell me what I've done.'

'I'll tell you. Didn't the kamcape say that you were a witch? See what you've done now. Your teacher – it is you and no one else who has burnt him. He is dying, if not already dead now.'

Mpona's wife, in spite of all her hatred of Aphunzitsi, let out a shrill cry – one of those shrill cries which, issuing from her voluminous person, could be a piercing cry of sorrow, a high-pitched note of laughter, or a war cry, a summoning to arms to finish off what might have been only partly done. Mpona could only gasp, 'How, how?'

'You sent your fairies to burn his house. Did you think we didn't know you kept fairies? Did you think we didn't know that Cimbutu, the most mischievous of your fairies, is still alive?'

'Fire!' exclaimed Mpona's wife. 'Fire!' she shrieked again and her big tears pelted the mat below her. 'His hair,' she exclaimed wildly. 'Hair! Hair! Burnt and all! Oh, Mpona, you are . . .' She broke down, weeping aloud.

'She knows, she understands,' said Lubinda, turning to Banda. 'Tie the pig up. He too must be burnt, just as he has burnt his Christian teacher.' Lubinda was good at sarcasm. 'Christian brother,' he repeated.

In the meantime, the crowd – all the women in the village and the men who were not at the teacher's house – was getting impatient.

'Bring the witch out,' shrieked one voice.

'He is a witch, he must die,' said a second.

They dragged him out by his feet, with his hands bound together behind his back. Even though the people outside had not heard the struggling inside, there had obviously been a fight because the old man's mouth was spouting blood as he lay on the floor. Yuda was there, even old Simbeya was there, borne thither on a makeshift hammock by his grandchildren. Old Mrs Simbeya was there too, seeking out her way with the eye of her stick. They were all there, the whole village, except Natombi, 'That foolish stubborn woman whose turn it will be next,' as Lubinda kept telling the people.

Old Simbeya lifted his eyes to look at the tattered remains of a once-noble Chief. His eyes blinked fast as they tried to dam the tears of sorrow. His mind went back in a flash to the day of that great debate when what he had said then, he was sure, had swayed the scales of justice in favour of the teacher. But he was too old now; the fire of debate was gone. In any case, this man was a witch. Simbeya's blood raced. If he had had a stick he would have struck the bag of bones lying there. He looked around him in frantic helplessness. There was no stick, and he had no hands anyway.

Natombi sat in her hut, awaiting news of her son's disappearance and, perhaps, death because of the misfortunes that had struck the teacher. Would the teacher live? Might there be hope even for her son? She had overheard women passing by and whispering things. What did they mean? Someone had said that when they carried the old teacher he was very heavy. This could only mean one thing. A shudder went through her body. 'The teacher is dead, and so may be my child!' She burst into tears. Those who passed by her house could hear her sobs.

'She mourns the death of her two fellow witches,' they whispered to each other. 'The teacher cannot live, and Mpona dies today.'

'Have you a spare head-band?' asked one woman of another.

'I have three to spare, one for the teacher, another for Mpona, and the third for Natombi. We shall mourn them all.'

Natombi lay on her mat, suppressing another bout of sobbing. It was all her fault that the teacher had come back. If he had not returned to help her people, there would have been no burning. Who had done it? But why should Mpona have done it – the man who had gone with her to the mission to see her child? 'My son Mwape, shall I ever see you again? Your teacher is dying!'

But for Lubinda the hour of triumph had come. For the second time in his struggle it was now or never. He could not miss it again.

'Put the man in clamps,' he rasped. 'He who lets him escape will catch it!'

They set him up and he offered his legs without a struggle. He was, after all, an old man. The women were looking at his bruised and bloody mouth for the first time. They could not help weeping. But did their weeping mean that what had been started must not be proceeded with?

'Carry him now, you men, to the burnt man so that we may hear who did it,' said Lubinda.

Yuda had already gone ahead. There he was fanning the flies off the teacher's body as the man writhed in agony.

'Who has done this to you?' asked Yuda of the teacher as the people stood round him, with Mpona in the clamps.

The teacher did not speak.

'I say, teacher, we are all your friends here. Tell us who has harmed you so that we can tell the white man at the mission. If you do not say, the white man at the mission will tell bwana D.C. to kill us all, except you, the teacher. You are a Christian, aren't you?' Lubinda had stepped forward; his psychological approach was working. The teacher stirred.

'Is it I?' said Lubinda, leaning forward. 'Is it Yuda? Is it any of your friends?'

The teacher did not stir, but merely looked blankly at the people before him.

'Is it this one, then?' asked Yuda, thrusting Mpona before Aphunzitsi's eyes.

The teacher's face became contorted. His eyes shot with blood and he turned his head to right and left as though looking for a weapon. It was too much; he burst into a cry of hungry revenge and then lay motionless.

There was no mistaking the sign. Even the doubting Thomases now knew that Mpona, his friend Mpona the witch, had done it, done it against an innocent friend. How could they all have been so blind to the goodness of the man, the man who had come back to them in their hour of great need? Now here he was lying helpless before them. Would they have the chance to make up to him for all that he had done for them before he died? It was too much for the women. They cried over him, cursing the day Mpona was born.

Even the Chief could not mistake these signs from a dying man. The teacher had spoken and named him as the witch. Why, why? the question pounded at his mouth. He had to tell the dying man that he was wrong, that it was not Mpona who had burnt him – that even his wife could speak for him: 'I am your own and only friend,' he stammered. But it was too late. Lubinda and some of the men were carrying the teacher away. To the mission. To Father Chiphwanya.

'This man is dying – why then worry about killing Mpona, a dead goat. It is not his death I want, but that he should serve under my rule,' reasoned Lubinda with himself as he led the group on their thirty-five-mile journey. 'At all events this man must arrive alive.'

For Natombi, the only one of the trio still at large, the events of the past few days had been mortally worrying. Knowing what Lubinda was, she did not for a moment believe that the Chief had done all the things that he was being accused of. But what could she do? She was only a woman. She would have to wait her turn. But she needed someone to talk to urgently. She thought of Silwamia and Simtowe. Neither of these men would be prepared to talk to her. Banda hated her, and as for Yuda, it was clear even to her that he was hand-in-glove with Lubinda. Simbeya? Yes, what about Simbeya? Could he who had been the most important member of the Chief's inner council really approve of all that was going on? So when the sun set again that evening she crept to his house. She had to talk to someone.

'I saw you yesterday. I know you don't believe that story.'

'What story, my daughter? Ah, if you mean *that*, how can you ask me such a thing? Not to believe that Mpona bewitched your friend the teacher? No, my daughter. It isn't right.'

'But, grandfather, surely it cannot be. They were both good men. The teacher, how he helped the village! And the Chief, how he ruled the village well!'

'It is you who says this thing. Not us, the owners of the village. You are only a foreigner to this village, Natombi!' Simbeya's voice rose in sudden anger, 'Natombi!'

'My grandfather,' she replied meekly. She could not remember when she had last spoken to any people other than the teacher and the Chief, and even less to the old man whom by force of circumstance she was now calling 'grandfather'. Had he not called her 'grandchild' when she first came to the village as a new bride, wrapped up in a black cloth, her hair matted in ochre? She had hardly been 'ripe' when Dulani had snatched her from her cousin at Cakuwamba village. She still remembered Dulani as she first met him; she would always remember. She was coming from the fields carrying a large basket of maize. Dulani, who had come that day from his village, when he saw her staggering under the load had said to her cousin Celiko, 'You, useless boy, how can you let such a child carry all this load?' Quickly he had run towards her in his nonchalant manner and lifted the load off her head. He had darted a glance into her face. Oh! how awkward she had felt. How she had blushed and run to her cousin.

'It is not possible,' said the old man. 'You cannot speak on their behalf. The Chief must die.'

'It isn't *that* I've come to see you about. You say he must die; let it be even so according to the custom if he is a witch. Oh, but it is cruel,' she began to sob. 'Can't you see?'

'There is nothing to see here,' said the old man impatiently. 'What is it that you want?'

'Something for myself. I plead with you, help me to leave the village where I have suffered so much,' replied Natombi.

'You can't leave, you know it yourself. You are a woman, my child; I may not speak about these things,' replied Simbeya. Even as an old man, there were certain matters upon which he could not speak.

'But I must go,' sobbed Natombi. 'I am now an old woman. Who will ever look at me, if that is what you mean?'

'You are still young, my daughter, and I know youth seeks companionship. Until you are purified we can't let you go. You would cause sickness in whoever married you. You . . .' The old man broke off; he had said too much already in the presence of this young woman.

'But I don't refuse to be purified. Why won't they do it and let me go?' replied Natombi.

At this point Simbeya's wife, who was also hard of hearing, and who had been straining to catch the conversation, stepped in. 'Aha!' she grunted. 'How can you ask a man such a thing?' Shouting into Natombi's ears, she said, 'No man will purify you, because your husband did not die a natural death. Didn't you bewitch him?'

'Then let me go,' screamed Natombi.

'I'm only telling you. Don't shout at me!' the old woman shouted back. 'Do you think I have no ears?' Then she leaned forward: 'You will stay here until you are purified. You will never be purified!'

Natombi stood up in anger. Her attempt at friendship had been rebuffed. The old man shouted at his wife for his pipe; following the directions issued loudly from his mat, the woman found the pipe and, tracing the barking voice to its source, located the mouth and firmly thrust it between the lips. Simbeya's jaws clamped down on it, and in a moment he was puffing away at his pipe, in cloud-cuckoo-land.

Chapter 13

Lubinda was welcomed on his return to the village like water to a parched throat. Plate after plate of food was brought to his house, with chicken and game meat for relish, and Lubinda shared it with the other people who had gone on the journey to the mission with him. Then there was the beer – no less than twenty years of good beer – brewed to celebrate his return. For three days the village plunged into festivity. The messiah had returned. From then on there would be no death from witchcraft. Lubinda himself took part in the festivities. After all, the beer, although it had been brewed to welcome them all, was really intended for him. It was a thanksgiving for his safe return, for all that he had done to rid the village of the witches. But, as the women's songs indicated, the end, although in sight, could still be far away. The women sang:

> *The Chief's garden, what a big one it was,*
> *There were his goats – as many as all the people on this earth,*
> *Then there was the stool itself.*

'Lubinda,' these women who were his cousins were saying, 'when will you set those hard buttocks, the buttocks which are as hard as those of a monkey, on that stool? You think you have achieved it, but we are watching you! If you give up now, like the wild pig that cried as the rope around its neck was about to snap, we shall do something to you.' Then they laughed, each one turning in her own direction, saying, 'And I will not be yours. It would even be better to marry Cumba.'

Lubinda watched the dance flanked by Banda on one side

and Juma on the other. Juma, although relatively unknown up to now, was shaping into one of his right-hand men. Banda was still a force to reckon with; so was Yuda, and so too was the old man Simbeya. But Banda was never on really firm ground. Lubinda suspected him of knowing that he had tried his best to win Natombi's hand, and that so far he had failed. He knew that if she was purified Banda might make her his third wife, as customarily the elder brother's chattels must remain within the family. This was why he, Lubinda, as the medicine-man of the village, had insisted on the issue of her purification not being settled for as long as he had hope – which was every time at dusk when he fancied that she was in his arms.

Today Lubinda was not drinking to get drunk. So he sat there, the man of destiny, canvassing support among the well-wishers by a skilful alternation of benevolent smiles and glumness. He was talking, too, telling them of how well his party had been received at the mission.

'That white man himself brought us oranges,' explained Banda, 'and Lubinda, what is that thing which is like money which he gave us?'

'There you go again,' Lubinda was saying, laughing. 'The white one did not give it to all of us.'

'True,' interrupted Juma. 'He said we should give it to whoever became our Chief. I have it here.' Juma excitedly untied a small string knot round his waist and revealed the little object that Father Chiphwanya had given them. It was a silver medallion with the image of the Virgin embossed on it. There was excitement among the crowd as the small medal, whose high value was taken for granted, went from hand to hand and then on to the women, amid exclamations of, 'Ha! white men are clever. I tell you!'

'So the white one understands our problems, then,' mused Simbeya, who had been brought out to the party upon Lubinda's insistence that he too, being the elder of the village and therefore 'the fountain of all authority legitimately exercised', should hear the report.

'Yes,' cut in Lubinda quickly. 'My friends, remind me, didn't he condemn Mpona when – who told him, my friends, that it was Mpona who did all those bad things to the teacher?'

'Even he, the teacher, it was the teacher himself,' replied Banda.

'Yes, I forget,' said Lubinda, 'some of us are getting old.' They all laughed. 'Yes,' continued Lubinda, 'he condemned Mpona and said that as his God lived in heaven, Mpona would die like a rat.' The white man sees more things than we can understand, each one said to himself.

'So, it must be so, my young men,' said Simbeya. 'I have always told you to obey the white man. He has more powerful medicines than we. Even the white one and his god agree with us, then. Let it be so.'

Just then a young boy – Banda's Aliyele – came up to Lubinda from the other end of the village. He was panting.

'What is it, Ali?' asked Banda.

'Tata, I have seen strangers at the end of the village. They have stopped at the school and they are writing something as they go round the building,' said the boy.

'What are they wearing?' asked Yuda.

'One dresses like those people who came with bwana D.C.,' replied the boy, breathless.

'Messengers!' exclaimed Yuda.

'Eh? Messengers?' asked Lubinda.

'Messengers?' asked Banda in a you-lie voice.

The women exclaimed as one, 'Messengers!' Incredulity filled every face.

There was no lower lip that did not fall nor tongue that dared interrupt the stupified silence that ensued. The dancing ceased and the song disappeared into the clouds of dust. A fly flew round and round the cup of beer which Lubinda was about to sip. It too, like the spirits of the people around it, drowned in the thick beer. There was no ripple in the cup. But for whose stomach was the fly destined? For whom had the messengers come? Simbeya remained motionless on the mat, his face criss-crossed with fear and surprise. Now and again his body twitched as he tried to chase away the horde of flies that were eating into his festering wounds.

'Impossible!' muttered Lubinda, breaking the breathless hush. All eyes looked up to him, the leader. But there was no assurance there, only fear, a greater fear than each of them felt was creeping into his own face.

The strangers swaggered haughtily into the village. The villagers could recognize the old senior messenger who had come with the D.C. last year. He was still fat; the mobile flesh around his waist was now hanging over his belt more like day-old biltong than ever before.

'It's me he's after,' said Yuda, abruptly hobbling away into the bush. 'They've come to take me to the hospital!'

No one else moved, and no one really heard him speak or run away. They all stood there, men and women, riveted to the ground and awaiting the inevitable. The white man had seen from many miles away how they had treated Mpona, they were sure. And now he had sent these men to punish them. So they kept quiet, waiting for the inevitable.

'Hahaha!' laughed the big messenger who was leading the other two people behind him. 'Hahaha!' he laughed again, this time with a curious grunting noise such as only those blessed with obesity can emit from the cavities of their throats. 'Have you forgotten, my friend?' he said, feeling his tummy with both hands. 'You are Lubinda, are you not?' And, without waiting for an answer, he asked, 'Where is that beautiful young girl who danced for bwana D.C.?' He ogled the faces and bosoms of the female audience. 'Ugh!' he said in disgust, 'there's no one here, only grandmothers. Lubinda!' Lubinda jerked forward, almost falling, as he answered, 'Bwana!' The other two men, who were in ordinary clothes, eyed Lubinda closely, but neither of them spoke. Lubinda could feel their gaze on him.

'Where is Mpona?' asked the messenger.

'Mpona, bwana?' asked Lubinda somewhat in a daze. He had not expected the question, even though it might have seemed an obvious one.

'Bring the criminal here. You are a foolish man, Lubinda. You think we have come here for nothing? The bwana wants Mpona, and we are going to take him away. He burnt the teacher, didn't he?' asked the messenger. The shortest man of the trio stepped forward with a melodramatic bounce. Turning round upon his heel, which he planted deep into the ground, he lifted his helmet, and with a mock bow said: 'I am detective Manda from Lusaka.' His head, as he bounced, gave the impression of a football because it was so round.

The 'tivitivi' was a terrible man in the white man's machinery of government. In Mozambique, across the Luangwa River, he did one thing; he whipped you, dead or alive, if you did not pay tax. Thus, whatever else might be said, you at least knew where you stood. But here the 'tivitivi' was more terrible. You did not know what he might be looking for. You might feed him and give him beer, thinking that you were being kind to a stranger, and yet all the time he would be gathering information upon which to arrest you.

There were stories of how these men wrote invisible things which even the teacher himself could not read. Had the teacher not told the pupils how easy it was for the D.C. at the Boma to hear all that was going on in the village, all the creeping of the children into the jars of bananas? There was a kind of glass the detective used which could see from hundreds of miles away what was happening in the village. Some of the people there could remember how the detective from Lusaka had found out about the death, five years ago, of a young child. In fact, it was Yelesani's cousin. Whoever knew that Yelesani's uncle had done it?

'Where is this criminal?' asked Manda in a peculiar singsong voice. There was something about his voice which Lubinda feared.

'He is not a criminal, bwana. Mpona is a witch,' replied Lubinda, trembling like a reed.

'Aha!' said the detective softly, 'under the Witchcraft Ordinance, there is no such thing as a witch, and if you insist on it, I will arrest *you*, my friend.'

'No, bwana, Mpona is not a criminal – I mean he is not what you say he is. But he has bewitched the teacher,' said Lubinda.

'Did you see him do it?' pursued the small man.

'You cannot see a witch bewitching, bwana,' replied Banda, 'but he did it.'

'Yes,' replied the whole crowd in whispered voices.

'Yes who?' queried the messenger, stepping forward.

'Yes, bwana,' replied the frightened villagers, this time clapping their hands slowly but distinctly. You had to be polite to these men. The small detective, who seemed to consider his cross-examination closed for the moment, smiled condescendingly at the crowd and drew back. But, even as he did so, a fat woman bolted out of a house at the far end of the village and broke into a run towards the crowd.

'My husband, he is not a witch. They lie, these people. Please take us, they are going to kill us, come and see what they have done to my husband!'

It was Mrs Mpona. Her husband had advised against going to the messenger and the strangers. She would only make matters worse, he thought. But she did not agree. So she came clumsily running up.

'She's mad, this one. Keep off, she will injure you,' warned Lubinda.

'If I am mad, you are mad yourself,' she replied, struggling to release herself from Lubinda's grip. By then more of the men had come to his assistance.

'Hold off,' commanded the detective. 'Where is your husband?'

'My husband? I have no husband but bones,' she said. 'Come and see what these people have done to him. They have kept him in that house like a thief, as if he was mad. For many days and weeks now he has been tied down in wood blocks. Please will you save him? He is *not* a witch.'

'He *is* a witch,' shouted several voices. They feared the white man's power in other things, but not in this one. What did the white man know about witchcraft or, for that matter, what did any black man who had turned into a white man know about it?

'He is a witch, Mpona is a witch,' reiterated several voices in reply to the silence from the men from the Boma.

'Shut up, you natives,' commanded the messenger. The small detective walked away with the woman to Mpona's home. The people could see him take out his notebook and scribble something as he came out of the house. It seemed that what he had seen there had not pleased him, because he came back walking slowly and shaking his head.

The messenger, who had clearly assumed the self-appointed role of social secretary, saluted him with the happy tidings that the village wanted to entertain the party as their guests for the night, and speaking in an undertone, he said, 'And that girl I was telling you about, she is available.'

The senior detective grunted under his king-size helmet, and then announced for all to hear, 'Right now I have work to do. I shall want to see you, Lubinda, alone. You have many questions to answer.' Lubinda was shaking. So were all the people. Would their popular leader be hanged for saving the village?

The interrogation started off in the usual manner. The small detective recited the number of murders which he had un-covered successfully in his career, as well as the number of people he had sent to the gallows. There was that chief head-man in Serenje who had ordered his kapaso to make a certain man 'disappear' because he had not sat down on the ground when he went to plead his case.

'It was, I think, a case of adultery and his wife was attempt-ing to bewitch him. That was really funny,' mused the little man, 'because I also found out that in fact the medicine to bewitch the fellow with was being given by the Chief himself, who wanted this woman to become his fifth wife. But the woman was having another affair with the headman's younger brother, who had hired another witch-doctor to cause the Chief to "disappear"! The attendants intercepted this fellow as he was leaving the Chief's village, and do you know what

196

happened? They dragged him to the dry stream, hit him with a hoe on the head and then buried him in the river-bed. To cut a long story short,' said the detective, 'the Chief is now in the Central Prison, and will remain there, I think, for some time to come.'

The small man paused to clear his throat. He thrust his hand into his bush shirt and the hand emerged with a pipe. He poked the fire before him and, with his hand, picked out a burning cinder and dropped it into the pipe. Carefully he pulled at it, covering the top with his thumb. The fumes began to rise into the air, and as they ascended higher and higher the man looked smaller and smaller below the chimney of smoke.

'And now you, Lubinda,' he said with finality, 'you must tell me who burnt your teacher; of course I know already.'

'It was Mpona,' replied Lubinda.

'Shut up!' yelled the messenger for the whole village to hear. A loud crack followed. The people, who were waiting in their houses to hear what would pass between the strangers and Lubinda, heard it too. They realized that Lubinda had differed with the strangers, and that he was being beaten up. Would Lubinda call them all to his rescue? They waited with bated breath.

'I do not tell a lie,' muttered Lubinda under his breath, trying desperately to recover his balance after this blow. His head was singing.

'You liar!' he heard the messenger shout. He looked up and saw the towering form of the messenger looking threateningly at him.

'Did you burn the teacher then?' asked the high-pitched, sing-song voice of the detective. 'You admit that you did it, don't you?' said the voice.

'No, I didn't, it was Mpona,' protested Lubinda.

Another loud noise of something hitting a fleshy object followed. This time it was a distinct thud and the villagers outside their houses knew that the blow had homed. As if to confirm it, Lubinda yelled out, 'Don't beat me, I am innocent.'

Again another blow, and then others in succession.

'You liar, tell the detective what happened, or we shall send you to the gallows,' yelled the messenger.

Fear gripped the gathered villagers as they listened to the noises. But no one would dare go to Lubinda's rescue. These men, although black, represented the power of the white man, and once you had that, no one could touch you. They would, therefore, first have to wait to hear the fate of their man, perhaps of the whole village.

The beating up, however, continued and Lubinda, who could stand it no longer, bleated out to the silent ears in the huts, 'You, my fellow people, you have left me alone!'

The small man, who was filling up his third pipe, stood up and said to the messenger, holding his arm lightly, 'That's enough.' Then he turned to Lubinda. Speaking in a fast, commanding tone, he said, 'You did it, yes, you did it, didn't you? Didn't you want to kill the teacher? Yes, yes, yes, you did. Do you agree? Messenger!' he exclaimed, 'beat up the . . .'

Lubinda knew what that would mean. So he jumped up, 'I did it – I mean, Yuda did it. It was he who forced me into it, into burning the teacher.'

The small one suddenly broke into laughter. He laughed and laughed until tears ran down his cheeks. The messenger naturally also laughed – though he didn't know what at. He nudged Lubinda firmly in the ribs and told him, 'Laugh!' So the laughter welled up until the whole hut resounded. The people did not know what to make of this.

The following morning the little man shook hands briskly – and amid smiles from both sides, said good-bye to Lubinda. 'She was a good girl, that one. If you had not presented her to me this day would have been different for you,' he whispered to him. 'Don't worry about the white man. He doesn't understand that crime and witchcraft are not the same thing.' Then he said sternly. 'But release Mpona.'

Lubinda was very happy. He recounted all that had happened, the beatings and the questioning, to his people.

198

But not the confession. Not the unholy sacrifice of the maid that had been offered to propitiate the anger of the white man's people. They only knew that the village had a hero, that Mpona had lost.

Back at the mission, the teacher's health was deteriorating badly. His burns had begun to fester, and had not been helped by the eggs which the people at Mpona had broken upon them – this being an emergency treatment for burns. The blanket which he lay upon, on the floor of the one-room clinic was becoming more and more oily from the pus of the wounds, and flies swarmed around him. To Father Gonzago, who visited him every day, it was clear that nothing short of a miracle would cure the man. So he prayed for him, and offered two masses each week for his recovery. To Father Chiphwanya, who treated his wounds, the teacher was just as much of a coward as Gonzago. If only he would practise a little hygiene he would soon get better. But that habit of expectorating on to the floor, never getting up to wash his stinking body, vomiting into his blanket – how could these help to cure him? He also suspected that the teacher was removing the medicine that he would dress the wounds with and rubbing in his own native medicines in the dark. He resented Father Superior's visits to the patient, and Gonzago knew it. Yet he went on because for him here was his Samaritan, falling among the thieves, being robbed and stripped of his clothes and being left for dead.

'We are ordained to suffer,' said Father Gonzago at one of his daily visits, looking at the deep sore in Aphunzitsi's stomach. 'These are the stigmata of those who must carry the Cross with Our Lord, Jesus Christ.' He crossed himself at the name and leaned over to the teacher, saying, 'Courage, my young man, courage.' He fervently embraced the festering skeleton that was the teacher. The old man was weeping. 'Can it be true,' he was saying, 'that the Chief did this to you?' he asked. 'You must forgive, because he knew not what he did.'

He stood up and slowly he recited the 'Our Father' for the teacher to follow even if he could not join him in forming the words. 'Give us this day our daily bread.' The priest's voice rose: 'And forgive us our trespasses as we forgive them that trespass against us . . .'

The old man turned and walked away from the sick-bed as quietly as he had come. Aphunzitsi's eyes trailed the small figure until the door closed behind it. He was feeling more sorry for that man whom he admired so much than for himself. For him the accident, if such it was, had been providential. At Mpona he had been an active Christian, a crusader. He had been a salesman for Christianity. But in the last few weeks that he had been at the mission, he had found a new richness, a spiritual uplifting which he could not describe. Every visit of the Father Superior shed something on to his sick-bed which made him feel grateful that he had been allowed an opportunity of suffering. 'If I am a witch – and the people say so – what is the use of my objecting? God knows all and I must have trust in Him. If people do not malign me now, when shall I be cleansed?' The teacher was not a thinker. For him thoughts were a series of impulses in succession, creating a sensitive picture of feeling.

As he was thinking about Father Gonzago, about how even though each of his visits left him braver, they also left him cursing himself for imposing so much sorrow on such an old man, Father Chiphwanya burst in. He pulled off the bandage from the wound on the stomach. Aphunzitsi winced at the pain. The wound began to bleed lightly on the sides until it was a raw mess of blood. 'Good,' said Father Chiphwanya, feeling it around the edges. 'Not rotten, eh? Good. Now sit up,' he ordered. 'Up, up! That's better. Eaten?' The teacher nodded. 'That's good,' said the priest, after administering medicine and bandaging it up. 'You'll soon be on your way back to those heretics. Would you like to go back?'

The teacher, who had been lying back flat on the bed again, tried to heave himself up. His arms were trembling from the exhaustion of the effort. But he wanted to answer the question sitting erect and not lying down. He wanted to say, 'Yes,' a clear and unwavering 'Yes'. Did the Father hear that he was determined to go back, back to that village to save Mpona and everybody else? Did he know that even if he were to die at the mission he would still want his soul to be sent there to preach the word of God? Aphunzitsi collapsed back perspiring – the effort was too much for his lacerated back muscles and the wound in the stomach. 'Yes, yes, yes,' he gasped.

'Good, then,' said Father Chiphwanya, tapping him lightly on the foot, and with that he left.

Father Superior had become very sickly of late. He had also been struck by a palsy which left him a trembling wreck from head to foot. But he could still go about some of his daily business as before. Those who saw him said he worked and prayed harder than ever. Was the old man staging a last act of defiance against death? But he had his moments of complete exhaustion when suddenly the world seemed to come to a still and quiet end, moments when even his breath would come in fits and starts. Sometimes at mass, right in the middle of the consecration, his hands would remain raised in the air for a long time as though he was waiting for Jesus Christ to descend with the chalice. There the chalice would remain in a tremble and the altar boys would ring their bells long and slowly so as to fill up the awkward moment of pause. Suddenly, the hands would drop down and the chalice fall to the altar. Father Gonzago, embarrassed by his own physical weakness, would thereafter hasten to make up for lost time. That was what had come to pass. Some people said that he had become too holy; there were others who swore to seeing him rise into the air above the tabernacle at the consecration. But Father Superior knew that his heart was failing, failing in the midst of so much work!

It troubled him to learn, a week after the detectives had been to Mpona, that the whole village was in danger of being punished for the burning of the teacher. To suffer is the role of the Christian, he would say to himself. No man, no government has a right to diminish this chalice for us by punishing everyone else. Even the Chief who had burned the teacher should not be punished. He had tried to discuss the matter with Father Chiphwanya to find out if he, as a young and educated man who knew the ways of the government, could intervene with the D.C. at Feira in this matter. But Father Chiphwanya had merely replied gruffly: 'The law must take its course.' Gonzago could not understand why Mpona had done what he had done to the teacher. Nor did he really want to understand. He merely prayed for mercy to be shown to all by the Almighty, mercy and not justice.

At the village, Mpona was still a prisoner in his own hut. The trip that Lubinda had made to the mission and the visit of the detectives had both ended well for him. At the mission, Father Chiphwanya had merely been concerned about the teacher, the future of the church, and the school. To him one native was as unreliable as the other, and if one of them harmed his teacher what was the point in maintaining him in a position of authority? The visit of the white man's men from the Boma had gone off singularly well. He was not clear as to what they had reported back to the bwana at the Boma, but he knew that it was not Lubinda they were naming as the man who had burned the teacher. So Mpona continued as a prisoner, permitted neither to go out without being watched nor to receive people in audience.

Although Lubinda and Simbeya had become friends of a sort it was clear that theirs was the brotherhood of the axe. You climb up the tree with your axe snugly tucked into your shoulder, but as soon as you have lopped off the tree branch you fling it away to the ground, and it drops – sometimes with a broken handle. Thus it was that as soon as Lubinda saw that his position was becoming strong he began to remember the power that Simbeya had wielded over the Chief. So he began to isolate him until in the end Simbeya was like an old bulldog with no teeth.

Simbeya remembered the old days when his advice to the Chief was invariably the order for tomorrow. He thought of the character of Mpona. Perhaps after all he was not a witch. Perhaps Natombi could even have been right in arguing that the Chief had not perpetrated the evil deed against the teacher. Perhaps . . . Then Simbeya remembered how many times in the past Mpona had been on the brink of abandoning the throne, how on each occasion it was his advice that had propped Mpona up and given him a new lease of life, of determination to conquer and to rule. Perhaps it was too late now, but there was no alternative but to try. As before, the kingdom still depended on Mpona continuing to rule. He would try. So it was that in the dark of one night he sent a child to call Simtowe and Silwamia. These two had always stood aloof from the controversy of the village. They had come to settle in Mpona because their custom was that a man had to follow his wife to her home. In no time, Simbeya was borne to the Chief's house secretly, and as soon as the two carriers had departed Simbeya broached his mission.

'You must fight back,' whispered Simbeya firmly. 'You must fight, even though it may be too late.'

Mpona listened to him, but he did not say a word.

'Mpona! Do you hear me? You must fight. You can't allow the tribal tradition to collapse under you like this.'

'Everyone in the village is against me,' replied Mpona, 'I can't fight.'

'You are mistaken about the village. You have friends here, even those who appear to be your greatest enemies. Who do you think brought me here to your house?' asked Simbeya. Mpona did not reply. He was feeling too weak to discuss anything. Besides, his mind was beginning to feel strange.

'Even if everybody in the village hated you, there are still the other people outside this village, the people in the kingdom. There are the headmen. Some of them have been to see me to ask what it is all about, what is happening here.'

'You've forsaken me too. You all think that I'm useless because I became useless once upon a time. Mad! That's what you called me,' replied Mpona, mumbling to himself. 'Mad!

Mad!' Then he broke off. His body was trembling and his eyes darting up and down.

'Stop this, stop it, please!' pleaded the old man, fearing that the worst had come and Mpona was going mad again.

'Eh! What? What? What?' exclaimed Mpona in a meaningless jabber. Then he jumped up from where he was lying and and grasped Simbeya firmly by the arm. 'I know, I know, I know why I'm being persecuted. It isn't because I'm a witch. No, no, no!' He was gasping. 'It's because Lubinda is afraid I know the truth, that I know that he slept with my young wife Ngoza and made her pregnant. It's he that killed her! Didn't he? Answer me.' Then he turned away from Simbeya and let go his arm. In a dreamy way and speaking to himself he said, 'She had warned me against marrying a young girl. She had mocked my trust in that girl. Didn't she die a week after I had gone, after Lubinda had handed her something? Yes, yes, my young wife's midwife! But she wouldn't reveal what my wife had revealed! Carrying such a heavy secret to the grave! Oh! Oh!'

'But this kingdom can't hold together without you, my son. Who can rule if you surrender? Don't you see that your own future and your wife's, and the future of the whole village, the whole country will vanish?' pleaded Simbeya. 'There are many people who know that only you can rule in peace. But you are throwing their trust to the hyena and treating their trust like the trust of a dog's tail that must follow its master. You are still a Chief; but listen to an old man. I have known many winters and summers come and go. I have known what it is to be rich and then to be poor. I have known Chiefs like you eat grass from the anus of a goat. But I have never known Chiefs act like children.' Simbeya raised his arm; it was all he had, the hand and fingers having gone. 'We, the Nsenga of the river, are brave people. Where is the courage in your belly? Where is the fire that sent your uncle across the hills and rivers to strike, conquer, wrestle, and subdue? You are a woman, Mpona! Woman! Woman! Woman! Do you hear me? Is it right for an old man like myself to put up with the insults of these young men? To act as though I like what is happening? My years are past. I don't care if I die today. I will speak my mind even though I am never called upon to advise these days. I . . .'

One of the young boys of the village passed by. Only a few months ago this youngster would have been sitting before Aphunzitsi listening to every word that he said, enjoying his stories. But today the young one bore the torch of terror against anyone who opposed Lubinda. There were several of these young gangsters around. Naturally Simbeya closed his mouth. The boy said as he passed by: 'These lepers, why doesn't the Chief simply kill them all? Yuda is the only good one among them.'

Simbeya was fretting with anger. He had seen those youngsters do harm to an elder, just like wild dogs. But no one had punished them even when they had wanted to beat him up – he, Simbeya, an old and sick man, the elder of the village and also the kingdom. This was what it had come to, so he simply shut up, eyed Mpona briefly, and lay back. The people who had brought him there were not going to risk their necks. Therefore, it was not until after midnight that he was taken back to his house.

It was not long after Simbeya had departed that Mpona heard something. 'Wife! wife!' he exclaimed as he shook her vigorously, trying to wake her up. It seemed to him as if Simbeya had only just gone. So the noises he heard must be the carriers whispering to each other. He was too tired to bother about Simbeya or care about the carriers. What did it matter to him now even if the people who had taken Simbeya back to his house supported him? You do not save a man after drowning. Where the grass is burnt you cannot burn again. He pulled at the cloth. His wife had tucked most of it under her, and that meant he could not hope for much more. She was so heavy and such a sound sleeper. So he slept. But within a short time he was awakened again by the same kind of whispers. Had someone been whispering into his ears? 'Wife!' he called out again, shaking her limp body as much as he could. 'Hmm!' answered his wife's body, and she snored on.

'Mpona!' said a deep voice. The wood fire had died down. The room was as dark as pitch. Mpona's heart beat faster. His hair stiffened. 'We are your friends,' said the deep, whispering voice. 'Let's go. Don't struggle, otherwise they will kill you. Your enemy Lubinda will kill you. We want to take you away.'

Mpona looked into the darkness. He could see the outline of a human head looming over him. There was obviously more than one person because the voice which had spoken had come from the other side of his mat.

'We have axes if you struggle,' said the voice.

Mpona felt the house going round, slowly at first, then his head spun round and round, and he passed out. His wife continued to snore. A goat cried 'Mee! Mee!'; a solitary dog barked 'Wu! Wu! Wu!' But neither the other dogs nor the goats nor the people took up the cry. The blanket of darkness closed on the night's events, and Mrs Mpona continued to snore.

A cock crew. Mrs Mpona stretched out her hand. She was dreaming. She dreamt that she was floating in a canoe on a vast river surrounded by clouds. The clouds descended low to the belly of the river. She was sailing through them but every time she tried to grasp them they disappeared. Now she was perspiring from the exhaustion of chasing empty clouds up and down the river. She was getting out of breath. I shall drown, she was dreaming. The canoe's nose tilted into the water. Her fat body pitched downwards like a swimmer about to plunge. Half the canoe had now nosed into the water. Her head would go in first. Stars began to dance round her, white stars, red stars aflame with the blood of fire, all whizzing around her. 'I die, I die!' she exclaimed. 'No one in the clouds to help me!' That was when she screamed, 'Mpona! Mpona!'

That too was the time when Lubinda's nephew, hearing the cry, rushed out of bed and ran to Mpona's house to see what the matter was. Simbeya had protested mildly to Lubinda that Mpona had a feeble body, and that after the treatment he had received he might try to commit suicide. Lubinda's nephew thought that might be the cause of the cry, as he sped on to the ruins.

'My husband is gone. Someone has taken him away to kill him,' jabbered the woman to Lubinda's nephew.

When Lubinda was called and found Mpona's wife mourning, he rasped, 'He hasn't been killed, he has only run mad as he did before. No one persecuted him here. Only his witchcraft troubled him. You sound as if you don't know that you married a madman!'

If Lubinda had had his way, he would not have bothered to mount a search for the Chief. If Mpona had disappeared, that was the method which the spirits had chosen to rid the kingdom of a witch. But Simbeya was obdurate. Against this tragedy, the situation which Lubinda was trying to precipitate by his ambitions was nothing. He, Simbeya, was the elder statesman, and even if Lubinda were to kill him or set his lunatic youths on him, he was going to demand that the Chief be found.

'You must mount a search party throughout the whole kingdom now,' said Simbeya, speaking firmly to Lubinda, whom he had peremptorily summoned. 'The Chief must be found!'

'What Chief?' rasped back Lubinda. 'Mpona was not the Chief of this kingdom.'

'You say "was" as if he were dead!' rebuked Simbeya. 'He is the only Chief that I know of, and for that matter, anybody knows of. He must be found.'

'How do you know he didn't disappear before last night?' asked Lubinda. 'The man is mad, and I have too many important matters of state to attend to to be looking for madmen.'

'I was with him last night, if you want to know,' replied Simbeya.

'Who took you there, you stinking leper?' Lubinda was angry. He had given instructions that nobody should visit

Mpona. But Simbeya too was angry. If there was one thing to which he reacted sharply it was being called a leper. He moved in his bed, and raising his arm, which looked like the charred end of a pounding stick, he shouted: 'I will kill you, you son of a millepede!' Simbeya was trembling with anger.

Lubinda could not afford this kind of shouting match. If too many people overheard it would encourage them to dare similar outrages. 'You'll see, you leper!' he cursed Simbeya. 'As for those who carried you to Mpona, they'll see how Lubinda, the son of the lion, deals with traitors.'

Simbeya stirred in his bed again. Anger was choking him. 'You . . . you . . . if you touch them you'll see. Son of a baboon!' But Lubinda had gone, gone to mount the search for Mpona.

Later on that afternoon, the search party which had gone out in the morning returned empty-handed, but with alarming news. The men had found drops of blood in a certain thicket that they were sure Mpona must have passed through – or had he been dragged there by someone? The blood of a man smells like the blood of an animal, so they could not know whether it was Mpona's blood. But, more serious, as the men had climbed out of the valley into the hills that bounded it, they had discovered that, at the door of the Cave that no one dared enter, a goat had been hanged with a thick rope. Its four legs were raised towards the door as if it were pleading for mercy. Its mouth was wide open and its eyes popped out like those of a dead elephant.

That was taboo. To find a hanged goat, and at the door to the Cave which no one dared enter because of its mystery! Could it be true what legend said about there being a huge monster man in that Cave? The world was coming to an end. These were the things that the old people of long ago had prophesied: *When you will see blood shed on the door of the Cave then know that the spirits are angry with you.* But how could they be angry when only a few weeks ago Chief Lubinda had offered sacrifice there, outside the Cave? Could it be that the spirits were angry because a white one dared come to the Cave? 'It was not our fault,' each was saying in his heart, 'we tried to stop him, but he wouldn't agree.'

Banda had been the first one to speak. 'What shall we do with this goat?' he asked in a whisper. He drew near to it and looked at its snout. 'Whose goat is this?' he asked. Suddenly it dawned on him, and he gasped, 'Lubinda's goat!'

The village listened to the men's story. The people sat dumbfounded. Simbeya remained in his house, still angry with Lubinda for calling him a leper that morning. He would not talk to Lubinda when he came to tell the story and ask for his advice. He had advised enough in the past, Simbeya had replied, but his advice had never been heeded. Only Mpona had always accepted his advice. Times had changed, he told Lubinda. The young no longer wanted to follow his advice. This was what it had now come to, a goat being hanged in the door of the sacred Cave which no one dared enter. It could only mean one thing, that the world had come to an end and the Chief was dead. 'The Chief, the *real* Chief, Mpona, is dead, hanged like that goat!' Simbeya yelled at Lubinda. Confused and frightened, Lubinda retraced his footsteps to where the people were gathered, with no advice to follow.

'He can't just leave it at that,' said Banda when Lubinda returned. 'It was he who was last with Mpona. Why did he stay so long there? What was he planning to do? It is he who must answer for what has happened to Mpona, not you.'

Women were wailing. They had all – except for Lubinda's wife – gathered outside Mpona's house. Even Yuda's wife and Banda's wife were there. They were mourning the death of Mpona because they were sure that he had died. A dark cloud settled over the fated village. What had they done to deserve all this?

Men and women were arriving one by one from other villages. Some were coming in large groups led by their headmen. Within moments of Mkando village coming, Ciwera and Cakuwamba had come. By evening, the whole village was teeming with people and fires rose high, higher and higher as people kept the vigil. But no news of the whereabouts of the Chief had been received. A third search-party, composed of men from a number of villages, had just arrived, but there was still no news. Could the Chief's body be in the Cave, people began to wonder? How could he have gone in there when there were so many poisonous snakes, bees, and other things, according to the legend? Would the nameless creature that scours the countryside not have eaten the body up by now?

Lubinda, as he went from group to group of the people assembled from the other villages, was jittery. 'How did it happen?' asked village headman Mkando.

'Don't ask me useless questions! I was asleep. We were all asleep, like yourselves!'

When the village headmen gathered, Simbeya agreed to be carried out to where they were sitting. Ciwera turned to him: 'Simbeya, we have been hearing many things about this village in the last year. You are the elder of this kingdom. Can you tell us why the spirits have acted in this way? What has been happening here?'

Simbeya replied: 'Ask Lubinda; haven't you heard that he is now the Chief here? Who am I to know anything, a lame old thing like me?' The old man was rubbing it in.

'Lubinda,' said Ciwera, turning to him, 'we have heard a lot about what has been happening here. You young men of this village seem to forget that the headman of Mpona village is also the Chief of the kingdom. No one can charge him with witchcraft unless by agreement with all the other headmen in the valley. Is it not true that you, a simple vagabond who is here because Mpona's grandfather took pity on you, are now behaving as though you were the head of this kingdom?' Ciwera paused to swallow. His throat was getting dry. 'I do not ask these questions to challenge your claims; I ask to seek answers, so that we may judge you and the Chief better.'

Some youths of Mpona's village moved closer towards the group of gathered headmen as they heard the sharp voice of

Ciwera. Simbeya shifted uneasily and then said, 'Today we cannot sit in peace. You, Lubinda, have organized all these youngsters against the hands that fed you. Mpona must be found. Alive!'

Lubinda jerked with anger. Abruptly he stood up and made a dash for Simbeya. All the headmen jumped up and held him. 'It is right,' said Mkando. 'You must explain everything. Your goat, why was it hanging outside the Cave? Whose sacrifice were you making? If it's a fight that you want, we shall give it to you.' Mkando cast his cloth away. His fists were as big as pumpkins. He was ready to fight Lubinda and all his supporters.

'You are spoiling this tribe. You are ruining it, Lubinda, for your own personal ambition. We don't want power struggles,' said Cakuwamba. 'We want peace so that the traditions of our fathers and forefathers can be maintained. Who are you? Where did you come from? Who was your mother that you should accuse others?'

'I am Mpona's successor,' yelled Lubinda, 'and when I take over you will see!'

'Is that why you have been trying to buy off some of our people, to get the support of our villages?' asked Mkando, who was now pacing up and down, disappointed that he had not been allowed to hit Lubinda. 'Our Chiefs are chosen by us, the headmen, through the wishes of the spirits of our ancestors. Not by one man who chooses himself.'

Lubinda looked around for Banda, for his nephew, for Yuda, but they were nowhere in sight. Then, from the other corner of the village, where the commoners were seated, a commotion developed. Someone was swearing at Banda. It was Yuda who was pointing at Banda with his walking stick and saying, 'It is he who has encouraged Lubinda to think that he is a Chief. Lubinda never listens to me or to the old man Simbeya.'

Lubinda looked in that direction and heard Yuda's voice shouting, 'Beat him up! Beat him up! They have spoilt the kingdom. Kill Lubinda!' All the headmen rushed there, just in time to stop Banda and Lubinda's cousin hacking each other to pieces.

Late into that night, after calm had settled on the confused village, the elders of the tribe were discussing the succession question: this had to be disposed of first, before any other matter such as the funeral arrangements could be attended to. Lubinda was there, not by his own wish, but by that of the headmen. 'If the Chief is dead . . .' said one.

'Don't say "if",' cut in another, 'he *is* dead.'

'But if that is so, why has the drum not been sounded?' asked the former.

'Yes, the drum!' gasped Simbeya. It could be beaten only on his orders. 'Shall the drum be beaten?' he asked uncertainly. There was quiet. If the Chief had died, the only evidence that could be accepted would be his body. Without it no succession was possible. That was why it was so important that if he was dead his body should not fall into the jaws of the lions.

Early at dawn, just when the second cock crows, there was again commotion, but this time from the direction where the women were seated, mourning, around the fire. A group of about five people were walking into the village slowly, obviously carrying something heavy.

'The Chief's body,' yelled the women in frantic mourning. 'Our Chief is dead. What shall we do now without him?'

Lubinda leapt up to the women. 'Stop this!' he rasped. 'If he is dead he is dead!'

The women wept all the more. 'Lubinda is a witch,' they cried.

The group carrying the load went on slowly past the tearful women, then on to the men, and set their load down. The load moved a little. There were exclamations from the men. The Chief had returned. He was alive. Sipopa – one of the village headmen whose absence had been forgotten, said simply, 'Here is the Chief,' and his men quietly took their seats among the others around the fire.

'Where did you find him? Why did you steal him? I demand to know at once!' said Lubinda, raising his voice as he stood up, his neck swollen with anger.

'My people found him in the bush near the village,' retorted Sipopa. Lubinda was furious. He had devised every possible means to oust Mpona from the Chieftainship. Now a method which he had never thought of, and which even if he had thought of he would never have dared try, had presented itself. Mpona had been abducted and presumed dead. Suddenly, he had reappeared. Whoever had done it, why had they found it necessary to implicate *him* by hanging his goat in the most suspicious place?

'It's you that did it,' he charged Sipopa. 'You abducted Mpona and hanged my goat. You're going to pay dearly for this,' said Lubinda.

'You're wrong, Lubinda. Only your guilty conscience makes you think that I organized this thing,' replied Sipopa.

'Why does he quarrel with a man who has brought the Chief back?' asked Simbeya in a 'see-for-yourself' tone. 'It must be the spirits that took the Chief away, because some people in this village were plotting to kill him.'

Mpona remained speechless as he lay on the ground. He was too tired, cold, and dazed to understand what was happening. After carrying him back to his house, the men left him there to face the inquisition of his wife. It was not until his wife realized that he was as good as dead that she let him lie in peace. But at the fireplace the debate continued.

'Everyone here accuses Lubinda,' said Lubinda himself. 'There are a lot of questions to which no answer has been given. How is it that it was Sipopa who found him? My people have been all over the valley. No one told them where he was. Why? There is a plot here to discredit me. Mpona was not carried away by the spirits but by Sipopa.'

'Are you saying that the spirits could not carry him away?' asked Simbeya. 'This is what it has come to. Even the medicine-man, the man who wants to make himself our Chief, does not believe in the spirits of our ancestors. How shall he keep the shrines? It's no use trying to find out how the Chief was taken away. The important point is that he's here. The important question,' he said slowly, 'is, what shall we do with those who have made him suffer, as though only *their* voices mattered in this land?'

'Mpona is a witch!' exclaimed Lubinda. 'How can you ask what to do with a witch? It's obvious. He must drink mwabvi so that we can see whether he is a real witch or not.'

'No! It isn't like that,' protested Ciwera.

'If Mpona is a witch, then what Lubinda says is correct,' said Mkando. 'He who drinks mwabvi will die unless he is not a witch, or is fortified against the medicine. When the kamcape condemned Mpona he did it only in the presence of this village, not of all of us who are the rulers of this valley.' He paused, but then resumed, 'Therefore, we need to see for ourselves. Let the kamcape be called again, and if he says that Mpona is a witch before us all, then I, Mkando, will despise our Chief. A Chief cannot be a witch and still remain a Chief.'

There was silence as each one of the headmen carefully weighed in his mind the complex constitutional problem that had arisen. Mkando, feeling the need for further discussion of the matter, said, 'I have no desire for the stool, the Chief's stool. Even though I am much closer to the Chief than many of you,' he was looking at Lubinda, 'I don't desire it. If Lubinda is the successor, let him succeed the Chief, but only if the Chief is proved a witch.'

A cold wind blew over the skins of the debaters. Someone stood up, yawned, and stretched himself, and shouted, 'It is daybreak! The Chief is well!' The people put out the fires, for there was no longer any mourning. But how could people go back to Ciwera or Mkando or Cakuwamba without understanding the events of that whole night of terror? So no one returned to his home; they were all going to wait for the kamcape to come before dispersing. He might take two days or even a whole week, but they were going to wait.

'Mpona is not only a witch, but he has also sold this country of ours to the white man,' said Lubinda in an effort to change the long procedure that had been decided upon. 'It was Mpona who agreed with the white D.C. that we should dig pit latrines. It was Mpona who allowed the white missionary to take Mwape our child to the hospital in Lusaka so that they could cut his tongue out. Perhaps some of you don't know, but the child has never been heard of since. Certainly he will never speak. How can a child born dumb speak if that is the way the spirits wanted it to remain? This is the man that you want to lead you, the man who made the white one bold enough to walk into our places of sacrifice, as if he was going round his banana plants. If that is what you want, bring him back. I am going to take my life. Yes, that's what you want from me. When Mpona was mad and I ruled for him, did I ever send anyone's child to the white man to be killed like a dog?'

'You can't kill yourself; this matter is for all of us to solve,' said Sipopa.

'He can if he wants to,' replied Simbeya. 'But why do we repeat what has already been decided? Someone is going to call the kamcape today, and until he comes we must all wait. No one should leave this village.'

Chapter 14

Father Gonzago sat on the step of the mission house reading his breviary. You could have known from the number of times that he raised his helmet as he read, the number of times that the name Jesus occurred in the book. His small arms had now shrunk even more, and the blue veins of emaciation were showing more clearly under the olive skin than ever before. As he read, he was rocking himself backwards and forwards so that he looked as though he was nursing the breviary to sleep.

Even though in the last week the teacher's health had improved greatly, and Father Chiphwanya who needed the bed for another patient was already talking of discharging him, Father Gonzago was still remembering the teacher as his lips muttered their way through the breviary. The old man always looked forward to a moment of calm when he could say his prayers, and when he found it he guarded every second of it jealously. It was from these brief moments of utter loneliness that he recharged his spirit. He had stayed too long in lonely places to think that a man could go on doing this and that, stirring the whole earth into ACTION. For a missionary loneliness was not something to run away from, because it was like being in a desert, where you could not escape. There you had to learn to eat the sand, and so a missionary also had to learn to live with loneliness. Once the initial hurdle had been overcome, what was once loneliness became loveliness, a moment for communion with one's inner self and with God. It was like walking up and down a valley of scented flowers, nectar honey, clear sparkling waters, and plenteous milk. Father Gonzago knew that that mystical experience of eternal wonder was not always an easy thing to achieve. In fact 'achieve' was not quite the word, because it was something which the Lord Himself either blessed one with or did not. Either way, as a priest you had to keep your nose to the grindstone. You had to go on believing there was water even though your whole life was strewn with red-hot rock.

For Father Gonzago this mystical experience was what really mattered. He knew he had finally got hold of it, and that was why whenever he turned to the breviary he prayed with bated breath lest he should be distracted. At these moments his soul was not in his body; it was away there in heaven communing with the saints, asking them questions about Paradise, daring them to state their joy in all its dimensions:

'You holy ones in Paradise, Your joy, is it a great one?'

To which the saints in his mind would reply:

'Our joy you cannot appreciate. By being with God we have everything.'

Father Gonzago's eyes would shine with happiness. He would still be looking at the breviary, without realizing that it had become dark.

That was why when Father Chiphwanya found him seated on the step in the dark, with the breviary still spread open before him, he observed, 'Apparently, Father, all your senses are failing except your eyesight.' Instinctively, the little man stood up. His dream had been shattered. He looked up at the fuzzy beard of Father Chiphwanya blowing in the gentle breeze.

'I am sorry to disturb you, Father,' said Chiphwanya, 'but it's about your teacher.'

'He isn't dead!' exclaimed Gonzago, grasping Chiphwanya's huge arm with his two hands.

'No, no, no!' said Chiphwanya, flinging him away. 'You might as well say *you* were dying. There is a man here from

Mpona. He has been sent by the people there. They want the teacher to go back with him.'

The Father Superior was puzzled. 'To take him back?' he asked himself, just to make sure that he understood. 'Why?' he asked, looking up at Chiphwanya. 'I don't like it!'

'You think like these natives, Father Superior,' said Chiphwanya. 'Maybe *you* might find out why. The man won't tell me.'

'Is he one of those who brought the teacher here?' asked Gonzago.

'No, certainly not. My theory is that the Chief has sent for him. Perhaps there's some trouble which he would like him to help in sorting out. You know what these natives are. When they're in trouble they will turn even to the people they have wronged. It happened to me once. The man who stole the wine for Mass came to me on his knees asking me to anoint his child who was dying, in the mistaken hope that it would live.' Father Chiphwanya warmed to the subject. He was suddenly finding himself to be as competent as any professor of anthropology in these matters. Father Gonzago must listen to him.

He was about to continue when the little old man said, 'Yes, if Mpona is really still there.' Then he went on, 'Extreme Unction can cure people. This is why we administer it, to cure the body if that is the Lord's wish, and certainly to cure the ills of the soul.'

Father Chiphwanya's voice rose with anger, 'What do you know about the Kaunga Valley to doubt what I say? Whenever did you visit it? Have you ever seen Mpona at his own home? All you go by is the gossip you gather here and there. A missionary's job is not to save himself but to save others. You may pray like an angel in your cell, but if you don't go out amongst the people, what is the point?'

The Father Superior winced under the attack. He could not understand why his little remark had provoked so much anger.

'I know more about the anthropology of these people than you do, Father,' continued Father Chiphwanya. 'Let me tell you this today, because you have been behaving as though by merely staying here so long you understood these people. You have been like a tree, even a pumpkin, decaying among them. You have never understood them! Since I told Mpona to keep the school open, neither Mpona, nor anyone else for that matter can close it. That's why they want the teacher to go back, because they know that if the school finally closes they'll be in trouble.'

Father Gonzago merely kept quiet.

'As for your anointing,' said Father Chiphwanya, 'you know it's a lot of nonsense. God wills, through the kind of medicine given and the time it is given, *ceteris paribus,* that a man shall live. In my work among these poor people, Father, I have gone through really difficult times, times of abject suffering among these people who regard death as the end of life, when I have wondered why God will not heal them. No amount of anointing has ever cured a single man, woman, or child who was clearly dying. Father, if you had been as busy as I have been, as involved in the misery of these people as I have been, you would have reached the point where religion becomes an instinct rather than a faith whose path is strewn with works of love and charity.' Father Chiphwanya stopped. He had burnt out his anger and he was now finding himself in the position of a master instructing his pupil in the rudiments of religion and realism. The waiter was standing by at a distance in his khaki uniform. He wanted to tell the two men that supper was getting cold.

'Let him go if he is well,' said Father Gonzago in despair.

They ate the meal in silence. Father Chiphwanya was still annoyed. The heavy schedule of things to be done the following day, the Feast of the Immaculate Conception, did not help his temper. He had to cycle eighteen miles to Kapoche, an old abandoned mission, to say Mass. Then there were a number of baptisms to be done, people to be preached to and others to be listened to with their petty problems. The Church was an authoritative institution. If those who had gone before him had emphasized this to these primitive people there would have been no need for the interminable interviews that followed each Mass. Each one of these people appeared to feel that he had special problems meriting dispensation from normal laws of the Church. Where there is truth, authority must be exercised absolutely and not diplomatically. He threw a sharp glance at Father Gonzago across the table. It is people like this one, he said to himself, who cause all this trouble.

During supper Father Superior began to vomit. He was vomiting a thick yellow stuff which poured out of his mouth like maize beer from the cup. Father Chiphwanya had identified the disease some months back as a mild form of jaundice and had advised the old man to go to the hospital in Lusaka for treatment.

Father Chiphwanya looked at the little man as he vomited at the door to the dining-room. 'You might at least go and vomit in the latrine, Father,' he said. 'I have told you over and over again to go to the hospital. Unless you go you will die,' he continued.

'This is no time,' replied Gonzago, after the vomiting had ceased and he had cleaned up the mess, 'to talk of death. I have lived in this valley for many years, many, many years indeed. I have learnt one thing, and that is that when death marks you it is better not to struggle against it, becaust in the end it wins. If death has not marked you for its own, then you will pull through. It is not necessary to go to the hospital, because even here there are many African medicines, Father, which can cure this yellowness which you consider to be a disease.'

The old man was tired. The words came out of his mouth in a slow and lifeless way. Every time he spoke it seemed as though he were paying for death in instalments. 'There is no time for thinking of death in this valley, Father. There is so much to do. So many people are dying without baptism. You do so much travelling, Father, and wear yourself out, and yet we do not reach them all. If only we had a truck!'

Father Chiphwanya ate quickly. He had to go to the vegetable garden, even though it was night, to see whether the furrows had been cleaned out. Ever since Brother Aruppe's death he had taken over all the chores at the mission in addition to his own work. There were the paddy-fields to be looked after; there was the wheat-field and the fruit trees. All these things demanded a lot of Father Chiphwanya. Every month an assurance had come from the Monseigneur in Lusaka that a brother would be sent soon. But up to now, so many months after Aruppe's death, no one had come.

He ate quickly. If he did not clean up the furrows the vegetables would not be watered properly the following day. Some change, perhaps not much, had come over him these last months. He had learnt to listen to his Superior quietly, but the same impatience remained, the same unwillingness to suffer fools gladly.

Immediately Father Chiphwanya left, the little old man began to vomit again. He almost vomited into the radio as he stood over it trying to tune in for the evening news. It had all come up so suddenly. Father Chiphwanya was called back. 'Perhaps my day is at hand,' said his Superior. 'They say there are people in this valley who have medicine to stop vomiting.'

'That is pagan, Father,' said Father Chiphwanya, speaking in a soothing tone as though he was speaking to a child. A dying man was a child and, even if he said stupid things, you just had to dam up your torrent of anger.

But the old man jumped up, 'Pagan! What is pagan about African medicine? How do you think I have lived all this time without touching your quinine, which makes my ears sing? Pagan? That is foolish talk, Father Chiphwanya.'

'It's not foolish talk,' replied Father Chiphwanya, all restraint gone. 'I waste my time teaching these Africans to come to hospital to receive medicines, teaching them not to scatter their fæces all over the place, to avoid disease, to be treated for leprosy, smallpox, and everything else. And here you are telling them that they have medicines to cure all these things. Do you think we would have been so busy at this mission baptizing corpses if you didn't undo my work?' He faced the old man. 'It seems to me you're something of a sadist, Father Superior! You don't mind these people dying provided they die in the "traditional" way. Everything about these natives is good and everything that I do is cruel, is unkind. I'm sick of fighting the natives to get them to change their ways, of fighting you because you won't allow them to follow what is in their best interests. I'm sick of it all!'

Father Chiphwanya was wrestling with anger. He knew it was not proper to talk in this manner to a very sick man. But if the sick man was a little idiot, what else was there to do? The cook, who had gone to call him, was very surprised that instead of helping the sick man, Father Chiphwanya was shouting at him. But the little man was undaunted. 'Father Chiphwanya, I am a dying man,' he said.

'You're not dying, for heaven's sake! Stop pitying yourself, Father,' cut in Chiphwanya.

'A dying man must carry truth with him to the grave,' said the little man, ignoring Chiphwanya's interruption completely. 'Therefore I seek only the truth from you. Tell me, how is it pagan to believe in African medicine? So many of our medicines are made from herbs, both in Europe and here. These people have medicines which will stop birth when they want. I'm not saying it's right, but the fact is that they can stop the arrival of unwanted children. That's all I'm saying. They have . . .'

'It's wrong, I tell you. It's pagan,' cut in Father Chiphwanya.

'I know it's wrong. Pope Pius XII defined the doctrine in this respect and I believe it entirely. But you miss my point: the distinction between the moral and physical,' replied the old man. He started to vomit again; this time an even thicker and much more yellow vomit tumbled out of his mouth. Blood followed. Father Chiphwanya could only stand and wait. It was not time yet to administer the Last Sacraments, which Mother Church conferred on its dying children. Father Chiphwanya doubted whether it would ever come to that.

That evening Father Superior did not eat anything, nor did he drink any water. For some time now everything he ate had tasted bitter. He had, nevertheless, been eating all along in order to keep up his strength and so as not to draw too much attention to himself.

Father Chiphwanya was edgy. It was too much trying to cope with his own work, that of Brother Aruppe, and now Father Gonzago's – the hypochondriac that he was. If he felt that he was dying, why didn't he agree to be sent to hospital? Who had told him that at the hospital they operate for every disease? Why did he think that Father Syminskov died – because he'd been taken to hospital? This was a strange attitude for a white man to take, no matter how long he had been in Africa. Listening to Father Gonzago talk, one had a feeling that he believed in witchcraft, that his disease was the result of witchcraft and that, therefore, it could only be cured, if at all, by the natives here.

'But it's jaundice!' exclaimed Father Chiphwanya to himself. 'He's afraid that he'd miss a hero's burial if he dies in Lusaka. That's all there is to it,' he said again, pacing up and down his room. He remembered the letter he had once written but never given to him. It was still lying in his drawer. That letter was still as true today as it was before. He should have handed it to him. Maybe then he would have mended his ways. Relations with the Boma had gone from good to bad, all because of Gonzago's insistence upon not assisting the D.C. in the investigation of the criminals who had set fire to the teacher from Mpona. He must have been told a lot more by the teacher inside the privacy of the confessional, which he could not pass on to assist the authorities.

He reached out for his breviary and, by the light of the candle, read the remaining part of the day's assignment. Then he turned to the rosary. For thirty minutes he knelt down, trying to fix the Sorrowful Mysteries in his mind. He was having great difficulty with prayer this night. So many distractions kept coming up: what his Superior had said, some strange phenomena concerning African bird-life – he must remember to make a note tomorrow. But Brother Aruppe's death was uppermost in his mind. It was because of that thought that he had chosen the Sorrowful Mysteries, even though normally on a Saturday he recited the Joyful Mysteries. It was for this reason too that he tried his best to fix his thoughts on the prayers. If he, who had been one of the two people who knew Brother Aruppe, did not pray for him, who would? With all his faults – and we all have them – Brother Aruppe deserved prayer. His thoughts wandered on to Gray's Elegy:

> Beyond these rugged elms, that yew tree's shade,
> Where heaves the turf in many a mouldering heap,
> Each in his narrow cell forever laid,
> The rude forefathers of the hamlet sleep.

He shook himself. The fifth mystery: *The Death of Our Lord Jesus Christ*. Than on to the *Hail Holy Queen*:

Mother of mercy. Hail our life our sweetness and our hope. To Thee do we cry, we poor banished children of Eve. To Thee do we send up our sighs, mourning and weeping in this valley of tears. Turn then, most gracious advocate, Thine eyes of mercy . . . O clement, O sweet, O loving Virgin Mary.

He snuffed out the candle. The wax had spread on the rough table. Somehow he was not satisfied with his prayers that evening. He had more than fulfilled his obligations, but he felt like a soldier who had marched many miles to no purpose whatsoever. Hadn't St Ignatius Loyola, the great soldier, talked about the doldrums of prayer, moments when the lips moved but the heart remained closed? But provided one went on doing one's best to pray, this in itself was prayer.

He had not been asleep for more than two hours when he jumped up from his bed in a shiver of sweat, yelling for help. He had had an awful dream. There was a huge fire, and all round it were mounds of earth which looked like graves. On one side of these mounds was the entrance to a large cave which was in the side of a hill. Drawn across the entrance was a purple cloth, which was being struck down the middle by a repeated flash of lightning, even though the sky was clear. But the cloth was not being rent in two. Every time the lightning struck it seemed to part, only to rejoin again.

A large crowd of people – all white and naked except for the hoods on their heads – stood silently by each mound of earth, and their backs faced the entrance to the cave. The light from the fire played on their naked bodies, making them look as if the bodies had been washed down the stream for many days. There was no movement: everything was as still as the mounds themselves. From nowhere a huge naked man with only one ear, and a band that came low down to the temples, walked to the centre of the gathering and stood beside the fire. The flames, which had been lapping up furiously, died down, and instead his body began to shine from the feet, gradually up to the head, and then more light formed a cone over his head. The giant spread out his arms slowly into the air. The charms on his arms and legs could be seen clearly and the red ochre on his chest stood out against the lifeless white flesh of his abdomen.

A bloated-looking woman with grey hair pottered towards the Big One. Behind her followed four young men, all of whom appeared to arise from nowhere, since there was no movement among the statue-like people around each mound.

'Our fraternity of witches,' said the woman, addressing the Big One, 'asks you to ordain these novices.'

'Do you know them to be worthy?' asked the Big One, shifting uncomfortably on the mound, which kept sinking and rising. The bowed hoods, speaking as one, replied:

'So far as human frailty may judge, we do know and testify that they are worthy to bear the burden of office, the office of witches.' There was a lifeless metallic tone about these voices which made Father Chiphwanya tremble as he lay in the bush, confronted with this scene. He squeezed himself into the earth lest they should smell him out.

The Big One, turning round clockwise, bowed in each direction. He looked like a big monster to Chiphwanya. As he bowed in the direction where Father Chiphwanya was hiding, the Big One winced briefly, as if he had been pinched hard.

But he continued revolving like clockwork. When he had turned full circle he stopped. He looked slightly confused, or was it upset? But the hoods remained bowed.

'You who are now about to be consecrated to the office of witches,' he said at last; 'endeavour to receive it worthily; with great care should we advance to so high a state. Care must be taken' (he repeated, 'must be taken'), 'that they who are chosen be qualified by their unworldly wisdom and magic.' Then he repeated the first part of his injunction. 'You who are now about to be consecrated to the office of witches, endeavour to receive it worthily (with great emphasis on 'worthily').

'It is not meet,' continued the Big One, 'that they who are called to this honour should display acts of self-interest, my dear brethren.' Then he raised a large shining axe from nowhere: 'For even this unmagical instrument of our art belongs not to any one man, even though you may have fashioned it for your own use. It belongs to all of you, but in the service of *me*, your supreme leader.'

He paused for a while; it seemed like ages to Father Chiphwanya, who was pushing his body more and more into the ground to avoid being discovered. 'Therefore, dear brethren,' concluded the Big One, 'be not selfish, for in advancing your own cause, you hasten your doom.'

The Big One stepped aside from the mound. The bloated old woman offered him a root, and with it he struck at the head of the mound.

'Come up, come up,' he said, 'you little man of the black people. You thought that you had run away from us by going to Africa. We have come for you now, all the way from your motherland. Thus the prophecy will be fulfilled that the witches of the fatherland shall collect all the bones of its children scattered over the globe, and eat them, so that the nation shall remain as one.'

There was a loud crack in the grave. A white body with hands bound behind the neck in a white bloody bandage came up. The head was in a mess, with part of it crushed and eaten. '*Multos annos!*' muttered the Big One as he struck at the band-

226

age. '*Multos annos!*' The little toy-like body stood up as the bandages fell away. It looked accusingly in the direction where Father Chiphwanya was hiding. All hoods, looking up for the first time, turned to follow its gaze. It was then that Father Chiphwanya, covered in perspiration and shivering, yelled for help. For before him stood the corpse of Brother Aruppe, just as it had been after the lion had mauled him. It was staring fixedly in his direction, eyes upturned and groaning like a goat, 'Worthy, worthy'.

'Worthy! Worthy!' exclaimed Father Chiphwanya jumping off his bed. He winced at his own pinch. So it must have been a dream. He tried to forget it, but the word 'worthy' kept coming back to his lips with a chatter. It was singeing his lips. What did the dream mean, he was asking himself. He had heard that word and those words somewhere. Where? Where? Where? The question pounded at his heart. Then suddenly he groaned, 'Ah!' His head was throbbing with the pain of full realization. 'My ordination!' he gasped.

The clear voice of Bishop Anselm rang through his head. 'Do you know them to be worthy?' It had been a bright summer day when he and his fellow ordinees – four of them together – had marched up the aisle to keep their individual appointments with Our Lord Jesus Christ. Bishop Anselm had stood at the altar smiling faintly as if to say, 'Keep courage, don't give up, Our Lord is waiting for you.' After the ordination, he had quietly said to Father Chiphwanya, 'Well done, Father Oliver, well done, Paul,' and patted him on the back. 'Be worthy of your calling,' he had added. Later, at the ordination banquet, Bishop Anselm, sitting opposite him, had told jokes about the Society, all strung round obedience, poverty, and chastity – the cornerstones of Jesuit morality. That quiet pat on the back, the relaxed manner of Bishop Anselm, had lifted so much weight off Father Oliver's shoulders and fired him with so much zeal to offer himself completely to Our Lord. That relaxed manner of the Bishop had concealed many years of subjugation to the will of his superiors and, therefore, to God himself. His mother had turned to him after the banquet, pride in her eyes, to whisper, 'Bishop Anselm is a good man. Be good, Paul, obey your superiors.' Then she had torn herself from him, weeping with joy and sorrow.

And now, what had he done? Was he still worthy? Had he obeyed his Superior? Had he recognized the authority of Jesus Christ in the simple little man who was his Superior? In a shiver he lit the wasted candle. There on the table was the letter he had written to him many months ago. The envelope, looking as fresh as if it had just been unpacked, was waiting to be addressed. He remembered the contents: he could have recited them all word for word, because he had felt so strongly about everything that he had written for all these months now.

'God!' he exclaimed, falling to his knees. 'Forgive me, a proud sinner.' He snatched the letter as if it would run away, and tore it to pieces, muttering, 'Forgive a proud sinner.'

The first bell rang. It was 5.30 a.m. In thirty minutes the 6.00 a.m. Angelus would ring. He must prepare for Mass. Then he remembered that Father Superior had been vomiting badly yesterday. Could it be possible that he was actually more ill than he had thought all along? Suddenly he saw in his mind how much the old man had wasted away during the last few months. Hurry! hurry! a voice kept urging him.

Father Chiphwanya knocked at his Superior's door. There was no reply, but groans of a man in great pain, and gasping for breath, could be heard. He rushed into the room – Father Superior never locked his door. He embraced the tiny shrivelled body of the old man and broke down in tears. 'Forgive me, a proud sinner,' he was trying to say. He heard the clear voice of Father Gonzago, much stronger than ever before, say, 'I leave my people in your hands. Pray for understanding. They are good men, these people. There is more love among them than in our society. Pray for them. Pray for me, for Brother Aruppe, for Mother Church.'

Father Chiphwanya sat motionless at the bedside. Before today these words of his Superior would have been distasteful, but now, how much they meant! His eyes strayed to the rough

piece of plank that was the superior's working table. There he
saw a small piece of paper neatly tucked into the corner. From
impulse he moved a step nearer to read it. The note simply
stated, in Father Superior's simple handwriting:

Devotions for the Week
    For Father Oliver's continued strength and health – 3 rosar-
    ies a day.
    For Chief Mpona, to be saved from the false judgement of
        the kamcape – 3 Stations of the Cross daily, 2 Our Father.
    For obedience to my holy assistant – 3 Litanies daily.

And then there was a note below this:

'I think Mpona is in trouble.
I will visit Mpona tomorrow, 15th August.'

Father Chiphwanya burst into tears. 'Forgive me, a proud
sinner,' he said again. He turned to the bed. Father Gonzago
was dead. In a few minutes the bell would toll to announce the
death of this little man. The bell would also announce the
Assumption of the Blessed Virgin Mary. But for the moment
he was alone, alone with his Superior. '*Vere magister meus
mortuus est,*' he muttered. '*Requiescat in pacem.*' Then he exclaimed: 'My God! I haven't anointed him!'

Father Chiphwanya would have to go through with the
Low and High Masses, because this was a great feast in the
liturgy of Mother Church. In the afternoon the remains of
Father Gonzago would be put away in the small room at the
cemetery where all the white people – and they were all the
religious ones – were shelved. The carpenter was busy making
the coffin. It had to be ready by midday, or the body would
fester.

At midday, just as the undertakers were lowering the body
into the coffin, Father Chiphwanya was looking through
Father Gonzago's papers in his bedroom. The old man
appeared to have a habit of committing small things to paper –

failing memory maybe – all small bits and pieces of paper torn out of the corners of exercise books. Then his eyes rested on one small piece of paper. He settled his glasses more firmly on the bridge of his nose. He could not believe his eyes. 'What?' he exclaimed. Then as if to reassure himself that he was reading what he was seeing, he read aloud: 'My dying wish. To be buried among the people in the ground.' Did he have to obey that? Why then did he not say so before he died? When did he write this? Father Chiphwanya looked at the note again. 'Fourteenth August,' he read. 'Only yesterday!' he gasped.

Around the time that Father Chiphwanya was sorting out the new situation presented by Father Gonzago's note, a stranger pottered into Mpona village. As he reached the edge of the village he tottered on uncertainly, never looking up at the faces of surprised villagers whose eyes had turned on him. He held his stick firmly in his right hand, and slung over his double-bent back was an old tattered blanket. The man walked with great difficulty and appeared to be in pain.

The people followed him with their gaze and then, when they could not understand, they slowly turned to Lubinda as if to say, 'Lubinda, this is your man.' Lubinda did not move. He too was looking at that bag of bones. The man walked on. He was going towards Mpona's house. He stopped outside the battered door to the ruins, coughed a little and whispered, 'Odi.'

After a little while the door opened. Mpona was standing in the doorway, leaning against the short pillar. 'Why do you come here? Why do you return to this village, this house?' asked Mpona. His voice was flat, and his eyes were looking to the distance as he trembled with hunger and exhaustion.

Mpona's wife had been outside looking for some firewood at the back of the house. 'Get him out of here!' she yelled. 'Go away! Go away!' Even she was looking weak and spent. 'Get him out of here, the cause of our suffering.' Saying this she grabbed him by the hand and pushed him off. The stranger was not strong. He fell like a dry mealie-stalk. The teacher –

for it was he – burst into a sob. Every time he tried to look up, Mpona's starved frame and bruised ankles met his eyes. Silwamia came from behind. He had to deliver his charge to Lubinda. 'Let's go,' he whispered to the teacher. 'It wasn't the Chief who sent me for you. It was Lubinda,' said Silwamia. There was no bitterness in his tone.

Chapter 15

The teacher walked straight into the jaws of the 'new men', and remained incommunicado for three days. The three days seemed to him like three years of waiting in Lubinda's other hut for the unknown which was being prepared to receive him. Youths went up to the house day and night, while the people who had come from the many villages of the kingdom looked on silently. Apart from Ciwera, who was soon disowned as a sell-out by the other headmen, anger mounted in the breasts of the people as they saw how Mpona, their Chief, the teacher (for whom they had cared little), and Natombi, now also a virtual prisoner, were being treated. But for them to intervene in the affairs of the private citizens of Mpona would have been tantamount to interference in the internal affairs of a brotherly village. This would have been to weaken the constitutional right of their headmen and therefore themselves to have a say in the vital matter of the future of the Chieftaincy. They were getting tired of living on Lubinda's charity. They resented it. But what could they do? If they left, then Lubinda would have said that they did so because there was no case to answer, and that Mpona was unfit to rule by virtue of the fact that he had been proved a witch.

Lubinda was impatient for a decision. It had now become so desperate to reach one that he was prepared to install himself as the kamcape in order to try the Chief. After all, he was the village's medicine-man, and because Mpona village was the seat of government, it could be said that he was the kingdom's medicine-man. So on the third day after the teacher's arrival he arraigned them all – Mpona, Aphunzitsi, and Natombi.

Lubinda began the charge against the Chief: 'You have betrayed the royal family of which we all had chosen you leader by deceiving us about your bastard origins. You have brought the basic institutions of the land into disrepute by consorting with white ones and bartering our traditions for the dirty goods of the white man. In the hour of the kingdom's maximum need, you deserted us on the scaly back of that reptile headman called Sipopa.'

Lubinda was working himself into a frenzy. He did not care now what any of the visiting headmen might say. The Chieftainship could only devolve on those who were not of Mpona village if there was no one available there. Lubinda had behaved like a Chief already and the time had now come to show his kingly authority.

Sipopa leapt up at the references to his name. He cast aside his black cikwembe cloth. 'I will fight you, Lubinda, you cheat! If you think you are Chief, come! Did I steal the Chief? You don't like my having found him, do you?'

Lubinda's eyes flashed with anger as he turned to face Sipopa. 'Come!' he yelled at Sipopa. 'Come, if you are a man. All of you here, come! Lubinda is doing nothing more than preserving this kingdom from witches. I don't want your filthy throne, the throne which once upon a time would have deserved me but now stinks with dirt, murder, corruption of the worst kind, humiliation of the citizens of this kingdom and – adultery. That is what this man whom you wish to continue to rule stands for.'

Mpona lifted his finger as though to protest. The lips moved, but no words came. He sank back into silence.

'You have sold our child,' continued Lubinda, 'to the white man. You, Natombi, you knew that Mwape was of this village, of the royal family, even though he was your child. You who once called yourself Chief, you knew you had a council of headmen to consult in these weighty matters. Did you ask these people if they agreed to the boy Mwape being sold into slavery, to be slaughtered by the white men in return for his dirty goods?'

Natombi was weeping. Lubinda spoke with such certainty about the fate of the child that it had to be true. He knew more than anyone else, and after all he had been to the mission more recently. 'My son,' she burst out weeping, 'Mwape, Mwape you are no more.'

The women in the crowd began to weep also. Lubinda let them weep on. The veins in his neck grew larger and larger with fury. Mpona collapsed. The news of Mwape's death was too much for him. The teacher remained standing, with his head bent. His lips were moving rapidly, maybe in prayer. But there was fear in his eyes.

'Do not weep, Natombi. You sold your child, your only child, because you do not have the heart of a woman. Mwape is dead. I know it. That is the reason for my anger,' Lubinda yelled above the heads of all, in a hoarse voice charged with emotion. He wiped tears from his eyes. The large crowd of people from all over the kingdom remained cowed, subdued with sorrow but angry – angry with Mpona, angry with Natombi, angry with the teacher – he especially, because he was the one who had brought the white man's ways into the kingdom through the school.

'Mwape was born dumb. This was the wish of the spirits of our ancestors. Can we cut open that which they have sealed? You man that was once a Chief, didn't I tell you so then?' asked Lubinda, spreading out his arms in a rhetorical gesture embracing the whole earth. 'We agreed to dig the white man's latrines. We of this village, my colleagues from other villages, we agreed to dig holes so that we could go to the same hole as our mothers-in-law. We agreed to be turned from self-respecting people into those animals which excrete in the same place – father, mother, children, mothers-in-law, fathers-in-law, grandchildren, everybody – every day of our lives. Why did we do so, I ask you?' asked Lubinda, once again spreading out his hands. 'Because we feared to stand for our old traditions. If you don't want the food that someone gives you, you don't receive it and then throw it away behind his back. That is the way of the coward. That is the way of the hyena,' he shrieked again. Then he lowered his voice, 'But that is exactly what we did. We dug shallow pits, put roofs on them, and thought we deceived the white man.

'We only deceived ourselves. Think of the liberties he has taken with us since then. Think of how he has held hands with this woman Natombi, before our eyes. Think how the other white one they call D.C. sat down turning up our women's cloths so that he could see their thighs. Such things are not of our tradition.'

Lubinda looked at Sipopa with a long and hateful eye. Sipopa's head was bent down. It was clear to Lubinda that he was winning. Mkando, the other difficult man, was hanging on his words, and you could see from the way he was narrowing his eyes that he was not only listening to what Lubinda was saying but was also seeing it all. Simbeya too, who had been dragged out of his house, was squirming restlessly on his mat. It was not with anger at Lubinda that he was wriggling like a snake being fried on the fire.

'And now, my fellow people, the death of Dulani. How can I explain it?' asked Lubinda. 'How can I explain the indignity of a member of your royal family going to the bed of death with a python? How can I explain the floods, the locusts, the strange whirlwinds, the frost? How can I explain anything?' he asked, screaming at the top of his voice, arms extended and shaking his head in despair.

Lubinda broke off. He strode away furiously, leaving the audience stupefied. Then there was a movement in the crowd. Yuda was hobbling like a whirlwind towards where Mpona lay. His axe was held high as he yelled, 'Kill them!' The crowd surged forward towards the three people in the ring. Just then someone shouted, 'Kamcape!' Yuda leapt round with a jump, the axe still held high. The whole crowd turned round to see. A prancing and dancing figure was reeling towards them, sprinkling medicine in its way as it sailed towards the crowd, laughing and jumping. The kamcape had come, singing his song:

> They say there is a witch here
> No, there are more, count them:
> Three, three I see in my mirror
> They call for the one and only kamcape
> Mwabvi is his drink
> The drink that is poison to the witches
> The drink that is water to the innocent
> Haha Haha Haha Hahahaha!

By then Lubinda had returned to meet the kamcape. He whispered something into his ear and the kamcape nodded significantly, and also shook his head significantly. Continuing this action of the head he struck up another song.

> The lion ran into a hyena
> The hyena cried Uwi! Uwi!
> Here I roar grrrr
> Here I roar grrr grrrr!

From nowhere drums struck and the crowd took up the song. The kamcape danced through the crowd and the crowd followed him in the witch-hunt dance. The three people in the centre of the re-formed circle remained still. Then he stopped, the drums stopped and the song and dance ceased.

'I know what has been happening in this village since I left,' the kamcape addressed the assembled villagers. 'I saw three people in my mirror walking towards the village. One carrying the leg, the other the chest, and the third the tongue of . . . is it the tongue of a man or a child?' There were exclamations of surprise.

Just then a great noise came from the bush on the eastern side of the village. Trees were bowing in the gust of wind. In a moment a huge column of dust moved like a furious lonely dancer towards the crowd. The dust gathered momentum, and before people knew where they were they had been sucked up

236

into the whirlwind and tossed in all directions. When the column of dust had passed, the kamcape was still standing where he had been before it came.

'Here, here,' he said, calling the people out of the clouds of dust. 'There was a plot, a plot, a plot, by my enemies in this village, to kill me before I can find out. But see what they have done.' He pointed to Lubinda's house. The roof had been sucked away by the wind and deposited several yards away, near Mpona's house. The people yelled with fright. 'If you eat rotten meat it returns to the mouth and you vomit it out. Do you see for yourselves?' continued the kamcape. 'Mpona wanted to kill me and Lubinda. But I was fortified, and now the roof has returned to his own door. Haha! He that married from the family of thunder does not fear lightning. Haha!' he broke off. Then he resumed, 'It is right. He that is a witch works at night. Let us allow the witches time to throw away their medicines.'

So saying, the kamcape took Lubinda by the hand and led him to his roofless house. In a moment, and after the kamcape had sprinkled medicine on the roof near Mpona's house, the men hoisted it back on to Lubinda's house. Then they were all sent back to their houses and camps for the night. Mpona was a marked man.

That night the kamcape did not sleep much. Nor did many other people. Even if you had never eaten human flesh, how did you know that you were not a witch? For some people, witchcraft is in their blood. Even if ten generations pass without exercising it, the witchcraft is still there in their blood. Therefore, if you wanted to be certain that you were not named the following day, you had to throw all medicines away that night. Even roots for making sure that your husband loved you and that your woman did not have ten eyes – you had to throw those away too.

Throughout the night, the kamcape kept chasing away imaginary voices in the bush. 'Don't throw your medicine near here! Throw it away at Mundo where the people whose heads you ate are lying!' he would shout out. Then the people would hear shouts of 'Uyo! Uyo! Don't struggle. Don't try to kill me!' into the late night and early morning.

So it was that when the dawn broke upon the village many people were already awake, having not slept throughout the night. From their huts they were listening to the incantations of the kamcape and wondering what the day would bring.

The kamcape began his day early. By dawn he had sprayed the boundaries of the village with a powder medicine. He had laid a root across each path into the village, to prevent any charms fleeing in or out of the village after this time. He had also sorted out the various charms which he was to use that day for the identification of the witches.

The question he had to answer was fraught with political implications. Was Mpona a witch? It was a simple question requiring a simple answer, not 'yes, but' or 'no, but' – but simply 'yes' or 'no'. From the brief time that he had spent in the village it was obvious to him that politically the best course of action was to declare Mpona a witch. But was the position as clear as all that? One headman – Sipopa – had spoken out openly against Lubinda. Mkando, whom Lubinda had already taken care of by bewitching him, had also shown hatred of Lubinda. Could it be that after they had gone back to their villages these other headmen would continue to support the old Chief? But then if that happened, reasoned the kamcape, his pulse quickening with excitement, it would be too late, 'because no man who is a witch survives my mwabvi'.

Lubinda's case against the Chief had one weak leg, thought the kamcape, who had been briefed by Lubinda – namely the allegation that the Chief was a witch because he was the son of that old woman who was a witch. What people would want to know when the dust had settled, was why the woman whom they all thought to be his mother behaved as if she was his mother. Mpona the Great One (the father of Chief Mpona) was not a man of 'many eyes'; he was faithful to his wives. How could they see him having an illegitimate child and successfully forcing it on his senior wife, and that child eventually becoming Chief Mpona, his successor? But the other leg of the case was strong. Why did Mpona offer that child to the white one? Who was this white one? Was it not possible that he was not a human being but a spirit? What human being could have wished to enter the Cave without fearing the consequences? They have eaten the child, he thought to himself. That is the explanation.

He had heard some time ago of the state of affairs between Lubinda and Natombi. 'Lubinda does not like her. She too must be a witch, to have agreed to her child being taken away.' And so he reasoned until it became obvious to him that not only the Chief, but also the teacher and Natombi had to go on trial. If the spirits had ordained that Mwape was to be dumb, what right had they to agree to the child being sent away, to be killed so that his tongue could be given to other white people? It was true that Natombi cried for the return of her son every night. But that was because she had run out of human meat. If the boy was alive, by now someone coming from Lusaka would have said so. Mpona had let the white man do some very unnatural things. For example, the latrine pits. All the other chiefs in this part of the world had refused to dig them because it was untraditional. But he had agreed to violate the custom; he did not mind about the spirits of the ancestors.

'I am ready now. Gather the people together, including Mpona, the teacher, and Natombi. All of them,' said the kamcape, with a small gesture of the hand. His forehead was perspiring.

'He doesn't look happy about this job,' thought Lubinda. But they had discussed everything the previous night. He could not fail to name the witch, he could not fail. But could he? Lubinda's knees started to knock against each other. He had not realized until now how much he had strained himself in the last few days. Now he thought he could win – but could he really? Everything hung on whether the kamcape would repeat to the public what he had assured him of in private. Could he trust him to speak as he had promised

The Chief's stool was brought out of Mpona's house and placed in the centre of the crowd. It had just been polished with castor oil and it was glinting in the morning light. That stool, after this day, might well change hands. Lubinda cast his eyes towards it. He swallowed and turned away. It was not meet to look enviously upon it. Mpona was brought out, at Lubinda's orders, by two men, one from Ciwera and the other from the village. When they set him down in the middle of the circle he tried to crawl towards the stool, but Lubinda's powerful hand stopped him. There was uncertain laughter from some of the crowd, though others buried their faces between their hands to wipe away welling tears. Long after the laughter had ceased, Yuda's loud voice was still booming with jeers. Simbeya, from his lying position, glanced at Yuda furtively, but did not say anything. A question was exercising his mind: was it right to treat a Chief in this manner? He searched history for a precedent, but there was none. Nevertheless, it had always been handed down as tradition that if a Chief became a witch he ceased to be a Chief. 'So let what will be done be done according to the wishes of the spirits,' he thought.

'You killed Dulani, you and your teacher and Natombi,' cried Lubinda, now prosecutor and preferrer of the charge. 'The white ones brought us hunger. You and Natombi caused Mwape to be dumb, and you gave him to the white ones so that they could kill him and you would share the meat. You killed Dulani because you wanted your maize to multiply in his blood.'

The crowd was silent. The heart of each one was thumping. 'And now, the time for judgement has come. Confess it yourself and you will be saved.' Lubinda passed quickly over the thought of salvation for Mpona. That would destroy everything. 'Even the white man at the mission, who was staying with this missionary you gave the child to, is also dead. He has been bewitched by you and the other white one. Mpona!' asked Lubinda, summoning all his energy, 'are you not a witch?'

The Chief shook his head. It was still beneath his dignity to answer charges preferred against him by a commoner and a rogue.

'You are the son of a witch and yet you will not say "yes"?' asked Lubinda with mounting anger. 'As far as we, the people of this village, are concerned – it does not matter what Sipopa thinks – you are a bastard son.'

Mpona's body twitched instinctively like an animal. They now remembered that twitch, which they had all forgotten about. With that twitch anger and authority always followed. As he squatted there on the floor, they all felt the full force of his compelling authority. But there was no anger in his eyes; they were not searching the distant hills, but simply downcast like one who has reached the end of the road, like the journey into nothingness of life itself. Then, like one in sleep, he suddenly blurted out with all the strength that he could command, 'You lie, Lubinda! You lie and you know it!'

'So he does not admit his guilt,' said Lubinda, with mock simplicity, and turning to the kamcape, he said brusquely, 'Do your work and find out who is the witch in our midst.' Lubinda sighed with relief. The first round had gone well. He looked into the eyes of the people gathered. They were blank. He looked into Sipopa's eyes. He could see fear in them. 'It is fear that I will give him mwabvi too, the idiot,' swore Lubinda inwardly.

The kamcape immediately swung into action. He ran round the boundary of the village. He was laughing like a hyena. He was roaring like a lion. 'Cross here and you die, you die like a rat that crosses the road,' he said at last, panting from the run. He waved his fly-switch at the drummers. The drums struck up. Howling and yodelling round the gathered circle, he led the introductory song of the diviner:

> *Uyu ndi uyu,*
> *Waufiti ndani?*
>
> *This one and this one*
> *Who is the witch?*

The lion dance followed in which the kamcape lay down

while they set a pounding mortar on his chest. His assistants pounded into the mortar while he squirmed on the ground, roaring and singing. The drums quickened; the men and women clapped their hands to the rhythm of the drums resounding with a husky tropical roar. At the wave of the fly-switch, the drummers stopped and the kamcape, still as cheerful as ever, started another song:

> *Lam'mawa suliona iwe*
> *Eya*
> *Lam'mawa suliona iwe mfiti*
> *Ulula*
> *Heya!*
> *Ulula.*

> *The morrow you will not see*
> *True*
> *The morrow you will not see*
> *you witch.*
> *Heya!*
> *Confess now.*

The kamcape reeled into the circle exclaiming 'Haha!' He danced in and out of the crowd. The drums beat to the rhythm of his dance and, when he raised his fly-switch to signify 'stop', the place was one huge dust-bowl.

Then he sat down with legs spread out and an axe handle between them. He was shoving the axe handle up and down.

'Go! go! go!' he said, tapping at its head. The people clapped their hands together. 'Is it envy?' he asked the axe. He continued shoving it up and down. 'Is it jealousy?' he asked again, looking at the axe handle. The handle continued to yield to his force. 'Has the hen sat on the larder?' he asked again. 'Has the rat sat on the bow?' The axe handle seemed to resist further pressure to move it up and down. The kamcape became excited, 'Ha!' he exclaimed, 'is it witchcraft then?' The handle would not move any further. He was struggling to shove it up and down. Beads of perspiration showed on his face. But the handle would not oblige. It remained glued to the ground as if concrete had been poured over it. 'Is it envy then?' he asked again. The handle moved up and down again as if it had suddenly been released from bondage. 'Is it witchcraft?' he asked again. The handle suddenly ground to a halt. He struggled with it, but it would not yield. He invoked the names of all the famous medicine-men and kamcapes of the past – Bonongwe, Mulopwe, Kazhila, Hamusamu – but the handle would not go. 'It is witchcraft!' he declared, jumping up and telling the crowd. 'It is witchcraft that is in this village,' he said. There were sighs of horror all round. Lubinda's heart beat fast and his mind registered 'second round – won'.

'Who is the witch now?' asked the kamcape. 'There must be more than one witch. That is why the handle becomes so difficult to move. Never seen this in all my life,' he declared. 'Too much witchcraft!'

He pulled out a rusty old mirror from his bag. Holding it before him he ran round the crowd barking 'Uyo! uyo! uyo!' He was chasing the witchcraft charm. He had scented it and now he was in full pursuit. He had now left the crowd of stupefied people behind and was heading for the houses. The crowd followed, singing after him. He stopped at one house – Lubinda's house – but clearly the horn stuffed with charms did not belong there. Then on to Banda's house. That was not its house. The horn seemed to have broken into a fast run in order to elude him as he too suddenly broke into an extremely fast run. He was running towards Mpona's house. The frenzied crowd followed, no longer singing but yelling incoherently. 'Help me! Help me!' he shouted to the crowd behind him. 'This charm is too big, too strong for me.' He ran round and round Mpona's house and then into the house. The people heard him struggle with something, trying to penetrate the big clay jars in the house. Then the kamcape rushed back to the door as if to bar something from coming out. Quickly he tugged at a knot on his waist and sprinkled its contents into the house. 'Agh!' he sighed. 'It goes! It goes, haha!' he said slowly as though he was watching a fire die down. 'He is the witch,' he declared, 'but there are also others, though they are smaller.'

The people, mad with anger, charged at Mpona, who had remained lying down where they left him. 'Kill!' Yuda was shouting at the head of the column. Even though his feet were covered in blood, Yuda was hobbling faster than anyone else could run. The crowd swept Mpona off the ground and was just about to tear him apart when the kamcape struck at them with his fly-switch. 'Stop! Stop! you kill a person.'

'Then give him mwabvi quickly,' yelled Yuda. 'This man is a witch,' he said.

Four men came to pull him. The Chief did not struggle. They dragged him on for a long distance until they reached the Big Cave, which was in the bowels of the hill. The crowd followed, this time not demanding his blood and hurling insults at him, but quietly. Quietly because they were approaching a sacred place. The sobs of Mpona's wife pierced the hill. The Cave threw their echo back until the whole area was like a world upon which barking dogs had been let loose. At the back of the crowd followed Natombi and the teacher, gagged and tied up. They too had been found guilty.

'Open your jaws,' rasped Lubinda when they finally reached the entrance to the cave and the crowd had gathered round. At the door the remains of the goat were still dangling. No one could touch anything that had come so far as to reach the Cave. If Mpona died after drinking the mwabvi his body would also have to be thrown into the Cave, never to be touched by any human being. If Mpona vomited out the mwabvi, this would be a clear sign that he was a witch and he would, therefore, have to be killed. If, on the other hand, he did not vomit it out, but drank it and died, then this would also show that he was a witch. Since he had behaved like a witch he would have nobody to blame for having been given the liquid to drink.

'Open your jaws!' rasped Lubinda again as two men tore Mpona's jaws apart. Blood oozed out of his mouth as his jaws were forced open. 'This is your last chance,' said Lubinda,

'Do you still deny that you are a witch?' Mpona's nose twitched as though he was trying to sniff at the blood that was dribbling out of his mouth. His distant eyes looked straight into the hills as though he was searching those rugged rocks for a honey-bird to lead him to the honey. Absent-mindedly he shook his head to right and left as if he was telling himself, 'Go home Mpona, there is no honey.'

'So you deny it?' asked Lubinda, seeking a clearer sign of denial. Mpona's eyes remained fixed upon the hill. His mouth was still open, and every time the two attendants tugged at his jaws to force them apart further his body twitched with pain. But he did not struggle.

The kamcape stood over Mpona. The day had been long for him. Throughout the day he had been trying to cast out of his mind fears and doubts about the affair upon which he was now engaged. The sun had turned to afternoon and in a few moments all would be over. But he had to resolve his doubts in an even shorter moment now. Was it right to offer this man the mwabvi, knowing full well that he would die? Would the white man at the Boma not hang him for the murder of a Chief? The white men at the mission – if the teacher died, would they not bewitch him with their prayers? There were people who had been cursed by these missionaries, thought the kamcape, and they were now lepers. 'What should I do? Should I say "No" to Lubinda, the man who will now be Chief? What will he do to me? His kingdom is a large one. Even though I come from beyond the hills, I cannot run away before I am caught. If – yes, this is a good idea – if I do not myself pour the mwabvi down his throat then the white man cannot accuse me. I will let Lubinda pour it down,' thought the kamcape.

'Give him the mwabvi,' said Lubinda to the kamcape. Lubinda was already assuming an authoritative tone. In a matter of minutes, after all, he would be Chief.

The kamcape searched the distant hills for an answer, for a way out. In a clear bright light of the bending sun those hills were not vague darkness but an avalanche of grit, sand, and stones which appeared to be rushing at him, scraping his brain until it was all blood. Those hills would see that which was about to be committed, and they would be witnesses unto eternity. He looked up at the branches of the tree near by. The fleshy leaves, blowing gently in the wind, appeared to droop towards him, their tips smelling, seeing and listening to what was being done below. They too, even if they might fall in the coming season, would remain witnesses. The sun too lingered around the scene, walking reluctantly backwards towards the horizon. It also seemed intent on recording the events of that day. The goat in the doorway to the Cave swayed to and fro in the sudden gust of strong wind. The doorway remained calm and expectant. The jaws of the crocodile . . .

He would have to act fast. Beyond the third hour of the afternoon it would be impossible to consummate the deed – to condemn, to destroy, to propitiate the spirits, to throw the corpse into the Cave and then to dip one's hands in the big jar of water at the entrance to the village from the side of the cemetery. It would not be right to leave the body of a witch overnight in the village. This would only bring more misfortune upon the troubled community. Beyond the third hour when the sun is in the middle of its afternoon journey, all these things could not be done . . . He looked at the people around him. There were no people there, but eyes, big wide-open eyes staring at him, eyes whose light burnt into his own sockets until they felt like pieces of metal melting in the furnace. They, too, would be witnesses to the thing which was about to be done.

He blinked. A tremor shot through his body. He lifted the gourd in his trembling hands, but the arms lowered again. His lips trembled as he tried to force them to move; they said: 'Kamcape does not pour the mwabvi himself.'

'All right then, I will,' said Lubinda firmly. 'The kingdom must be purged of witchcraft.' He snatched the gourdful of mwabvi from an attendant. He held down Mpona's mouth with his left hand. He lifted up the gourd, raising it high for all to see. Slowly it tilted. Soon Mpona's mouth would be full of it. 'He is a witch,' the people were saying. 'Let him die.'

Then – then suddenly there was a stir in the crowd. Lubinda's heart missed a beat. The crowd was running towards the road. What was it? What was it? Was it the D.C.? Lubinda's hand was shaking. Then suddenly Cumba jumped sky-high towards the on-rushing crowd. 'I've brought Mwape! Mwape!' Cumba yelled. Mwape dived into his mother's arms crying: 'Mama! Mama!'

'Mwape speaks, Mwape speaks!' yelled the people frantically. The hill threw back their echoes, 'Mwape speaks, Mwape speaks!'

The gourd crashed to the ground. 'Horrible!' was all Lubinda could say as he stood aghast with fear.

The crowd dived towards Mpona, weeping ecstatically. As one, it tossed him up and down, joy and sorrow streaming from all eyes. 'Our Chief! Our Chief!' cried the people. 'Our Chief! Our Chief!' The cry rose higher and higher as the people ran around the village with Mpona borne sky-high. 'You are our Chief! say "Yes", Mpona!'

When Mpona finally found his mind and voice he whispered, 'I cannot be. Leave me alone. I cannot be your Chief.'

'Do not desert us in the hour of our need,' cried Simbeya as the mad procession passed him. 'We did not desert you when Lubinda drove you mad.'

'Be our Chief,' cried the men as they held the stool of Chieftainship high before the panicky crowd. Faintly Mpona whispered, 'I will, I will.'

'Swear! Swear you will not desert us! Swear by the stool,' cried the surging crowd of excited people. Mpona rested his hands on the stool of Chieftainship held before him and whispered, 'By the spirits of our ancestors, by this stool, I swear.'

Just then, the sound of a motor-cycle crashed through the crowd. But the crowd went on shouting, 'Be our Chief!'

Father Chiphwanya screeched to a halt and jumped off his cycle. He had come to pay Father Gonzago's visit. He looked at the crowd of rejoicing people still bearing Mpona high above their heads. Suddenly he remembered Father

Gonzago's assignment: for Mpona, 3 Stations of the Cross and 2 Our Father. He threw himself down and cried aloud:

> *Our Father who art in Heaven,*
> *Hallowed be Thy Name. Thy Kingdom come,*
> *Thy will be done on earth as it is in Heaven.*
> *Give us this day our daily bread,*
> *And forgive us our trespasses,*
> *As we forgive them that trespass against us;*
> *And lead us not into temptation,*
> *But deliver us from evil. Amen.*

The teacher had crept to where Father Chiphwanya was kneeling, and was praying with him. The crowd jabbered on, 'Be our Chief.'

'I will, I will,' said Mpona as he was lowered to greet the priest. Natombi was still seated where the crowd had left her, crying over her child Mwape with joy. For the hundredth time Natombi swept Mwape into her arms. She could not believe that her child could now speak. She looked up and saw Father Chiphwanya standing a little way off.

'There, there he is, your saviour,' she gasped to Mwape, and the boy ran full tilt, laughing and shouting, up to Father Chiphwanya.

At the sound of that voice, Father Chiphwanya's heart leapt up with joy. He could not believe his ears. Then the words of the prophet Isaiah burst through his mind and his lips trembled with emotion as they repeated after his heart:

> *Then shall blind men's eyes be opened, and the ears of the deaf*
> *unstopped. Then shall the lame man leap like a deer and the*
> *Tongue of the Dumb shout aloud . . .*

'Deo Gratias,' gasped Father Chiphwanya stretching out his hands in an attitude of prayer, 'thanks to be God.' And again, but this time in Latin, he recited the 'Our Father':

> *Pater noster qui es in Caeli, sanctificateur nomen tuum.*
> *Adveniat regnum tuum, fiat voluntas tua, sicut in terra et in*
> *Caeli . . .*

Then the excited crowd remembered Lubinda. 'Kill him! Kill him'! it roared, calling for his blood. But Lubinda and the kamcape had vanished.

Two weeks later a traveller from another part of the country reported coming across a dead body, its flesh eaten out by vultures. The Chief despatched a party there immediately. It was Lubinda's remains. His powerful arms were still stretched out as though he had been repulsing something. His bared legs were thrust apart as if astride an animal. A leopard's skeleton lay by his side. Lubinda had been a fighter to the end.

'How shall we bury him?' asked Yuda. 'He was a bad man.' The Chief eyed Yuda briefly. 'As a member of your family?' asked Yuda.

'Yes,' replied the Chief quietly, 'he was my Councillor.' He looked at Sipopa. Sipopa knew that the Chief was thanking him for his loyalty. When the grave had been dug and the bones lowered, a python crept into the grave from nowhere. It fell limp on to the coffin.

'A poisonous snake,' says an old proverb, 'bit my mother-in-law. It died – of poisoning.'